# Into the Open

## Urushalon Part II

### Cindy Koepp

Lumen Anime
Citron Concassé
Aberdeen, Washington, USA

# Into the Open:
## Urushalon Part II

For permissions and queries, contact the publisher at:
citronconcasse@gmail.com

PRINTING HISTORY
First Edition
April 2020

ISBN-10: 0999592755
ISBN-13: 978-0-9995927-5-5

CREDITS
Cover Art by: Matt Ostrom

PUBLISHER'S NOTE

# Into the Open
## Urushalon Part II

One

Amaya Ulonya *Kiand* strode into the *kiat's* waiting room and took a quick look around. The nautical decorations hadn't changed since her last visit a few weeks ago. The floor was sand and bivalve shells encased in a hard resin that reflected light coming in from the windows spanning the whole front of the building. The curtains over those windows were twisted strips of dark green material hanging from a rod draped with a fishnet. A pair of squashy turquoise armchairs at right angles to each other occupied the corner to her left.

She frowned. There was such a thing as excessive decorating, and her superior's office had passed that mark long ago.

At the seashell-studded desk across the room, the secretary sat—Teviya, wasn't it? She wore a skin-tight, seaweed green dress. Her hair, dyed to match, hung in braids of various diameters. Her make-up had turned her face ocean blue with dark green vertical stripes. She made no effort to acknowledge Amaya's arrival but continued affixing dark green fingernail extensions while humming a tune Amaya didn't recognize.

Amaya crossed her arms over her chest. If one of her subordinates ever treated a guest in such a way, retraining and disciplinary action would be shortly arranged. Rudeness, however, was clearly an expected job skill in the kiat's employ. Did Teviya's attitude extend to all the *kiandai* or just to her for having the audacity to want to help her human *urushalon* protect his people? She rolled her shoulders to dispel the tension building. If she had to absorb some rudeness to keep Ed and the rest of the Las Palomas police department safe, she would do so for as long as it took. Her adopted human deserved at least that much.

Movement drew her attention. Pavwin Vueltu *Kiand* of the Falcon's Wing station rose from one of the leather chairs and joined her. He clasped her right arm and pulled her into an embrace. "So, he's pulled you in on this, too." He stepped back.

She tipped her head to one side. Were they both here for the same reason? Assigning multiple stations to a task wasn't unheard of. With only six *kiandarai* per station, sometimes more manpower was needed, but why include her station? She was still training up four *kialai*. Although two would promote to full *kiandarai* soon enough, two of them were barely out of basic training.

Amaya followed him back to the chairs near the wall. Sitting in these, she might as well sit on the floor with her knees closer to her ears, but there were no other places to sit and pacing would give the impression of impatience. She leaned closer to Pavwin and whispered, "Any idea what this is about?"

He shook his head and made a quick nod toward the secretary, Teviya.

Half a second after their rear ends made contact with the blue-green leather, the secretary stood. "The *kiat* will see you both now." The smirk on her face precluded any suggestion of coincidental timing.

Pavwin rolled his eyes as he stood and adjusted an equipment pouch on his belt, which only added a hint of a sneer to the secretary's lips.

Keeping her own annoyance out of her face, Amaya used the arms of the chair to push herself up. She followed Teviya and Pavwin down the hall behind the secretary's desk. Muted blue and green lighting had been added since her last visit. The flowing blobs of color reminded her of a disorientation training session back when she was still a *kiala*. Given the number of people who were nauseated by these visual effects, Emyrin's choice of lighting puzzled her, but he didn't seem like the obliging, welcoming sort.

The secretary waved her hand past the sensor plate near the door decorated with porpoises then strutted back to her desk as the door slid open. Pavwin gestured Amaya in ahead of him.

The waiting room's decorator had been given a free hand in here, too. Dense, sand-colored carpet was deeper in some areas than others giving the floor a rippled appearance. Artwork on the walls showed off reefs and their flurry of brilliantly colored wildlife.

Emyrin Koral *Kiat* sat at his mahogany desk, typing furiously on his keyboard. As hard as he hit the keys, Amaya marveled that the keyboard was still intact. How often did he have to replace it? Older than both her and Pavwin by at least two decades, their superior had close-trimmed gray hair a few shades lighter than their uniform. Permanent wrinkles marring his pale face suggested that he'd neither smiled in ages nor spent any time in the sun. His copper collar tabs sported a new orange crystal for successfully completing the demolitions course, a curious choice for someone who didn't do field work anymore, but the protocol allowed *kiandarai* to choose studies that interested them, even when they weren't too practical.

Eyes still glued to the boxy computer, Emyrin pointed to the blue leather chairs with seashell-studded, wooden legs. "Sit."

Amaya settled into one of the padded chairs while Pavwin took the other. What was next? A treat or a pat on the head to celebrate their obedience?

Emyrin scowled and jabbed the screen's off switch. He turned a hard stare on them. "You'll both need to prepare to receive Rinulyn Tolu *Tura*."

Amaya shifted in her seat but schooled the amazement from her features. What could possibly interest someone of his station in one of the smallest enclaves in Texas? Woran Oldue had no major features or facilities that might cater to the ultra-wealthy. The aquarium was tiny relative to others in the state. No unique cuisine called this enclave home. Sure, the beach might interest some, but there were larger enclaves with more to offer that also had an impressive beach. Worse, she'd never been close enough to see a member of nobility in person. How did one act in the presence of an Eshuvani baron? The most basic protocols for such an event eluded her, and now she had to prepare to receive him as a guest of the enclave? The family of her *kiala* Vadin traveled in that social group, or at least closer than she'd ever been. Still in the middle phase of his training, would he be up to the task of training the rest of them? If not, she could borrow the social hierarchy specialist of another station for a crash course.

Pavwin raised an eyebrow. "Nobility? Here in the buffer zone?"

"Yes." Emyrin leaned back in his chair. "He's meeting with the governors of the human states that overlap our territory."

Amaya looked up at a corner of the room and recalled an overlay map of human and Eshuvani territory. "So, that'd be Texas, Oklahoma, and New Mexico."

Pavwin squinted for a moment and nodded. "Yes. We overlap parts of each."

With the *tura* coming from the Texas Panhandle and the governors coming from Oklahoma City, Austin, and Santa Fe, somewhere in central or western Texas would make more sense. Was there any way to talk them out of this? Ill-equipped with undertrained staff, any other station would be a better choice. "Good to know, but Woran Oldue and Las Palomas are small as cities go." Amaya steepled her fingers. "Wouldn't a larger city have more of the facilities they'll likely need?"

Emyrin waved a hand in dismissal. "It's enough for you to know you need to be ready for his arrival."

If he thought he could brush her off that easily ...

Amaya squinted and frowned. "If you want me to protect him with limited resources and half-trained personnel, I need more information than that."

Emyrin's ears turned pink.

5

He drew a breath, but before he spoke, Pavwin leaned forward and cut him off. "It would be helpful to know why they chose to meet here of all places. Neither the enclave nor the city has much to offer such august persons."

Amaya glanced at Pavwin and nodded. Aside from some tourist-trap establishments, Las Palomas was as sparse as the enclave on the matter of fascinating things to do.

Emyrin twisted to face Pavwin directly. "The wives of the four delegates will be here and two are bringing their children. There's talk of visiting the beach, our aquarium, and the humans's museum."

This got better with every passing second. Three governors, the *tura*, their wives, and children? "They're bringing their families?" Amaya's left hand drifted down to her right shirt cuff, but the bracelet was gone. After coming to terms with her grief, she'd given her wedding bracelet to Ed to regift or dispose of. The bare twinge of sadness was still there, even if the bracelet was not. She rubbed her wrist for a moment then steepled her fingers again. *"Kiat,* we should advise a different coastal town. I've only been training the Las Palomas police for almost a month, and they're not yet equipped. Nor have we gotten the local crime wave under control. We'll have a hard enough time securing the *tura* and three governors, never mind wives and children."

Emyrin wagged his finger at her as if she were some petulant child. "Your only concerns are the *tura*, his wife, and his children. Let the humans take care of themselves."

How terribly mercenary. Would the *tura* agree with that? "Then I'll coordinate with Las Palomas police to make sure all is in hand." A visit with Ed would be imperative. His captain might have been freer with information.

Emyrin slammed his palm on his desk. "You will not leave the security of the *tura* in the hands of humans!"

He could pound the furniture all he wanted. If she had to prepare, then she would take full advantage of all available resources, including LPPD.

"But if we don't communicate with the humans, we'll trip over each other in our efforts." Pavwin shook his head and tapped his fingers on the seashells studding the arms of the chair. "We may even take contradictory actions and interfere with each other's plans."

"I suppose." Emyrin glared at Amaya. "But keep your priorities in order."

She had every intention of maintaining "priorities," but he shouldn't be too surprised if hers failed to align with his. "When should we expect the delegations to arrive?"

"Fifteen days."

Pavwin tugged a small notepad out of his shirt pocket and jotted the date on a blank page. "And what will the *tura* need from us?"

"He will contact you when the time comes. Pavwin, you'll have control of the situation at the aquarium and the beach. Ulonya, you have all Buffer Zone and Las Palomas activities. Serve with diligence." Emyrin turned away from them and jabbed the power button on his monitor again.

Referring to her by only her surname was a petty insult worthy of grade school children, which was roughly what she guessed to be his level of emotional maturity. Amaya concealed an eyeroll by standing and turning away from Emyrin.

She indicated the door with a nod and led Pavwin out. Once the door closed behind them, she turned to him. "Well, that—" She stopped. In all likelihood, Teviya was fully the servant of her master, which meant that anything spoken in her hearing would be taken out of context, twisted around, and used in the most damaging way. "— was highly informational," she finished. Anyone with a few milligrams of character would have left such a politics-crazed environment long ago. Well, she had danced through these interpersonal quagmires before.

"Yes, very." He leaned closer and whispered. "Outside?"

Amaya nodded.

They entered the waiting room. Teviya's smile was as real as her dark green hair color. She glanced up from rearranging strips of green cloth on her dress. "Serve with diligence."

Amaya nodded once. "Serve with diligence."

Once the outer door slid closed behind them, Pavwin guided her to the side of the building, out of sight of the windows. The parking lot, paved with reclaimed plastics, was large enough for a few cargo haulers or a half-dozen couriers. A larger lot behind the building would accommodate larger vehicles. Spindly oaks and yaupons formed an intermittent ring around three sides of the parking lot. From where they stood, the ugly blue-gray box of the local training center was clearly visible.

The sun beating down on them would cook them in a few moments. Amaya led Pavwin to the shade of a cluster of nearby oaks.

Pavwin leaned against one of the trunks. "I have to say I'm impressed by how little you react to Emyrin's insults."

Amaya shrugged. "Part of my specialization. I pretend I'm dealing with humans."

"They're that rude?" He tipped his head to one side.

"No, but in some environments, they don't find offense in addressing someone by surname only, and many take pride in 'staying calm under fire.'"

"I see. Useful when dealing with that one." He nodded toward Emyrin's office. "And on the matter of human reactions, if you can find a block of time, my staff and I will need some instruction on how to handle them before those human governors arrive. I don't even know how to greet them properly. They seem so aloof."

Amaya smiled at the common misconception. Humans, by contrast, often found her people "too emotional." "They do come across that way. Humans have stricter expectations of permitted physical contact. Some cultures more than others, especially between men and women. I'll look at my schedule and send you some options."

"We'll find a time and place." His comm system beeped. He clasped her right arm and pulled her into an embrace before he stepped away and tapped the dark blue comm crystals on his silver collar tabs. After a short, intense conversation, he jogged across the parking lot toward his avi.

To stay out of the way, she watched him go before hustling to her own avi. She stepped up into the pilot's seat and set her trauma kit behind her. For a welcome change, the avi started up the first time she triggered the ignition. The wings extended with a creak before she lifted off and turned toward Ed's house. No better time to start coordinating than now. Once clear of the trees, she rolled the accelerator forward.

Ω

Officer Mark Hollis pulled into the parking lot of a gas station and rolled down the window. A caller was supposed to meet them here and fill them in on the possible trespassing problem. Calls to this end of town were a mixed bag. He'd handled everything from some goofy kid trying to snitch a candy bar to a double homicide. The sporadic scattering of derelict buildings meant this was prime real estate for all manner of shenanigans.

His partner, Officer Robert Kirby, leaned across and pointed. "There."

Hollis twisted toward the station. A grease monkey came out of an open door wiping his hands on a badly stained and faded red towel. Hollis tried to get a read on what sort of call this was going to be. Smudges of dirt and old oil marred the man's face and overalls. Graying hair peeked out of the edge of a Houston Astro's baseball cap. The grease monkey, favoring his right leg some, moseyed toward the car and smirked. He leaned over and rested his elbows on the car's door then recoiled and winced.

If he didn't know it already, the old timer would soon find that the summer of 1965 was going to set heatwave records. Even the white part of a black-and-white could be used for a griddle, and it wasn't even July yet.

"Y'all sure got here quick." The mechanic rubbed his arm before resting both hands on his knees.

That was a new one. So often, people complained that the response time was too long.

Hollis nodded. "We were in the area. So, what did you see across the street?"

"Tall fella. Coulda been a player for the 76ers. Y'know the type. Didn't get a good look at 'im, but he jus' might be one of them Eshuvani. I been watchin' that place since I saw 'im sneak 'round back, an' he ain't come back out." He indicated the building across the street with a nod.

"How long ago?" Kirby stretched one arm across the back of the seat and leaned forward.

"Jus' before I called." He shrugged. "So, what, ten minutes mebbe?" The old man scratched under the edge of his ball cap. "Whaddya figger someone'd want in a closed up five 'n' dime, anyway? Ain't nothin' left in there 'cept maybe a coupla ol' shelving units and enough dust to grow taters."

Hollis frowned. They did not need more Eshuvani criminals in Las Palomas. The last had killed some officers and wounded several others. Although not a total surprise, Hollis's guts turned just thinking about the prospect.

"No telling." Hollis checked the boarded up, tan brick building in his rearview mirror. No obvious activity now. "You stay put over here while we check it out."

"I'll keep my eye on the place, but I don' want nothin' t' do with no Twig."

Eshuvani were tall and thin like twigs, but they were nothing to make sport of. Hollis hadn't met one yet who couldn't take a human apart like rotten wood. Fortunately, they weren't all bad news. Like most groups, a few problematic ones gave them all a bad name. He nodded. "Fair enough." With any luck, the grease monkey's attitude would keep him from trying to "help."

The old man backed away. Hollis shifted the car into reverse and headed for the now defunct five-and-dime.

"They're breaking into abandoned buildings now?" Kirby turned around for a look at the store front.

Hollis glanced at Kirby as he parked. "Maybe he needed a place to hide."

"His real target is—" Kirby twisted around and aimed his thumb at the gas station across the street.

"Maybe." Hollis left the keys in the ignition and tugged on the door handle. "I'll keep an eye on the back door. You watch the front. We'll wait for the *kiandarai* before we go in."

Kirby blew out a breath. "Right."

For the briefest moment, Hollis reconsidered the plan. If the suspect really was Eshuvani, splitting up might get one of them hurt. Their recent training wasn't that far along yet. With only two of them, though, they'd only cover one exit if they stayed together. Most criminals were smart enough to figure out how to use one exit when the other was being watched. Without additional backup, this was the only way.

Hollis slid out of the car and jogged around to the back of the building, staying well away from the cinder-block wall. The wooden door was splintered and broken inward, probably the result of a couple well-placed kicks. He found a reasonable hiding place behind some chest-high Johnson grass growing up through uneven cracks in the pavement and watched the back door.

The rhythmic hum of an avicopter grew louder. A clang came from inside the building. Moments later, an Eshuvani male with pale eyes and sparse, dark hair slipped out of the broken door. He carried a length of pipe and slid a palm-sized, angled object into his pocket.

A tremor built up in Hollis' hands. He'd seen the results of a human officer taking on an Eshuvani criminal alone. That never went well for the human. His mind flashed back to his own one-on-one encounter years ago. He never wanted to be looking down the barrel of his own gun again. Several years had passed, and he was older, wiser, and better trained now.

He drew his gun and aimed at the suspect. "Freeze! Face down on the ground. Now!"

The Eshuvani took one look and bolted across the back of the building. Hollis took off after him. The suspect dodged around stacked milk crates and delivery trucks behind the grocery store next to the defunct five-and-dime. Hollis had started only a couple strides behind but steadily lost ground—at first. Taking full advantage of his greater human endurance, he closed the gap as the suspect's stamina dwindled.

As Hollis came around the corner of a large dumpster, a strike on his right wrist sent the gun flying. A gray blur in the corner of his eye moved toward his head. He ducked, and the length of pipe whooshed past. Hollis kicked the Eshuvani's knee, making him stagger backwards. The suspect spun and stumbled the last yard or two to a small blue and yellow avicopter parked behind the dumpster. Hollis pushed off from the ground and came back up to his feet, but the suspect was already seated in the pilot's chair and extending the wings.

As the blue and yellow avicopter lifted off, Hawk's Nest's gray and silver courier cast a shadow on the pavement. If only they'd been here just a few minutes sooner. They might have had the suspect. He leaned against the warm metal of the shady side of the dumpster to catch his breath.

Blaming the *kiandarai* was no good. Unless they'd been on a call somewhere in the city, they would've been coming from a few miles beyond the far side of town. The way their dilapidated equipment malfunctioned; they'd caught a lucky break to have an avi actually working right. For a change.

Hollis rubbed his wrist. The sharp report of the initial hit had faded down to a heavy ache. Although he didn't think anything broke, he would have to get it checked out and fill out an injury report. Joy. More paperwork.

He shielded his eyes with his hand and looked up. The courier ship chased after the blue and gold. When they were out of sight, he looked around for his gun and found it next to a clump of grass. He retrieved it and holstered it.

"Hollis!" Kirby hollered.

He drew a deep breath and shouted back. "Here! I'm okay!" He threaded his way back toward his partner.

Kirby jogged around a delivery truck and slowed when they made eye contact. He returned his pistol to its holster, and the creases in his forehead smoothed out. "What happened?"

Hollis met his partner halfway. "An Eshuvani came out of the building with a hunk of pipe and took off running." Hollis grabbed his aching wrist and moved it through the range of motion. A twinge shrieked at him when he bent his wrist back. That was going to smart when the adrenalin wore off. "I got whacked on the arm as I came around the corner, but I ducked the follow-up."

"All that training with Hawk's Nest is paying off." Kirby absently rubbed his sternum.

"I'll say." He recalled about a month ago when a suspect had nearly killed Kirby with a shellfish knife. If Osborn hadn't shown up with his Eshuvani *urushalon* right about then ...

Kirby sighed and shook his head. "Y'know, it'd be real handy if we had a way to stay in contact when we have to split up."

"Yeah, yeah, I know. Osborn and Amaya are working on getting us collar tabs like the *kiandarai*." He nodded toward the building. "Let's see what we can figure out from the building."

"Sure you don't need a hospital?" Kirby glanced down at Hollis's wrist.

Hollis winced at the sharp sting as he slowly flexed it. Yeah, an ER visit was going to be in order but later. Otherwise, Kirby would likely get to check out the damage in the defunct store alone. Not a safe proposition by any means. The pipe-wielder might return with or without friends. "Let's get this dealt with first." He headed back to the broken door.

### Ω

Ed Osborn leaned back in the green, floral-print armchair in his living room. Amaya sat at the nearest end of the matching sofa and sipped the lemonade Esther had made that afternoon, no ice of course. The pitcher had been sitting out on the counter for an hour so Amaya could have a drink without getting muscle cramps, like the worst ever brain freeze dead center in the chest.

While he listened to her description of the impending gubernatorial meeting with the

Eshuvani baron, he watched her movements. To an outsider, she would look serene, but there were tells, small gestures that only he would know. That touch on her right sleeve when she spoke of the delegates' families meant she was worried they would be hurt if someone decided to move against the *tura* or governors. Her pale gray eyes, several shades lighter than her uniform, only narrowed when she spoke of Emyrin, a clear indication of her opinion of her superior. Ed had met the man and totally agreed with her dislike of the *kiat*. He came by the nickname "old piranha" honestly.

The most telling, perhaps, was the way the tension across her shoulders made her uniform wrinkle in a different way. Eshuvani were already only two-thirds the width of an athletic human, which made them look like they'd been squished, but when Amaya was stressed, that tension only added to the effect.

She wound down her description of the meeting with Pavwin and Emyrin. In addition to a good estimate of Amaya's mental and emotional state, now he had an idea about what tomorrow's staff meeting was likely to be about.

They should have been given more notice. Schedules would have to be rearranged and security checks would have to be done. For love of Christmas, why did they never have enough time?

He ran his fingers through his hair, catching for a moment on a tangle in the natural curls. Time for a haircut. "Fifteen days, huh?"

Amaya shook her head, and the wide pupils of her eyes narrowed to thin slits before widening out to circular when she looked at him again. "That's all, and we weren't exactly blessed with copious free time to start with. Have you heard anything about this?"

"Rumbles that something was in the works but always with a promise of more information to follow. A staff briefing is set for tomorrow morning early. I'm guessing that's when we'll get the official word."

She sipped her lemonade. "We need to get both Las Palomas divisions equipped as soon as possible."

Sure. He'd just add that to the list of things they needed and hope the brass listened this time. He snorted. "You can't afford it. You're barely keeping your own staff equipped, and half of that gear was new when you were still a *kiala*."

She smiled. "*Kiandara*, but not by much. I think the oldest equipment we're using was new one year after I graduated. Ultimately, I suppose it is good that even the youngest ones on my staff learn how to do without modern technology."

That still meant some of her gear was older than he was. She'd been *kiand* for forty-five years now.

"Does your department have funds?" She leaned forward and rested her elbows on her knees.

"Maybe." Las Palomas PD was in better shape for sure. Convincing those who held the purse strings would be the trick. "The most critical equipment would be what? Comm crystals, so my people can directly contact yours and handcuffs that would actually hold an Eshuvani?"

Amaya turned one hand upward, and her long, spindly fingers unrolled like a curled paper. "With the fire department handling most rescues and EMS taking care of medical issues, that might do it. Your pistols have sufficient stopping power. The infrared goggles for night vision are actually worse than your natural sight."

Esther leaned into the living room polishing a fork with an embroidered dish towel. "Dinner's ready, dear."

"Thanks, honey. We'll be right there." Ed stood and tugged downward on his pants legs.

Amaya stood, nodded in the direction Esther had gone, and whispered, "She seems to be recovered from the encounter with Wylin."

Ed grimaced and matched her volume. "Mostly? She's not having nightmares anymore, but she turned down a church event on the beach that she's done every year. When the kids want to go swimming, she takes them to the park, not the beach."

"Ah. Her recovery will take time." Amaya gripped Ed's shoulder. "Being kidnapped by Wylin and left to drown would—"

Movement beyond the door to the kitchen caught Ed's eye. He held up his hand to stop Amaya mid-comment then waved her on ahead of him and spoke louder. "Get me the price for comm crystals and cuffs, and I'll write up a proposal to see about equipping at least the senior partner of each pair."

Amaya nodded. "Not ideal, but that may be all we can do this soon."

Ed followed her. He was sure he could make a case for the new equipment, but with recent threats of budget cuts, it'd be a hard sell. He took a step down the hallway to the bedrooms. "Kids! Dinner!"

Nick whooped and charged out of his bedroom fast enough to just miss a collision with Lois, who gave him scrunched-faced glare.

"Walk, please. Keep the running for outside." Ed herded the pair into the kitchen.

"And no shop talk at dinner, please," Esther called from the kitchen.

Ed rolled his eyes and followed Lois through the door. "As if we ever."

"True, but there's obviously something intense going on." Esther set the last of the silverware on the table. The embroidered tablecloth matched the towel she'd been using. "You two have been talking about nothing else since she arrived."

"I might be on duty at all times, but I do know how to find other topics to discuss. I shall demonstrate." Amaya settled into the chair, without banging her knee on the underside of the table this time. "So how was the movie, Esther? What was it called again?"

Before she could answer, Nick beamed a smile that could be seen from the next county. "*Willy McBean and His Magic Machine!* It was the best!" Nick launched off into a retelling of the movie.

Lois leaned closer to Amaya. "I liked the monkey."

Ed sat in his customary place and tried to put work out of his mind for a while.

## Ω

Vadin took a deep breath to quell his jittery stomach. This was a staff meeting, not an execution. He rolled his eyes. A simple meeting shouldn't make him this nervous, but Amaya had left her meeting with the *kiat* and went straight to Ed's house. Warning number one. Whatever was going on was going to need coordination between Las Palomas and Woran Oldue. Then she'd come back to the station with tense muscles and narrowed eyes. Warning number two. He could've read the tension from orbit. Before retreating to her house, she'd scheduled this meeting. Warning number three. With four of them still in training, she didn't interrupt their studies for anything silly.

Something was wrong.

Whatever it was, he wouldn't be any wiser standing out here in the corridor. He blew out another breath and stepped into the briefing room. The largest room in the station, after the hangar that is, was irregularly shaped. Mismatched wooden or plastic chairs in various states of disrepair were arranged in a semicircle around a makeshift table composed of cinder blocks and a roughly rectangular hunk of well-sanded plywood.

Amaya had perched on the edge of the table, and the rest of their little group was scattered in the chairs. Some of the tension he'd seen earlier had faded, but that did little to settle his queasy stomach.

Normally, Vadin would be mortified to be the last one to join the meeting, but he'd been on the dispatch desk. Staying there until everyone was assembled then transferring the calls to his personal comm system was expected.

Amaya gestured for him to find a seat and launched off into a recap of her meeting with the *kiat* and the pertinent parts of her visit with Ed.

Vadin steepled his fingers and leaned his chin on them while she described the impending arrival of the *tura* and the human governors. Protecting them and their families could be tricky. He knew how to comport himself with that level of the social hierarchy–he'd better. Not only was it his specialization, but he'd grown up not far below the *tura's* level — but he was going to need a lot of training on how to protect dignitaries. He glanced at Nurinyan. With his martial arts specialization, he'd probably be the one to train them all on defending people. With any luck, Jevon's demolitions specialization would not be necessary.

"Do we know where the meeting will be?" Orinyay adjusted one of the pins securing her hair in the braided bun.

"Not yet." Amaya shook her head. "When pressed for the details, Emyrin was not forthcoming."

Vadin nodded. "Depending on who the *kiat* named as the person in charge of the arrangements, the *tura's* secretary, Halyuwin, will contact either you or Pavwin to work out the details."

Blowing her bangs out of her face, Ishe crossed her arms over her chest. "You watch. They'll put the meeting here."

Oh, that would be a fine disaster. This place hadn't hardly managed Consecration Day, and that was relatively informal compared to a visit from the *tura*.

Nurinyan leaned over and took a swipe at Ishe's ponytail. "Don't say things like that. We'll all suddenly have enough chores to keep five stations busy."

Amaya snickered. "If they do decide to host the meetings here, we'll deal with it, but I can't imagine the *tura* and governors would pick Hawk's Nest. There are better facilities to be had." Amaya brushed the concern away with the sweep of her hand.

That was the understatement of the millennium. Vadin hid a smirk behind his hand.

"I don't suppose equipping the human officers will be done in time?" Jevon scratched the side of his head and slouched in his chair.

"We're still working out where to get the funds to afford collar tabs and proper handcuffs for them." Amaya sat up straighter, a sign that usually meant she was concerned. "I'm hoping we can get the equipment issue figured out in time, but if not, we'll just have to find another way. Other questions?" After a few moments, she hopped down from the table. "Then, that's all I know for now. The *tura*, three governors, and their families will be meeting somewhere in the area of Woran Oldue and Las Palomas. As I know more, you will know more."

Vadin watched her go. All at once, not the huge disaster he'd expected and yet a much bigger mess than he wanted to deal with. He returned to the dispatch desk and restored the incoming calls to the main system before he started compiling a list of things that might make this place presentable. Amaya was right. The meetings would most likely be held at another site, but the dignitaries might want to be introduced to Hawk's Nest. A few touches here and there might make a better first impression.

Ω

Amaya landed the cargo hauler at the edge of the grocery store's parking lot, the only spot nearby that was big enough. She preferred the courier for these sorts of city calls, but Jevon was working on the necessary maintenance that kept the smaller avi in the air.

Ads in the store windows boasted of grapes for fourteen cents per pound and carrots for nine cents per bunch. The construction site across the street looked quiet, but most human establishments closed on Sunday for a day of rest and worship.

Nurinyan, the oldest of her four *kialai* and the one who simultaneously had the most potential and caused her the most worry, turned toward her. "Are you sure we're in the right place?"

The site was awfully quiet for an "unexpected disturbance" call. She consulted the note Vadin had given her on the way out, to make sure she'd landed in the right place. The addresses matched. Maybe the source of the weird noises had left. "This is the address the dispatcher gave Vadin."

"Yes, but–" He turned back toward the construction site. "–There's no one here."

If there were contests for conclusion jumping, Nurinyan would win. With a bit more training, that could develop into remarkable intuition. She opened the avi door and grabbed her trauma kit. "There's no one visible. We can't see the entire construction site from here, can we? Nor can we see into the large shell of the building from the air. So, we have no knowledge of whether there's anyone in the area. There's no one out here because we've arrived before the police, but this is the place."

Still, the "weird noises" reported coming from within and the "loud, mechanical hum" someone had reported had to come from somewhere, and the most likely source was an avicopter somewhere in the construction site.

After closing the door behind her, she slid the backpack onto her shoulders and walked around to the other side to wait for Nurinyan.

A black Pontiac Tempest sped by. A woman in heavy plastic glasses and curly hair leaned out the passenger window. "Go home, Twigs!"

Nurinyan's jaw tensed, and he bared his teeth. His ears turned red.

Amaya watched his reaction build. With such a vital meeting impending, she needed him to show the "grace under pressure" that humans valued. If he could get that riled up by a simple insult, she'd have to consider a trade with another station for the duration. Finding another martial arts specialist who spoke English would be tough in such a short time.

Gradually, the tension in his jaw faded. "Isn't she nice?"

Good. Amaya smiled and clapped his shoulder. "There will always be detractors."

When the traffic was clear, Amaya jogged across the street with Nurinyan close behind. She kept her voice low to avoid carrying to any listening ears on the other side of the fence. "It's hard to blame them. We hid in our enclaves for centuries. That generated distrust. Many humans fear what they don't understand."

"Yeah, but there was a reason to stay in the enclaves." Nurinyan shielded his eyes with his hand and stared down the street.

"True, and I don't think we had much choice, really, but now we must work to correct that distrust." She checked the lock on the gate. The chainlink fence surrounding the site had pieces of plywood bolted to it, blocking visibility into the area. It was still secured and intact, which meant little. Avicopters and helicopters could land inside, and this fence would not be hard to climb over. "America is dealing with many issues of equality even within their own species, so we should not be surprised to see their misunderstandings aimed at us as well."

"At least the police have accepted us." He pointed to the black-and-white rolling toward them.

The car stopped a few feet away. Mark Hollis and Robert Kirby slid out.

Amaya smiled and waved them over. Ever since their joint effort to capture Wylin Leonan, she'd grown close to those two. Mark's eyes were heavy-lidded and the skin below them looked darker. His newborn must have been interfering with his sleep. That would pass.

Robert, on the other hand, had a bounce in his step and a brilliant smile. Once they settled the matter of where the noises came from, she'd have to ask him how his jazz band audition had gone. She'd never heard him play any instruments but the rumor mill at LPPD said he was particularly skilled.

"Anything?" Mark put his hat on as he joined them.

"All quiet." Nurinyan nodded toward the construction site and spoke in English. "Dis is de place?" His accent was still dense in English, but fortunately, most of the human officers didn't appear to struggle with it.

"Yep." Mark nodded and checked his watch. "Twenty minutes before the owner can get here with a key, though."

Nurinyan looked at the eight-foot chainlink fence and snorted. "Dis fence? Not even a challenge." He took a step in that direction and reached upward.

He was still very "ready, fire, aim." Would he ever learn caution? Amaya pressed her hand on his shoulder. "Are you not the same person who doesn't think we're in the right place?"

He looked over his shoulder at her. "We will not find out standing here."

"There's no cause to enter the property yet." Amaya pulled him back. Not for the first time, she wondered if she should contact the training center and delay his promotion. She needed him to become a full *kiandara*, but was he really ready for that?

For that matter, had she been ready for hers? He couldn't stay a student forever. She leaned closer to him. "Even the witness wasn't sure the avicopter landed in the construction site. We didn't see it from the air."

"Yes, but dere was dat big shed." He pointed toward that corner of the site. "You can hide at least one avi in dere."

A loud clack and a rumble like a metal garage door echoed off the half-finished structures inside the fence. Amaya turned toward the construction site and tipped her head to one side, listening for the next sound.

Nurinyan shrugged away from her. "Now we have cause." He reached for the fence.

"Wait!" Robert kept his voice down but took a step toward him.

Amaya darted forward and caught Nurinyan by the collar the moment his knees bent for a jump. Nurinyan grabbed at his throat and stumbled back into her. She caught him, set him back on his feet, and whirled him around to face her, glaring while he coughed and rubbed his neck.

She spoke Eshuvani and pitched her voice into a range only rare humans heard. "If I have to put three darts in your hide to keep you from doing something fatally stupid, do not think for half a second that I will refrain. Do you understand me?"

"I'm sorry, Amaya, but I don't stand around and do nothing well." He pressed his fist to forehead. "Obviously there's something going on in there."

"Cultivate patience." She mimed thwacking his ear. "Show me that you're really ready to graduate."

He winced. "I'm sorry. I know better. Darting in there might get me, you, or one of the humans killed. I will do better."

"You must. You are much more interesting alive than dead. I don't want to assign you to permanent dispatch duty, but if that's the only way to keep you alive, I will. Now, stay here."

"But–"

She let her scowl speak for her.

He slumped. "Right."

Amaya jumped and caught the top edge of the plywood. She pulled herself up just far enough to see over and hung there by her fingers. The half-constructed building inside consisted of a skeletal framework and the beginning of walls on two sides. A small red and white shed sat off in the corner, some fifty strides away and far removed from the main construction area. The door, the sort that rolled upward into the ceiling space, was wide open, and a length of heavy chain was piled on the ground. The other, larger shed they'd seen from the air was blocked by the main construction.

She dropped back to the ground and relayed her findings to the others.

Robert's tie flapped in the breeze as he looked toward the corner where the shed was. "That's probably where they keep harsh chemicals." His Mexican accent, inherited from his mother, was more a matter of cadence than pronunciation. It became more obvious when he spoke softly.

"Explosives?" Nurinyan shot a glance that direction.

Robert shook his head. "Not likely in town, but a little creative chemistry could concoct something."

Mark drew a breath between his teeth. "We could be in for a wild time." He checked the bulky, square watch on his wrist. "Still a quarter-hour until the owner's expected, and if they have an avicopter in there ..."

"There's no way we'd catch them in the cargo hauler." Amaya sighed and looked first at Nurinyan, then at their avicopter. If only she could be sure he'd follow her lead and not his "instincts." "The noise in what's supposed to be an empty construction site at this time of day is sufficient cause for *kiandarai* to check it out. We can fly all four of us over the fence in the avicopter."

Mark shook his head. "Really a gray area. We should wait for the owner."

As much as she understood his protocols, that plan risked the possibility of dangerous criminals getting away with the chemicals to make something obnoxious. With the impending conference, that would never do. She nodded once. "I understand. I'll check it out and report back." She fixed a stern look on Nurinyan.

"No, I am not keen on dispatch duty for life." He pressed his fist to his forehead. "I will show de proper professional discipline."

"Stealth is the key right now. We don't know how many there are." She pointed to the fence. "The avicopter's engines would be heard, so we're going up and over. Be mindful of your landing."

"Message received."

Noises of cracking boards and grunts came from the shed.

Amaya jumped and caught the top of the plywood again. The chainlink fence rattled some, but not as badly as she'd expected. She hauled herself up and over, then hung by her fingers for a few seconds before landing on the other side with a slight crunch of the gravel.

Nurinyan planted one hand on the top of the fence and tried to vault over but caught his foot on the top. He landed face down with a loud thud and a much heavier crunch of gravel.

Amaya cringed. So much for stealth.

## Two

She darted back to him and rested a hand on his shoulder. "Are you hurt?"

"Yes." He spoke in Eshuvani through his clenched teeth and squeezed his eyes closed. "Hurt my knee, and I feel like I'm going to be sick."

Amaya winced. That was probably a broken bone somewhere in or near his knee.

A barely audible comm system chimed from within the shed. "*Kiandarai* closing ... out of there!"

"I can't find ... I don't think it's in here," a man's voice replied.

"Plan Two will do the job. Move it!"

Amaya thumbed the start-up switch on her pistol. It whined through the power-on self-test.

An Eshuvani man of average height, dark hair, and pale eyes ran out of the smaller shed and headed for the larger blue one. Amaya led the target and fired. The first shot went off clean and struck the man in the wrist. She led the target again.

Nurinyan pushed her shoulder, wrecking the aim of her second shot. "Go. I am not going anywhere."

The suspect turned the corner and disappeared behind the partially constructed building.

Amaya growled, pushed off from the ground, and ran after him. An avicopter wound up in the distance. She ran through the open part of the building toward the larger shed. A blue and yellow, four-seater avicopter flew out. The passenger door swung open. The suspect's right arm hung limp from the shoulder. He was only a few strides away from the avicopter, definitely too far ahead for her to catch. She slowed, increased the shot power to her gun, and took quick aim.

She squeezed the trigger twice, and the darts flew. He caught the edge of the door frame as the first shot struck his thigh. The second slammed into the door when it swung into the dart's path. Another passenger hauled him onboard as the avicopter climbed at a dizzying pace.

Amaya groaned. She could still hit him at that distance, but what good would it do? If he fell from that height, he might not survive. If his friends kept him in the avi, she would have just wasted a shot. She powered down her gun and returned it to the holster. At least they hadn't found what they were looking for.

As the avi turned, she squinted into the sunlight and tried to read the ID numbers on the tail. Nothing. They'd either been painted over or removed. Most likely, the avi had been stolen.

She wiped perspiration from her forehead and jogged back to Nurinyan. He lay on his left side and clutched his right knee. He quivered as he rocked back and forth. His face was scrunched up in a pained grimace. This was the consequence for the exuberance of youth. She squelched her annoyance. Wisdom came from experience, mostly bad experience. She'd made more than a few errors in her youth, too, but at this rate, he would become one of the wisest people she knew.

Amaya crouched beside him. In addition to whatever had happened to his knee, scrapes marred his face and hands. "All right. Let's have a look at your knee. You might have broken it, so don't try to move it." Amaya slid off her backpack, took out her transdermal viewer, and flicked the power switch.

"Amaya, what's going on over there?" Mark peeked through a gap in the fence boards barely wide enough to reveal his eye and a sliver of his face.

"Suspects escaped in an unmarked blue and yellow avi. Nurinyan's down. After I've treated him, I'll check the shed."

"Right. Still waiting on the key over here." Robert, the more athletic of the pair, did a chin-up and looked over the top of the fence.

Amaya glanced toward the shed. "No hurry now."

The viewer chimed to indicate its readiness. She picked it up and scanned Nurinyan's leg, changing the viewing depth as she completed each pass. The tendons looked good, so did the ligaments. One particular bone, however, showed a small but distinct crack.

"You must have landed directly on your knee. There's a crack in the patella." She set the viewer aside. "You're fortunate you didn't break something more severely."

Nurinyan groaned. "Still not what I needed."

She bit her lip to avoid chastising him. His carelessness had caught him this time, but she made a policy of never hitting a man when he was down.

"Umhm." She pulled out a pouch of regenerative salve and an applicator. "The good news is, the break is simple, so I don't need to set it."

"And the bad news?" He squeezed his eyes closed.

"You're out of active duty until tomorrow at this time."

He slumped. "I was afraid you were going to say you were planning to write me up for discipline."

"Because you tripped?" She smiled. "Even I'm not that harsh. Keep your knee at just that angle." Amaya unsnapped the seam of his pants and dug a pair of plastic gloves from the side pocket of her backpack. Although there was some elasticity to the gloves, they squeezed her fingers uncomfortably. Still, that was better than accidental contact with the regeneration gel. She did not need another bout of anaphylactic shock any time in her remaining lifespan.

After tugging her shears off her belt, she snipped the corner of the gel packet off and dipped the scoop-like applicator into the bag of gel. She slathered the clear goo on Nurinyan's knee. It sank into his skin. The pained look on his face faded. She picked up the scanner again and checked the progress of the repair. The crack narrowed and gradually faded.

Amaya turned off the viewer and slipped it back into her kit before pulling out a sterile water pack and a piece of gauze. She cleaned out the scrapes and applied the remnants of the gel to the worst of them. "The rest of your injuries are minor, and you'll have to wait until tomorrow to use more gel." She stood and spoke English. "Mark, Robert,

33

Nurinyan's injuries are healing. I'm going to check the shed."

"Be careful in there," Mark called.

"Always." She shouldered her backpack and started for the small shed, keeping her pace slow enough to be fully aware of her surroundings. The avicopter might have left, but that didn't mean they were alone in here. Aside from a couple mockingbirds, a seagull, and a male grackle, the site didn't appear to be occupied.

As she came closer to the buildings, the loose gravel became compacted and packed hard into the pale tan, clay-ladened dirt. Heavy vehicle tracks marred the surface. When she reached the shed, she leaned against the side used the flat of her knife as an impromptu periscope. She didn't expect to find occupants, but checking was safer than assuming.

When the reflection showed her nothing but wooden crates stacked two deep and four high around the perimeter, she sheathed the knife and slipped into the shed. "Ceramic tile" was printed on the crates's labels along with lot numbers and colors. The few crates that were open verified that contents were as described. If Robert had guessed the purpose of the blue and gold avicopter's occupants, they'd made an unfortunate error in their assumptions. That might have been good news, except for the mention of a backup plan.

Amaya jogged back to Nurinyan.

Ω

Amaya flew the avi over the station. Below her, the arrangement of houses forming a half-circle behind the main building gave the appearance of an eye and eyebrow. Orinyay had the largest house closest to the hangar. Normally, Amaya would have been there because of her rank, but Orinyay had a family. She needed the extra space, and Amaya was quite comfortable with less. Ishe was directly opposite, furthest from the hangar. Amaya spotted her own house almost directly behind the center of the station. She preferred that location for its easy access to the main building. Nurinyan and Jevon had the two spots between her house and Orinyay's, and that left Vadin the one between Amaya and Ishe.

She landed the avi in the hangar and climbed down. After slinging her backpack over her shoulder, she jogged around to the other side. Nurinyan opened the door and slid out, landing on his left leg. He took a tentative step forward and grimaced.

Was he seeking more wisdom? Amaya offered her arm. "Don't be too ambitious. You did break your kneecap."

"It's a little stiff. That's all." He leaned on her and hobbled.

"I'll help you to your quarters." She couldn't get him past the living room, but that'd be a good start. Vadin or Jevon could help him to his room later.

"Really, it doesn't hurt. Not half of what it did earlier."

"Umhm, and if you're too ambitious, you'll be out a week instead of a day. I'm going to need you before then."

He sighed. "True enough."

She helped him limp down the long hall that connected the hangar to the entryway.

The door into the briefing room was on the left, exactly opposite the foyer. Straight ahead, the kitchen. Beyond the briefing room, another hallway led to the storeroom and the back door that opened into a yard between the station and the individual houses. A separate corridor led from the foyer past the front of the kitchen to the infirmary — hardly more than storage for first aid supplies at the moment — and holding cells, empty for now.

Vadin jumped up from the dispatch desk and leaned on the half-wall that separated the foyer from the corridor leading to the hangar. His pale complexion came from his lack of time outdoors. His erect, almost stiff-looking posture accentuated his height, already most of six-and-a-half feet tall. "What happened?" When he spoke, each word was distinct with final consonants over-pronounced.

Even without knowing his background, she would have concluded he was much higher born than average.

Nurinyan sighed. "I tripped and banged my knee."

Amaya set her pack by the wall. "You'll be fine by this time tomorrow, if you take care of yourself today. Vadin, you'll be with me on calls until Nurinyan recovers."

"Yeah, okay." The slang sounded unnatural in his speech, a forced effort to fit in. Vadin slid his shoulder under Nurinyan's other arm. "How about I put him in bed?"

Nurinyan frowned. "Am I that pitiful?"

Amaya waited until Nurinyan had transferred his weight before stepping away. "Yes, until this time tomorrow, if you rest."

"Fine." Nurinyan rolled his eyes.

"Just think of it as an opportunity to catch up on your reading." She gripped his shoulder and accompanied them as far as the dispatch desk in the foyer. She'd have to work dispatch until Vadin returned. A welcome change of pace from constantly going out on calls.

As they wobbled off down the back hall, a well-tuned avi's engine thrummed ever closer. Who would that be? Located in the middle of the eastern Buffer Zone between Woran Oldue and Las Palomas, Hawk's Nest station rarely received visitors in person. Amaya beelined to the window. A blue and gold avi, a much newer and sleeker model than the one she'd seen at the construction site, settled in on its landing struts in front of the station. Markings on the side showed the heraldry for one of the noble houses, but Amaya didn't know enough to tell which.

Could that be Rinyulin Tolu *Tura*, the Eshuvani baron who would be meeting with the human governors? If so, he was ridiculously early, or she'd been given the wrong date. No, it couldn't be the *tura*. Even if she had been given the wrong date, the *tura* was coming with his family, and that avi wasn't half big enough for the *tura*, wife and kids, a pilot, and whatever entourage he traveled with.

She blew out a long breath and rubbed the back of her neck. Amaya pressed one of the blue crystals in her collar tab and started Pavwin's code but stopped and tapped the cancel. There wasn't much he could do to help.

The blue and gold avi tucked in its wings and shut off. Both the doors opened, and the pilot stepped out. Short hair framed an angular face. He wore a pale blue uniform and carried a pistol on his belt, but his stiff posture wasn't the same as Vadin's well-trained erect stance. The pilot was more likely closer to her own social rank and trying to fit in with the expectations of his job. The unnatural tension would slow his response to any threat. Was he all show and no function? New? Untrained? Deliberately camouflaging his ability?

A shorter, older man exited from the passenger compartment. He wore his gray hair longer and bound back into a tail, after the fashion in vogue some twenty years past. His uniform was similar to the pilot's, but the elderly man carried no obvious weapons. She knew better than to assume he was unarmed. Unlike the pilot, the elderly man's board-straight posture was natural for him. There was ease in his mannerisms, not forced rigidity.

The younger man fell into step behind the elder. Amaya triggered the door as the pair drew near. The pilot entered, backed out, and followed the elderly man in. Amaya bowed her head and turned both hands toward her visitors. Her stomach felt emptier than the void of space.

"Grace be unto you, *Kiand*." Like Vadin, the final consonants in his words were over-pronounced. The older man stepped far enough inside to allow the pilot a space.

"And peace, from God, the Father of our Lord. I am Amaya Ulonya *Kiand*." She looked up, first at the pilot then at the older man. "How may I serve?"

"I am Halyuwin Cavera, secretary for His Transcendence, Rinyulin Tolu *Tura*. I have come to see the status of your meeting facilities and advise improvements as necessary." He tugged off a pair of pale gloves and tucked them over his belt.

The *tura's* secretary had come all the way from the panhandle to tour the station? Must be nice to have that much spare time in the day. Apparently having the money of a small country at one's disposal changed priorities. Where was Vadin? More than ever, she could use his expertise. He'd grown up in the blazing light of nobility. She wasn't even sure how to address such a person.

Amaya arched an eyebrow. "Meeting facilities?" If they were holding the conference right here at Hawk's Nest, that might have been nice to know sooner.

He squinted. "Have you not been informed of the impending coordination meeting among His Transcendence and the three human governors?"

He might be surprised to know how little she knew about the coming events. Just getting Emyrin to let them know who was on the guest list had been a huge challenge. She took a half step back and sublimated her annoyance with Emyrin before it could show in her face. "The meeting, I was aware of, as well as the need to provide protection for His Transcendence and his family for all events in the Buffer Zone and Las Palomas. I was not aware the meetings would be at *Uloniya Varoosht.*"

"Curious." His eyes narrowed. "I was assured you had been informed. Well, this is neutral territory. Where better?"

Behind him, the pilot smirked and looked around.

Yes, she was well aware of what the station looked like. Amaya nodded. "Of course." This had to be Emyrin's doing. Had he deliberately staged the conference here without telling her? To what end? He had to know she wasn't equipped for onsite security. Emyrin had, after all, purchased her station's materials and staffed it before her arrival. Why then send nobility here?

Her empty stomach churned. Surely, her superior wasn't in on some nefarious plot against the *tura.* The governors, maybe, but not their own nobility. She'd have to tell Pavwin. Yes, Emyrin had only charged him with security in Woran Oldue, but his station was actually equipped properly. Between them, they had to figure out something. Would it be appropriate to warn Halyuwin? Did one trouble the upper echelons with such trivialities as safety concerns?

Secretary Halyuwin frowned as he ran his hand along the scarred and battered wall paneling. "Is this a particularly old station, *Kiand*?"

"No, built within the last month." He should have seen the exposed wiring, piles of sawdust, construction debris, and loose furniture pieces. She'd since made considerable strides toward updates through creative engineering. At least the wiring was tucked away, and the junk had been carted to waste disposal centers.

He grimaced at his fingers then brushed his hands off. "It's rather rustic, isn't it?"

Surely, he meant run-down, dilapidated, and unimpressive. "There was a need to get the station online as quickly as possible." Enough about this disaster. She needed to know more about the impending one. "What will His Transcendence require for these negotiations?"

He huffed. "A room with sufficient accommodations for the gentlemen to meet, of course, and some manner of lounge for the ladies and children." Halyuwin walked past her and pressed his hand against a wobbly chair whose padding had long since dry-rotted away. "Naturally, you'll want some means of detecting intruders before they become a threat. As for meals, His Transcendence will take morning and evening meals at his hotel, but midday meals will be here."

So, had Emyrin planned to inform her before or after the meetings? She turned toward the kitchen and frowned. Before returning her attention to the secretary, she forced a more amicable expression onto her face. "I'll show you what's available." But in all sincerity, they'd do better somewhere else.

The back door squeaked open and closed. A few moments later, Vadin entered the foyer and rushed to the secretary, never once losing the straight-spined posture. They clasped right arms and embraced. "Halyuwin, such a wonderful blessing to see you!"

The pilot shifted his weight and pointedly avoided watching the two.

"Vadin, I didn't realize you'd completed your apprenticeship." Halyuwin stepped back and looked Vadin over. "How are your parents? I haven't seen them in weeks."

"Very well, thank you. They're traveling abroad right now."

"Are you liking your new post?"

Vadin smiled. "The people are wonderful!"

"I'm glad." The secretary gripped Vadin's shoulder. "I won't keep you from your duties. If you can get word to your parents, let them know they've been missed. Serve with diligence."

Amaya watched the exchange and smiled. Vadin's social hierarchy specialization and his family's upper echelon connections would become even more valuable than she'd originally thought. In this case, Emyrin's attempted sabotage could serve her well.

Vadin returned to the desk and slid into the chair.

Halyuwin caught the gaze of his pilot. "You may wait here." The man nodded and sat.

"Come with me, please." Amaya conducted the secretary to the briefing room. An assortment of chairs in various states of disrepair and a table made from cinder blocks and a piece of sanded and painted plywood were strategically arranged around the room. The plastic tubes containing the huge, rolled up maps of the area took up one corner.

His eyes narrowed. "And how well isolated is this room from distractions?"

"Not at all." Amaya stepped further into the room and turned back, pointing to the different locations. "From here, you can easily hear the hangar doors. You can also hear anything going on in the hallway and foyer. Likewise, anything spoken here above the level of casual conversation can be heard from the entryway and hallways."

His frown deepened as he inspected the chairs, makeshift table, and repaired park benches. "Well, it will serve for the ladies and children. The negotiations will need more privacy, though."

In a functioning station? That might be too much to hope for, but there was one small possibility. "There's the safe room, but it is considerably smaller. I'll show you that next."

He gestured with a sweep of his hand. "After you."

Amaya led him out to the entryway and down the back hall, through the storeroom to what looked like a part of the wall. She passed her hand over a section of the wall, then returned to the door they'd just come through. After moving a plastic storage box aside, she tapped a pattern five centimeters above an x she'd drawn there. A wall panel at the far end of the room slid open.

She followed the secretary through into the safe room. With reinforced concrete walls, floor, and ceiling, it was built to withstand anything short of nuclear detonation. "This room is soundproof and can be secured."

Halyuwin surveyed the empty, undecorated room no larger than the storeroom itself. "With four suitable chairs and a table big enough for all or smaller tables for each, this will serve, I suppose."

It'd have to work. Aside from meeting in someone's house, the only other options would be the holding cells, which were deliberately not private, or the infirmary, which might be needed for its primary function.

She led him out of the room, secured it, and walked back to the foyer with him. "And as regards meals?"

Halyuwin peeked into the kitchen, no less rustic than the rest of the place. "Yes, well, of course, His Transcendence won't expect first tier accommodations but suitable for his station."

And if she hadn't grown up two millimeters above the poverty line, she might know what that meant. She prayed Vadin had a solid grasp on what they needed to know. She glanced his direction.

Behind Halyuwin, Vadin pivoted away from the computer and tapped his forehead.

The tension in her shoulders lightened some. Amaya nodded. "I'll take care of it."

"Excellent." Halyuwin smiled. "Is Vadin available to walk out with me?"

"Of course."

Once the door had closed behind Vadin and the secretary, Amaya perched on the dispatch desk and blew out a breath. "We needed this additional challenge?" She snatched up a notepad and jotted the list of requirements Halyuwin had given her and frowned. She pushed off from the desk. "The proximity alarm has to work."

She trotted to the storeroom and scanned the shelves. The blue emergency lights were stashed in a box stuffed in a corner. The plastic storage container next to them was labeled "proximity alarm." Amaya pulled it down and carried it to the entryway.

Vadin walked in, let the door close behind him, and leaned on it.

"That bad?" Amaya asked.

He winced. "He, uh, guessed you were not high-born."

Amaya chuckled. "True. Any lower and my family would be subterranean." Which had been ninety-five percent of the reason why she'd joined the *kiandarai* in the first place. "Did I do something wrong?"

"Yes." Vadin drew in a breath, held it, and blew it out again. "You gave him commands, changed the subject of conversation, and escorted him into new rooms improperly."

She smiled and raised her eyebrows. "All that? What should I have done differently?"

"Instead of, 'Come with me, please,' ask it as a question." He perched on the nearest chair. "'Would you like an introduction to the station?'"

She nodded. That slight change would be easy to manage. "And I'm not allowed to change the subject of a conversation?"

"Not with someone who outranks you. The choice of subject is his privilege." He stayed still and waited.

So now he was demonstrating that by waiting for his senior officer to change the topic. She needn't have worried about whether he could teach the rest of them. He was a natural. "And there's a right way to enter the room?"

"Yes." He smiled and nodded. "The lower ranked person steps in first to make sure the room is safe and acceptable then backs out to let the higher ranked person enter."

So that was why the pilot and walked in, backed out, then followed the secretary in. She mentally compared what she had done to the expected behavior. "So, overall, I was too assertive and not sufficiently deferential."

"Correct."

Vadin looked away from her. "Halyuwin wanted to know if I had enough rank to take over preparations for the meetings here."

Was he kidding? She'd been half a heartbeat away from assigning the task to him. She sat in the chair next to his and pulled him into a one-armed embrace. "You don't need rank. You need willingness. Understanding how to deal with the entire social hierarchy is your specialization, after all. Are you up for it?"

He nodded. "Sure. At least, I think so."

"Then I'll let you. That'll leave me with site security here and in Las Palomas." The security at the museum in particular would be a challenge since it was clearly a human establishment. They wouldn't recognize her authority. She walked over to the box, opened it, and rummaged through the old parts and frayed wires.

Vadin joined her and leaned over the box. "Nurinyan and Jevon are better than either of us at electronics, and Nurinyan wanted something to do."

That should keep him from reinjuring his knee before tomorrow. "He could do the initial rewiring safely in a seated position. Take this to him, and I'll get what wire we have."

She handed the container to Vadin and headed for the storeroom.

Ω

Deep within Woran Oldue, Teviya secured the front door of the *kiat's* headquarters. She drew the curtain made of curled strips of kelp-colored cloth across the entire front entrance and called out for the windows to darken. They went nearly black, which triggered the automatic lighting system. Like the corridor down to Emyrin's office, the blue and green colored blobs swirled around the room. Not exactly the ocean feel of the rest of the décor, but it was cute.

Her spike-heeled shoes clicked on the resin-enclosed sand of the floor as she strutted back to her desk and opened the largest drawer. The secret compartment occupying the back third of the desk would need her key. Her dress today, brilliant blue with white lace to represent a cresting wave, had no pockets. She looked around her desk. Where had she put the key this morning? She really needed to find a consistent hiding place for days when she didn't have a pocket to tuck it into. She moved the pencil caddy, human-style telephone, and a photo of her and her hairdresser before she found it under a paperweight made of a glass-encased sea urchin.

Teviya smiled. She pressed the key against the lock and waited for it to click. The latch popped open, and the lid slid out of the way. She pulled out the communication system, untraceable and more robust than anything a typical *kiandarai* station would have, and put it in the middle of the desk.

Down the long hall, the lock for the back door clicked and beeped, signaling she was safe for her last task of the day as Emyrin's secretary. She tapped a code into her communication console then tapped the ID number for the team leader. The relay clicked again and again without answer.

"Come on, you moron. Answer the call," she muttered. To this day, she couldn't figure out why Emyrin insisted on using hoodlums. There were plenty of competent, skilled Eshuvani citizens who would have happily helped with this first step in removing the human control rod in the reactor of Eshuvani greatness.

Emyrin joined her and perched on the edge of the desk.

Her eyes narrowed. Really? Did he have to park his rear on the surface where she worked and ate her lunch? Were there no perfectly good chairs to be had? Teviya dismissed her irritation. That quirk of his annoyed her, but really, was it that important? She cleaned her desk with disinfectant daily in part because he mistook it for a chair.

"Yeah." The voice matched the team's leader, but he didn't usually sound so winded.

"You really should keep those collar tabs with you. They're designed to attach to your collar." Teviya inspected her fingernails, decorated with blue paint and fine, white lace to match her ocean wave-inspired dress.

"Uh-huh, and some of the tasks I do in a day react very badly to radio frequencies. Get to your point." His already deep voice dropped a couple more pitches. "We're not just sitting out here anxiously awaiting your call."

She turned her harsh look toward the idiot on the other end of the communicator and the annoying power drain Emyrin had recruited to "help" before drawing a deeper breath.

Emyrin's firm hand landed on her shoulder. He shook his head.

Teviya rolled her eyes and contained the very direct answer coming to her mind. "Did you get what we needed?"

"No." The team leader snorted. "There was none on the site."

"What? There should have been plenty." Teviya leaned closer to the mic.

"The bigger building was all tools and small vehicles. The smaller was flat, square ceramic pieces. There was nothing we needed. Then the *kiandarai* showed up and we had to leave in a hurry. As it was, they almost got one of us."

She shook her head and struck her forehead with her palm. "Then you'll have to find another site and try again."

"We've got a better option," he said.

"A better option?" She squinted at the speaker. He'd been such a fountain of enlightened ideas already.

"Yeah, a better option. Just you remember who's on this team and what we're each good at." He snorted and spoke so softly his voice almost disappeared under the wind. "Unless, of course, you want me to broadcast the details over the comm system."

She frowned. "No, of course not." The system was supposed to be perfectly secure, but some local *kiandarai* were reputed wizards at sorting out tricky electronics problems.

"Then stop interrupting us. We have a lot to do."

The connection went dead.

Teviya huffed and shook her head. "Who does he think he is?" She reached for the console to code in the collar tabs again.

Emyrin massaged her shoulder. "Let it go. They're a tool to achieve a goal, nothing more."

The firm waves of pressure released the tension that always built up when she had to deal with the hoodlum brigade he'd recruited. She closed her eyes and smiled. He could do that for hours, and it wouldn't be too much.

She toggled the button on the comm equipment and put it back in its hiding place.

Some day after these buffoons had served their purpose, they'd be the next to go. Humans first, morons second, then the best of the Eshuvani would recover the glory lost when the generation ship had crashed here. Teviya only hoped it happened in her lifetime. Unlike Emyrin, she wasn't content with re-creating the Eshuvani technology for their children's generation.

Teviya brushed all that aside. She patted his hand and stood. "Ready to go?"

"How about the Blue Snail tonight?" Emyrin offered his hand.

That dive again? Fine. They did make a Crab Duel on the Beach that was fairly palatable and beautifully presented. "Perfect!" Teviya entwined her fingers with his and leaned on his shoulder. Her heels clicked on the resin floor all the way to Emyrin's newest silver and red avicopter behind his office.

$$\Omega$$

In the days after Halyuwin's visit, Nurinyan had rewired the sensors while Jevon had worked on the main control system. It should be working, at least that's what all the diagnostics had said. If the actual defense of their guests was going to fall on him as the martial arts specialist, he wanted as much advance notice as he could get.

With the sun beating down on him, Nurinyan pinched the clip for the proximity alarm's sensor and secured it to a convenient juniper branch. He glowered at the sensor. "Stay there until we're done with our test." He stood and wiped the sweat from his brow. Next time, he would get to stay inside and watch the lights. Jevon could come out here and get baked. Nurinyan had no doubt that he'd been volunteered to place the sensors as some sort of vengeance for their old rivalry. They'd been in the same classes, taken an interest in the same gal — who'd wanted nothing to do with either of them — and vied for the same apprenticeships. Now they were at the same station. Sometimes he wondered how much Amaya knew of their old rivalries. That first night at the station, she had noticed the friction between them and issued her warning. They had to be pros, seek other stations, or get ready for discipline and retraining. So far, none of that had been necessary.

Nurinyan turned toward the station and tapped Jevon's code on a dark blue crystal.

"Jevon."

"Nurinyan. The sensor's in place." He stared at the sensor and dared the clip to let loose.

Jevon growled. "Well, I knew it couldn't be that easy. You're not triggering it."

Nurinyan walked several strides away from the station. "Maybe I stayed too close after I turned it on. I've backed off. I'll walk past it now."

When he walked past another juniper, a small, gray rabbit darted out from under the shrub and sped past the sensor. Nurinyan skittered back a few steps and shook his head.

"Blue light!" Jevon exclaimed.

If only it were that easy. Nurinyan frowned. "No good. That was a rabbit, not me."

"A rabbit?" Jevon muttered something impolite under his breath. "That thing registered a rabbit?"

He leaned aside and spotted the beady little eyes staring at him from under the edge of another shrub. "Yep. Cute little critter I spooked out of a bush."

Jevon growled. "Would taste great barbecued. We can't have this thing reacting to wildlife."

"We'd spend half our days chasing birds and squirrels."

Amaya would be thrilled. If they couldn't make this work, she undoubtedly had some no-tech solution to teach them from around the turn of the last century when she'd gone through training. If they ever figured out how to time travel some sixty years back, they'd just about blend in now.

"All right." Jevon hit something hollow-sounding. "Bring it back in. We'll have to see if we can adjust it."

"Message received." Nurinyan retrieved the senor and headed inside. The dry grass and last fall's leaves crunched under his boots.

His first stop would be the kitchen. A pitcher of water had his name on it.

Three

Vadin snatched up his clipboard. With practiced ease, he positioned it at exactly ninety degrees to his forearm and stepped outside his house. This early in the morning, the cool breeze off the coast held the ungodly summer temperature at bay. He stretched and drew in a deep breath of sea air while a nearby mockingbird went through a litany of different bird calls.

Texas had such a grand assortment of birds. He smiled at the one perched on top of the station. Vadin crossed the dry grass to the rear door of the station and entered. The hallway's overhead lighting was dark, but enough light filtered in from the clear windows in the foyer for him to see his way. He ran his hand along the wooden wall, careful not to round his shoulder forward, and noted the smooth and ridged alternating panels. True, this place wasn't as nicely appointed as the garden shed at his parent's home, but some day it might be. Until then, he had a place to live and a useful job to do. Until his coursework for his specialization had introduced him to the opposite end of the social spectrum, he would never have appreciated this.

In the foyer, Nurinyan and Jevon crouched next to an open, plastic crate and sorted electronic parts on the floor around them. Nurinyan, the only blonde in their group, was pale enough to pass for high-born, but the way he carried himself was sloppy. Jevon, the second oldest of the *kialai*, was worse. As he dug through the box, his back and shoulders were so rounded, he looked short, in spite of being the tallest at the station. Amaya stood nearby and watched. Her tanned complexion confirmed what he'd known from the start: her family was peasantry. Still, she'd made full *kiandara* by the time she'd been Vadin's age and blew through that to *kiand* some forty-five years ago. If they ever got past the current crisis and she resumed her coursework, she'd be one of the youngest *kiati* ever. What she lacked in social standing, she made up for in ambition.

Jevon looked up at Amaya and grinned. "As near as I can tell, all the parts are here."

"Excellent." She twisted around to Ishe at the dispatch desk. "Pavwin said this was a gift from Wolf's Teeth?"

Although Ishe's family was middle class, she had a complexion worthy of peasants and a posture worthy of nobility. She wore eye makeup, red today, almost too bright to fit within the protocol. With her weight, if working for the *kiandarai* didn't work out, she would have no trouble finding work as a model. "Umhm. He said he'd been out there checking in with a specialist they have of some kind about something or other." Ishe rolled her eyes. "He was almost that detailed in his explanation, but anyway, while he was there, they were installing and testing a new perimeter alarm for their station, and they were going to junk the old one, but Pavwin mentioned that ours was going off for wildlife. Not sure how he knew about that—"

Amaya smiled. "I posted a request for troubleshooting assistance when ours misbehaved."

"Oh." Ishe shrugged. "Well, anyway, he asked if they'd be willing to send their old system to us, and they said, 'Sure!' So Pavwin dropped it off on the way home. Nice, huh?"

Vaden smirked. And so the other *kiandarai* stations had thwarted yet another of Emyrin's efforts to weaken *Uloniya Varoosht*. Nurinyan picked up a part and inspected it. "He didn't happen to say what was wrong with this system that it needed replacing?"

Ishe nodded. "He sure did. No image projection."

Vadin joined them and looked over Nurinyan's shoulder at all the parts. "So, it'll change our lights blue but it won't give us a hologram for what it's seeing." That was handy, but was it really necessary? Proximity alarms had only added hologram projectors for common use about twenty years ago. Nobility had access to it not quite a decade before. He'd been thirty when Dad had purchased the first projectors for their house.

Jevon glanced around at all the equipment and frowned. "Yep, that's what's missing."

"Combine the image projection from our current system with this one, perhaps?" Amaya suggested. She picked up one of the sensors and inspected it from all angles, smiling as if she'd encountered an old memento. What sort of interesting caper had she been involved in that had used an old proximity system?

"I'll try to rig that, but I don't think the tech is compatible." Jevon studied a large box and tapped each input and output port.

Vadin had no idea which one did what. Dad had always hired maintenance work done.

A gray and white courier avicopter landed outside.

"Don't lose sleep for it. If this system forgoes informing us of the odd rabbit or deer, it's a lot better than we had." Amaya stood and arched her back. "I'll retrain everyone on the pre-hologram protocols, if necessary."

Vadin rocked forward and backward on his feet, absorbing all the movement in his knees so his upper body didn't move. He always looked forward to Amaya's vintage protocol lessons. Accomplishing tasks with technology was easy. Using brain and braun was unfamiliar, exciting territory.

Amaya leaned over and gripped Nurinyan's shoulder. "Your ride's here. You'd better get to your test."

Oh, yeah. He was headed for his final assessments. If he passed, he'd be a full *kiandara*, and Vadin would start learning field work from Amaya, a prospect he both anticipated and dreaded. He knew Amaya had to walk him through his field work and teach him the practical side of the job, but he didn't feel ready. Not yet. There was too much he didn't know, but that was the point of the training, wasn't it?

Nurinyan looked at his watch, and his eyes widened. "Oh, right. Wish me wisdom."

Vadin waved. "God grant it to you in abundance."

Nurinyan darted out. The door slid closed behind him.

"So, um, he's going to pass. You know that." Ishe leaned her elbow on the dispatch desk and her chin on her palm. "So, who's your next partner, Amaya?"

"Vadin." She pointed.

Ishe slumped and groaned. "When is it my turn?"

Vadin's gut clenched. Physically, he was only a few months older than Ishe, but emotionally, she acted younger than his little sister. Amaya had made no secret of her training plan from the beginning, and her patience approached absolute zero with unprofessionalism.

Amaya's eyes narrowed. "Two things must happen first. Vadin must graduate successfully, and you must demonstrate more professional maturity than that. When both of those things happen, you will begin your field training with me."

"Sorry." Ishe pressed her fist to her forehead and turned away. She brushed her eyes with her hand.

Vadin's chest ached in sympathy. Sure, he could understand Ishe's keen anticipation, but Amaya had set up the training plan deliberately. She hadn't steered them wrong yet, even when she'd been blinded by her grief. Was that really less than a month ago? It seemed so much longer.

"Forgiveness will be granted when I see the degree of your repentance," Amaya recited the standard acknowledgment for an apology. She leaned over and patted Jevon's shoulder. "See what you can do today about getting this system tested. If it's in good order, we'll need to get it installed and soon."

"If this was Wolf's Teeth's system until yesterday, it should be pretty straightforward." Jevon started gathering pieces. "I'll get on it."

Vadin crouched, set his clipboard aside, and helped pile the parts in the plastic crate. Amaya went to one knee and helped load, too. Some of the pieces were heavier than expected and others had hardly any mass to them at all. Once the last piece was stowed, Jevon flipped the lid closed and carried the crate out through the back door. Vadin stood and dusted his hands on his pants.

Amaya smiled. "Good morning! How does the day find you?"

He offered her a hand up. "Great. If you have a minute, I need to talk to you about food during the *tura*'s visit."

She accepted the offer but didn't lean on him much. Amaya pulled back the edge of her sleeve and looked at her watch. "I have about ten minutes before I need to leave for Falcon's Wing."

"That should be fine." He started for the briefing room.

"Amaya?" Ishe sniffled.

Amaya gestured toward the briefing room doors. "I'll join you in a moment, Vadin." She walked over to the dispatch desk and perched on the edge.

This was sounding like a private conversation. Vadin hustled into the other room.

"I guess I just get too–" Ishe began.

The doors slid shut behind Vadin, muffling the words.

He found a wooden chair to sit on. It had never been designed to have padding, and those were more comfortable than the ones that were supposed to have a cushion and didn't.

Going back through the notes, he verified that he had everything properly listed with the right grammar and syntax. This assignment was the first major task Amaya had given him, and he would rather cease to exist than let her find it subpar. That was silly, and he knew it. If Amaya were so hard to please, everyone except Orinyay would be gone by now. Everyone had erred terrifically at least once.

Vadin reached the end of his notes and flipped the papers down. The menu would be reasonable for His Transcendence, but would it also be acceptable for the governors?

The door slid open and Amaya entered. She flipped a chair around to face him and sat. "What do you have for me?" For someone as low-born as she was, she didn't slur her words as much as he might have expected. Her diction was still too faulty for the circle his family traveled in, but each word was clear.

He took a deep breath. She had to see the menu sooner or later. "My aunt is a caterer, and some of her frequent clients are at or above the *tura*'s level." He turned the clipboard so it faced her directly before handing it to her. "These are her recommendations for our menu. She recommended three courses per meal. A main course, soup or salad to follow, and a dessert of some kind. She isn't accustomed to cooking for humans, though, so we weren't sure if this would be acceptable for them."

"Logistically speaking, humans in this part of the world generally have the soup or salad prior to the main meal. To be accommodating, we may wish to alternate our own general practice with theirs." She flipped through his list. Her sole reaction was a raised eyebrow.

Was there a problem, or did she approve? The back of Vadin's neck tensed. "Is it okay?" She winced and looked through everything again, flipping the pages at a rate too fast to be reading them. "I really can't determine that from this. Do you have a translation?"

"To English?" Had she spent so much time with her *urushalon* that she struggled with their own language?

She smiled and shook her head. "To plain Eshuvani. My culinary language is not up to the necessary speed. Take this first day's lunch. Bird's Nest on Bark? Twig and Beetle Soup? Eggs in Snow? The only one that sounds edible is the last, and not terribly appetizing at that."

Vadin laughed and covered his mouth. She had said her family was barely above the poverty line. What did they consider special food? "I'm sorry. My coursework hasn't covered culinary differences yet. I assumed that this was common information."

"No, no, I'm afraid not." When she turned her chair to sit next to him, it creaked as she sat down again. Leaning forward, she held the clipboard where they could both see it. "It was only after I began working in the *kiandarai* that lunch, or dinner for that matter, consisted of more than a bowl of noodles or rice, beans or lentils, a few pieces of vegetables, and — only on rare occasions mind you — a few small pieces of meat or cheese. Often, we had the same meal most nights, but we were grateful enough that we were blessed with something to eat."

His jaw dropped open. Even the servants in his parents' house ate better than that. "Oh, well, Bird's Nest on Bark is shredded carrots and sweet peppers arranged on a piece of steak. It often has a spicy cream sauce. Twig and Beetle Soup has rice and mushrooms in a vegetable broth. Eggs in Snow are round pieces of fruit on ice cream."

Amaya sat more upright and set the clipboard in her lap. "That all sounds agreeable, but it'll be important to remember that humans in general, at least in the cultures around here, do not spice their food as much as we do. Sauces and spices may need to be available but not on their food." She scanned through the next day's menu and tapped the Pond Soup. "So, who will be cooking?"

"We thought you would do that." He squelched a chuckle and watched for her reaction. She would find it funny, wouldn't she?

She grinned and cast him a sideways look. "Not a good idea if we want this to be edible."

He snickered. "My aunt. We got my aunt."

"What does she expect in exchange for her service?"

"She wanted a genuine *kiandarai* antique at least fifty years old. She's a collector." And what a collection she had. Looking at — but never touching — her assortment of pieces had originally turned him on to the idea of becoming a *kiandara*. He nodded toward the foyer. "Ishe found an old box of Model Three pistol rounds in the bottom of a storage crate, a little dusty but in good condition. Orinyay looked it up, and those were–"

"Last used–" Amaya looked up at the corner of the room. "–fifty-eight years ago. I was there. Make sure they're neutralized before giving them to a civilian."

Vadin nodded. He should've remembered that Amaya had been in the *kiandarai* back then. "According to the protocol. My aunt was ecstatic. She already had a pistol and a maintenance kit. The darts were the last thing she needed to complete that set."

"Excellent." She checked her watch and frowned. "I'm out of time. If you could translate this for us low-born sorts, I'll verify the rest upon my return." She offered the clipboard without first turning it to face him.

Vadin took the clipboard without complaint about the unintended social gaffe. In his coursework, he'd learned that such meticulous detail was considered irrelevant among the low-born. He stood. "I'll have that done by the time you get back."

"Very good. Thank you for handling this." She checked her watch again and jogged out.

As soon as door latch clicked, Vadin allowed himself a moment to slump in his chair. Dad wouldn't be impressed by such a pathetic display, but after a few seconds of indulgence, Vadin straightened again and situated the clipboard at the proper angle to his arm before he strode to the storeroom to get some paper.

Ω

Amaya landed the courier in the lot next to Falcon's Wing. Since Orinyay would be handling the station's calls for the next few hours, Amaya had let her choose the avicopter she wanted to use. For some reason Amaya would likely never understand, Orinyay preferred the cargo hauler. Convenient, because that left Amaya with the courier. It had its faults, but she preferred how it handled.

The main structure of Falcon's Wing was built of natural stones set among a frame of heavy, wooden beams. The color was all wrong, but the texture brought back recollections of the mine and the death of her partner, her friend. She didn't know why he'd descended into that shaft alone by rope instead of using the lift, but at least she could acknowledge the choice had been his own. She hadn't ordered him, forced his choice, or encouraged such a foolhardy maneuver.

A momentary wave of sadness swept by her and left behind a memory of his smile. She marveled that, with the Rite of Final Memorial past, she could think of him without getting swamped by her grief.

Amaya powered down the avicopter and shouldered her backpack. The front door of the station slid open, and Pavwin stepped out. Until today, every time she'd seen him in the last month, he'd been completely hairless from the eyebrows up. Today, this bald head showed black stubble. Interesting. She'd thought the lack of hair had been a biological phenomenon, not a matter of choice.

As she stepped out of the avi, he ran his hand over the top of his head. "I thought I'd see if I preferred no hair to thin hair. I didn't."

She clasped his right arm and embraced him. "Fortunately, that's not a permanent change."

He chuckled and ushered her inside. "It'll be a while growing back out."

She smiled. "Less time for you at the barber." That reminded her. Her own hair was almost touching her collar. She'd once again have to decide if she would start wearing it up or go get it trimmed again. Her hair hadn't been longer than her collar in over fifty years. Given the heat in this part of the world most of the year, she'd probably continue the trend.

The inside of Falcon's Wing had been plastered and painted a pale blue. The dispatch desk was behind a wooden beam and stone half-wall. The well-polished, wooden furniture had been constructed in a simple, sturdy style, and all the pieces matched. The plaque near the door marked the Consecration Day a mere thirty years ago. Corridors led straight back from the foyer and off to both sides just like Hawk's Nest. Neat, black paint on white, wooden signs pointed the way to the hangar, storeroom, kitchen, medical ward, and jail. A door a few strides behind the dispatch desk was marked the briefing room.

The *kiandara* seated at the dispatch desk was a young man with blond hair and a pale complexion. His silver collar tabs showed a gray-blue stone surrounded by swirls of metal, an engineering specialist. He came over and gave her a quick embrace before returning to his station.

"You'll recognize the layout." Pavwin took in the room with a gesture. "The light switches and so on are much closer to the doors, however, and generally all in the same relative place."

Amaya walked further into the foyer. "Are all of the stations of Woran Oldue built on this floorplan?"

"Only the ones since Emyrin came on as *kiat*. The rest have more character." He turned one hand toward the ceiling and uncurled his fingers. "It's functional."

She glanced back at him. "Curious, considering the lavish decoration of his own office."

Pavwin nodded. "The funds for that had to come out of somewhere."

That made sense, actually. A *kiat* did have a free hand in allocating budgets. Most of the ones she knew, however, didn't spend so much on decorating their own offices.

"And using the same design for all the stations means he doesn't have to hire an architect to check over new plans." Amaya took a couple steps further in and looked around.

Reusing a functional design would save the Woran Oldue *kiandarai* a lot of money, but that raised other questions. Her own station budget required her to account for every part of the funds. Surely, the *kiat* was held to the same standard by the Council of the *Kiati*. How had Emyrin gotten away with misdirecting funds for so long? Cooking the books perhaps? Outright lying to the council? Allies in the council who turned a blind eye to his extravagance?

"Exactly." He led her to the briefing room. The door's proximity sensor opened the door as they approached, and he gestured her in ahead of him. "Two of my people are returning from a call, so we'll start the class when they join us. In the meantime, let's review what I found out about the mysterious collar tabs in your grieving criminal's possession."

Hardly a fortnight ago, the rescue mission to retrieve Ed's wife had taken them to Wylin's camp in the ruins of Woran Juvay. There, they'd found an old set of *kiandarai* collar tabs formerly registered to Orinyay, Amaya's own data analyst, which she'd reported missing long ago.

The briefing room door slid closed behind them. Although the size and shape of the room was identical to her own briefing room, the dark blue couches at the far wall and padded chairs clustered around sturdy wooden tables looked more inviting than the cobbled together mess in Hawk's Nest.

Perhaps the *tura* and the governors should be meeting here rather than in her own station. This might not be neutral territory, but it certainly had a more professional demeanor.

She descended the short run of steps and settled into one of the blue chairs around the wooden table. It didn't even wobble under her weight.

Pavwin flipped a chair around backwards and sat facing her. "There are five potentially false names, all with collar tabs that have recycled numbers from someone who reported a set missing. All five are *kiandarai* tabs."

Five sets? Did that mean they had at least four more adversaries? That couldn't be good. Wylin alone had killed one officer and endangered many others. If these other four were working together, the coming meeting would become a disaster on a scale equal to the Palm Sunday tornado outbreak in the Midwest.

"What do the records say for the potentially fake names?" Amaya folded her hands on the table.

"When I looked them up and the five people who reported lost collar tabs, the records all look normal. Apprenticeship and *kialai* training records are there. A history of stations. Some even have minor disciplinary issues." He glanced away and leaned closer. "Then there's this. Each of the ten — both the five who lost the tabs and the five with suspicious names — have a section of the file hidden by a coded block. For some, it's in the current assignment, and for others, it's in a past assignment."

Amaya shook her head and leaned back in the chair. "If they once served or are serving now in a special task force, then such a block would be expected, particularly if the task force had been involved in undercover work. Orinyay isn't in one now, but—"

He held up his hand to pause her. "That's what I first thought, too, but the block has a code. I went to Wolf's Teeth yesterday to speak to their personnel specialist. It's a 'training center administrative block.'"

She bit her lip and tipped her head to one side. Why would the training center block part of a record? "I don't understand."

He shook his head. "I don't either. I tried to inquire at the training center, but they told me that since the *kiandarai* in question weren't part of my station, the information would not be released to me. I didn't have 'valid reason.'"

"All right. I'll have to go. With Orinyay working at Hawk's Nest, I have a 'valid reason' to make the request." She tapped her fingertips together. "This is producing a peculiar odor."

"Extremely."

Amaya fished the collar tabs Ed had found in Wylin's tent out of her pocket and studied them before she set them on the table. "I only see two ways down this path. Someone with the authority to requisition a basic set of collar tabs is using deactivated numbers to equip criminals, or Orinyay and the others had their tabs lost or stolen by these criminals, but then how are they getting into secure areas to steal the tabs?" She pressed two of her dark blue crystals and recalled the potentially false name now assigned Orinyay's old collar tabs. "One potential way to find out."

"Dispatch."

"Amaya Ulonya *Kiand.* Please connect me through to Ianolin Simiala *Kiandara.*"

"One moment."

Amaya waited for the relay click, but the comm stayed silent. Her crystals glowed blue, so the connection hadn't closed.

"I apologize, *Kiand*, but Ianolin Simiala *Kiandara* is on a no-contact list." The tone of the dispatcher's voice matched the raised eyebrow on Pavwin's face, and the creases Amaya felt forming on her own brow.

She modulated her voice to show none of the suspicion in her thoughts. "Thank you for your diligence. Message received."

A click marked the end of the call as her blue crystals went dark.

"How terribly convenient." Amaya frowned. She should have known that finding "Ianolin Simiala," if he even existed in real life, wouldn't be that easy.

Pavwin ran his hand across the dark stubble on his head. "That raised more questions than it solved."

Amaya rose and paced away from the table. Worse than the no contact convenience was the potential safety hazard. "This could have something to do with the meetings here. Collar tabs would allow the criminals, if there are any others involved, to communicate during whatever they have planned."

Pavwin stayed seated but sat up straighter. "True, and whatever they had in the works, you have decreased their numbers by two: Wylin and his brother."

She tapped her finger on the holster of her pistol. "Maybe, but they have had enough time to reset their plans or even recruit other help." If these plans had been in the works since before she got here a month ago, elaborate arrangements with multiple levels of redundancy could be in effect. There was no other way around it. The meeting had to move somewhere unexpected. "We need to warn the *tura* and the governors. Advise a change of venue."

"I agree with you, but–" He shook his head. "I already tried that. My social hierarchy specialist contacted Halyuwin and explained to the secretary that Woran Oldue and Las Palomas might not be suitable. She went into the recent issue with Wylin targeting Las Palomas officers and posing unacceptable threats. She even explained that with your station in operation for such a short time, you hadn't had time to train *kiandarai* on humans nor humans on *kiandarai*, which would make for a potential hazard."

"And ...?"

He shrugged and rolled his eyes then effected the clipped, hard-ending consonant accent of the high-born. "I'm quite certain the *kiandarai* will be more than adequate for the task ahead."

Amaya snorted and gripped the back of her chair hard enough to risk leaving a permanent dent. "Of course. We work miracles daily, twice on the sabbath."

"There's more. Woran Oldue has the only buffer zone station in the *tura's* domain. Halyuwin says that all four of our visiting dignitaries wanted to meet close to home in a neutral place close to city attractions so the wives and children could also get together as a demonstration of friendship between our peoples. That means a buffer zone."

Amaya squinted. That couldn't be right, but there were no suggestions of deception in his demeanor. "Buffer zone stations are as common as pine needles up north. You mean I've got the only one in three states?"

Pavwin nodded. "Down here, with the exception of Las Palomas, humans built their cities far removed from the enclaves and made sure they grew in the opposite direction. Remember that Woran Oldue is the replacement for Woran Juvay after the hurricane flattened it. When Woran Oldue was built, the Texas revolution was happening. Las Palomas officials asked the enclave to protect them."

Her grip on the chair lightened up as she recalled the history of the area. "In hopes that the Mexican armies would leave it alone to avoid hostilities with Eshuvani. That's why Woran Oldue completely encloses Las Palomas."

"Right. In addition to protecting Las Palomas, the enclave slowed the Mexican army down, which allowed the Texian rebels to gather near what's now Houston." Pavwin leaned forward and crossed his arms on the table.

"So they won't move because of the symbolism of a 'neutral meeting place.' Meanwhile we have at least four more criminals to hunt down."

Worse than that, these weren't going to be the average sort of criminals, if there were such a thing. These were getting help. The question became how advanced was the help they were getting if they had a means to get old *kiandarai* gear, modern collar tabs, and altered records?

"We'll have to keep the security stringent." Pavwin clenched his fist.

"We can try, but are the twelve of us enough? I'd like to know if we're chasing ghosts or real threats." She returned to the table and sat. "I'll see what I can learn at the training center."

He flipped his chair the right way around. "Yes, but don't be surprised if you make no headway there, either. And be careful. You already have high-ranking enemies and Orinyay has a family. I wouldn't push too hard at this point."

Should Orinyay hide her family? She was a data analyst, which meant she knew enough to interpret information they found. Was she in on the plot? No. She couldn't be. She wouldn't have the clout to create false records or modify legitimate ones that severely.

Amaya rested her chin on her steepled fingers. Who had the authority to do all this? "You don't think it could be Em-"

"Emyrin?" He crossed his arms and nodded. "That occurred to me, too, and while I don't say it's impossible, I don't see him risking His Transcendence. He wasted no love on humanity, that's certain, but would he dare risk our own *tura*?"

"If he could blame it on the humans, maybe, but the *tura* may be in no danger even if Emyrin is pulling the strings." Amaya shook her head. She thought back through some of her marksmanship training and some particularly dicey missions that involved using that skill. "From the right angle and at the right distance, it's possible to pick a certain person out of a crowd, especially if collateral damage isn't a concern." She'd done it even when collateral damage mattered. "Still, you may have-"

The briefing room door opened with a hiss. When Pavwin reached for her hand, Amaya stopped. She spun toward the door. The five *kiandarai* of Falcon's Wing entered. Amaya stood and got ready for her lesson. The issue of the collar tabs would have to wait.

## Ω

Amaya paused to see if any of her students had a last, burning question, but all six members of Falcon's Wing stayed silent. She didn't harbor any grand illusions that they were all instant experts on human relations. If anything, she had overloaded their minds with new protocols. They would need time to process before questions surfaced.

She scanned the room, reading facial expressions ranging from bored to overwhelmed. "If you find you need further clarity on something, send me a message or contact me through the comm system. If necessary, we can meet again later in the week to review the information. With some notice, I might be able to arrange something with the Las Palomas Police Department to give you some practice time."

Pavwin nodded. "That might be prudent." He turned to face his own people. "We are trying to arrange things so at least one person from Hawk's Nest is at all of the functions. If we find ourselves at a complete loss, we can ask the Hawk's Nest personnel or follow their example. For now—"

When Amaya's comm system chimed, her muscles twitched and her breath caught for a moment. She stepped outside the briefing room door before she pressed the dark blue crystal on the left collar tab to answer. "Amaya."

"Ishe. There's a call in Las Palomas. Orinyay and Jevon are already on another one and Nurinyan isn't back yet." Her muffled pronunciation suggested she was snacking. That girl was perpetually hungry. Still, her weight stayed consistent, so she must have had a hummingbird's metabolism.

"Brief Vadin on the emergency. I'm on my way." The calls in Las Palomas might be related to the collar tabs, and even at the fastest, she'd be a few minutes getting to the site.

"Message received."

The connection clicked closed.

She jogged a couple steps to the dispatch desk where she usually left her backpack then rolled her eyes. She wasn't at Hawk's Next. The matching furniture and decent-looking walls should've been her first clue.

Her rubber-soled boots thudded on the hardwood floor as she darted back to the briefing room. The door opened at her approach, and Amaya slipped back into the briefing room.

A conversation in progress stalled. The six members of Falcon's Wing stared at her as if she'd interrupted something personal, hopefully not aimed at her.

Amaya snatched up her backpack. "I'm sorry. I have an emergency call."

Pavwin rose and walked her out to the parking lot. "My social hierarchy specialist is concerned that you may not have the experience you need to deal with the *tura*. She'd like to offer equivalent lessons to your staff."

An astute observation on his specialist's part. Amaya's lack of the formal social graces probably blared at anyone who knew what to do with people as elevated as the *tura*.

"I may not be personally ready for the *tura*, but I have a hierarchy specialist whose family travels at that level. Perhaps your specialist and mine should compare notes and arrange something." Amaya darted through the outside door as soon there was enough space for her. "Let me know if your people need a second lesson."

Pavwin nodded. "They do. I'll send you another set of potential times for that review session."

"Thank you."

The outside air temperature, even at mid-morning, was sufficient for baking pastries on the avicopter's dashboard. Marquette only rarely got this hot, and by all accounts August here would bring worse.

Amaya blew out a breath. "Once we settle on a couple options, I'll work with Las Palomas to see if a few off-duty officers would help us, or perhaps some of their wives would be willing to help." She opened the courier door and stepped back, avoiding the wall of searing heat that always hit her like a heavy-handed fist.

Pavwin backed away and waved his hand in front of him. "This one has a functioning air cooler, doesn't it?"

She smiled and stepped up into the avi, putting the backpack behind the pilot's seat. She planted herself and winced. The cushion was hot even through her pants. "Yes, a little overzealous at times. A boon in this weather."

"Indeed." He closed the door and retreated a few steps.

Amaya tapped the avi's ignition button. The engine groaned and clicked before it went silent. With Pavwin watching, she resisted the urge to offer the recalcitrant machine a little encouragement in the form of a whack on the dashboard. She frowned and hit the ignition again. The engine repeated its previous performance but wound up at turtle pace. She flicked the switches for the other systems, starting with the air cooler.

Pavwin tapped on his collar tabs. Amaya's comm system chimed.

She extended the wings and lifted off before she tapped the blue crystal on her collar. "Amaya."

"Pavwin. Have the mechanic in your group check the battery linkages. They need tightening."

"I will. Thank you." She watched the avi-shaped symbol on the navigation screen until it was aimed toward Hawk's Nest and rolled the throttle forward.

Jevon would not be thrilled about the addition to his To Do list.

The terrain of dried grass and scrubby junipers and yaupons sped past below her until she landed in front of Hawk's Nest. Vadin ran over and hopped into the other side. The tension across his forehead would give him a headache if he didn't loosen up.

Amaya pulled up on the collective lever at her side to lift off and pushed the control stick left until the avi pivoted midair, releasing the pressure only when they faced Las Palomas. "Bring the details of our call into the open."

"It's a hardware store on Tenth Street near Cottonwood." Vadin twisted toward her and spoke at a significant fraction of lightspeed without losing the familiar heavy final consonant. "A shoplifter. Eshuvani."

"In custody?" As the edge of Las Palomas passed below them, Amaya tugged the control stick to the right to tweak their course.

He turned one hand upward. "That's the odd part in all of this. The dispatcher said the officers needed help apprehending the shoplifter, but when Ishe asked which way he was fleeing, they said he wasn't going anywhere. What does that mean?"

If they'd had time, she'd walk him through the logical conclusion. Next time, though. Amaya glanced at him. "It sounds like he boxed himself in." She deliberately picked a human idiom to see how he handled it.

"He did wh–?" His brow furrowed for a moment. "Oh! He has no viable exit."

"Right."

That could be tricky. Few creatures fought harder than one that perceived itself trapped. This would have been a better call for Nurinyan. His martial arts training might have proved its worth, but the hazards on these calls were not always predictable, and Vadin needed to know how to handle them, too.

The cityscape zipped by below them. When they flew over the construction site she'd visited earlier in the week, she pulled the control stick to the right again and made another course correction. Red police vehicle lights reflected off windows. Officer Robert Kirby waved up at her as she flew over. He had dark glasses on today, a necessity in the intense summer sun. The other uniformed officer on site was too dark-complected to be Mark. That was most likely Officer Nigel Parrish. Where was Mark? Ed almost never shook up his partner assignments. A few other people were gathered at a distance, but everyone was staying well back from the building. Another pair of officers were hiding in the landscaping behind the building. She only spotted their uniforms because of her height. Amaya throttled down to bring the avi to a hover and lowered the collective to bring them in for a landing in an empty corner of the hardware store's lot. She flipped all the switches down and pressed the ignition. The hum of the engine wound down and went silent.

Reaching behind the seat, she grabbed her trauma kit and hopped out. With Vadin a couple steps behind, she jogged over to Robert and Nigel. Nigel was just a hair taller than Robert. His black, tightly coiled hair was short enough to see his scalp through it below the edge of his hat.

Vadin stepped in past her and offered Nigel his hand. "I am Vadin Tara *Kiala*."

Nigel shook Vadin's hand. "Officer Nigel Parrish. Glad you two could come."

Amaya smiled. Nothing in Vadin's body language or mannerisms conveyed any surprise or unease about Nigel's remarkably dark complexion. That was exactly how it should be, and she made a mental note to make sure she explained the concept of "races" to Pavwin's people. Nigel wasn't the only one in Las Palomas PD whose ancestors came from Africa, and skin color variation covered a much narrower range among Eshuvani, the results of a genetic bottleneck after the generation ship had crashed.

Vadin turned to Robert. "Is Mark well?"

"He's fine. Traded a shift with another guy today. Baby check-up, and Ruth doesn't drive. The neighbor who usually helps out with that is on vacation in Aruba." Robert led them over to the hood of their patrol car where he had a paper map weighted down with a small rock in each corner. "Nigel's stuck with me today."

Nigel snorted. "Yeah, poor me."

Vadin's eyes narrowed.

He needed to work on cross-cultural humor.

Amaya leaned closer and whispered. "That was a joke."

Vadin smiled. "Oh!"

The map showed the general floor plan. There was a large sales area in the front. A long corridor started in one corner and ran the length of the building ending in another large space marked "storeroom." A couple smaller doors led off the corridor into an office and a restroom.

Amaya nodded. A fairly typical set-up, differing only in the minutiae. That made the job easier, both for her and for the suspect holed up inside. The familiar arrangement meant fewer surprises, but if they had to go in after the suspect to get him out, she had the whole, wide open corridor to traverse.

"The shoplifter bolted when he saw us coming in the front and went here." Robert traced the whole length of the hallway to the storeroom.

Nigel leaned closer and tapped the square marked "office." "If he'd just turned in here, he could've gotten out, but there's no exit from the storeroom and no windows, neither."

"Not even a small one?" Amaya turned toward the building and studied the store. Signage covering most of the windows advertised gallon cans of paint in an assortment of colors for one dollar and furnace filters for forty-nine cents.

"Naw. I walked all the way around thinkin' we could chuck some tear gas in there and flush him out, but it's all brick." Nigel pointed to the storefront. "That's all the glass in the place."

Amaya looked at Robert. "What's in that storeroom?"

Robert turned toward the small group of people nearby and waved. "Mr. Jameson."

A heavy-set Caucasian man who came to the height of Robert's shoulder waddled over. Even that short distance had him huffing and puffing. He crossed his arms and glared. "Well? Are you getting that creature out my shop?"

Amaya raised an eyebrow at him. Creature? So, being not human made Eshuvani sub-human. "We need more information."

"Why can't you just go down the hall, open the door, and get him out?" He waved at the building.

She faced him and stepped back to avoid staring down at him at such a steep angle. "Depending on the contents of your storeroom, that may be an option. What do you keep in there?"

Mr. Jameson rolled his dark eyes. "It's a hardware store, lady."

Vadin looked at the ground. "Forgive my ignorance. I do not understand what a 'hardware store' would sell. Apparently paint and some manner of air filtration, but surely more than that."

A valid question. He'd doubt himself less as he gained experience. Amaya clapped her hand on Vadin's shoulder.

Jameson propped one hand on his hip and aimed the other at the store. "Nails, screws, ropes, pipe, y'know, hardware."

"Any chemicals, fuel, ammunition?" Robert asked.

"No, of co—" His eyes went wide. "Cleaning supplies. I keep those in there." He grabbed Robert's arm. "And camping gear. At this time of year, I sell some of that, too. Y'know, for the tourists."

"Then if he's knowledgeable, he can make something toxic or explosive." Amaya frowned and wiped the sweat from her forehead. "All right. We'll try the easy way first. Vadin, join the officers in the back. I'm going to try to talk him out of there. He may try to run out through the office."

Robert glanced at his temporary partner. "Do you want Nigel and me with you?"

She turned to the group at the edge of the lot. "One of you should probably stay here and handle crowd control."

"That'll be me." Nigel raised his hand. "I've already been thrown around once. I'll let Kirby have a turn."

Robert smirked. "Hey! I had my turn, too."

"You got stabbed in the chest." Nigel shook his head. "That's real different from being thrown at a pile of pallets."

Humans never ceased to amaze her. Both of them had been in very real danger not that long ago, and they could actually joke about it.

Vadin darted off toward the back of the store while Nigel led Mr. Jameson back to the group at the edge of the parking lot. Amaya walked with Robert toward the glass-fronted store. What parts of the windows she could see through showed closely-packed, head-high shelving in rows. Amaya drew her pistol and thumbed the switch to power it up. She kept the settings at low power for such close quarters.

She stepped inside and darted to an end cap. Robert came in next and went to the end of a different shelving unit. The inside of the store had an overpowering stench of fake pine and an undercurrent of ammonia. She looked at Robert. He gestured for her to go around to her left then pointed to himself and back the other way.

Amaya nodded and crept to her left, keeping the pistol aimed wherever she looked while she scanned down the aisles from the top shelf to the floor. When she reached the wall, she ran to the other end and peeked around the corner. Robert reached the far side seconds later. She pointed to him then to the opening of the long hall. He hustled, pausing long enough to look behind the checkout counter. Amaya followed. She swapped places with him and drew her knife. Using the reflective surface, she peeked down the hallway and recalled the map. The doors for the office and the restroom were flush to the hallway's wall except for a couple inches of door frame. That would offer negligible cover. Those two doors and the storeroom were closed. She handed Robert her knife and let him look down the hall. He nodded and passed the blade back to her.

She drew a deep breath and made the mental language change to her native one. "In the storeroom. This is the *kiandarai*. Exit empty-handed with your hands in plain sight. Noncompliance will be deemed willful defiance of *kiandarai* directive."

The sounds of banging and scraping came from the other side of the storeroom door.

Robert put his hand on her arm and whispered, "I don't like the sound of that."

She shook her head. "No way to know what he's really doing in there."

"I'm sure it's not in our best interests."

"Safe bet." Amaya used her knife to look down the hall again. Nothing apparently different. "In the storeroom. This is the *kiandarai*. Exit empty-handed with your hands in plain sight. Noncompliance will be deemed willful defiance of *kiandarai* directive, which is punishable by prison time or a fine or both."

A loud bang shook the building. It had no sooner ended than another one occurred and rattled things off the shelves. Robert pulled her against his chest and covered her head with his arms as another explosion created a mini-earthquake. Glass, likely the storefront, shattered.

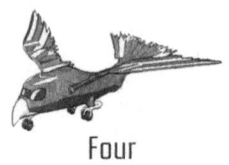

## Four

Amaya tensed, waiting for another explosion. The butt of Robert's pistol pressed against her shoulder. His aftershave and the sweat inevitable from the weather mingled in her nose. She suppressed the urge to struggle against his hold. His culture demanded that he attempt to shield her, even if his effort would be in vain if the ceiling over their heads came down.

When her collar chimed, Robert released her.

Amaya pressed a blue crystal. "Amaya."

"Vadin. Are you okay?" He spoke in Eshuvani, not the right choice.

She looked Robert over and switched to English. "We're fine."

"He has blown a hole t'rough de wall." Quick breaths punctuated his words, in English now. "Foot pursuit."

Good. He'd matched her language choice, but with his upbringing, physical training would have been frowned upon. He was going to need help.

She rose, gestured for Robert to follow, and picked her way through the debris. "Stay with him. I'll spot you from the air. Leave the comm system open."

"Right."

She smirked. That wasn't exactly proper comm protocol, but best he focus on his breathing.

"Need extra eyes?" Robert followed her out, gingerly picking a way through the broken glass from the storefront. Through the comm, a dart pistol discharged four times. He caught her arm and held up four fingers and mouthed, "Four?"

She nodded. He clearly understood the implication. If that fourth shot had hit the target, Vadin would be in for some major disciplinary action, and there wasn't much she'd be able to do to help him. "Vadin?" She powered down her gun and holstered it.

His breathing came in hard gasps. "He is–he is down."

She hoped that was "down" and not "dead." Only rare people could survive a fourth dart, and she prayed to God that he'd missed one. "Stay with him. What is your location?"

"T-T'ree–" He swallowed hard. "T'ree blocks due west."

Yes, physical training needed to rank higher on his priorities. Eshuvani endurance was not half as impressive as a human's, but he shouldn't be that winded after running three blocks.

"I'm on my way." She turned to Robert. "I've got the courier. Seating is limited."

"Okay. I'll stay here and help Parrish with the reports." He glanced over his shoulder at Nigel, who was talking to the wildly gesturing storekeeper. "I'd better help Nigel calm Jameson down first."

"Very good." Amaya glanced west. "We'll get the suspect taken care of."

He looked past her for a moment. "Um, I appreciate your diligence."

She smiled. The human officers were already learning to adapt to Eshuvani, and quickly, too. "Thanks for your help."

Amaya jogged to the courier, used the handhold on the side of the avi to pull herself into the pilot seat and slid her backpack behind her. She tapped the ignition. As before, the engine groaned and clicked but didn't start. After giving it a stern look, she jabbed the ignition the second time. The engine wound up, and she pulled the lever at her side to lift off. Once higher than the buildings in the area, she nudged the cyclic to the left and oriented toward the west. A large billboard she passed showed a massive cartoon tiger pumping gasoline into a car. Vadin sat next to an unconscious Eshuvani man in the middle of the half-vacant parking lot of a clothing store. She set down in the back third of the lot. Once the avi was powered down, she grabbed her kit and jogged to him. As she came close, Amaya tapped a blue crystal on her collar once to sever the comm connection. The thief lay face down on the pavement. Three darts stuck out of his back with no apparent grouping. There was no sign of the fourth one. Sweat streamed down Vadin's face.

Amaya knelt next to him and pulled the flap on the side of her pouch. The hook-and-loop closure crackled as it came loose. She withdrew the nutrition bars and sorted through them until she came to a berry-flavored one, his preference. She peeled open the wrapper and handed it to him then tucked a second one into his shirt pocket. "Here. You'll want this."

He took a small bite. "Thank you."

"Where did the fourth dart hit?" She pinched the fletching on the darts stuck in the thief's back and removed them.

Vadin pointed to a car. "Bounced off the hood of that car when he stumbled." His eyes widened. "You thought I shot him four times?"

"That did occur to me. Your shots were in rapid succession." She patted the suspect down and checked pockets. "Did you see them all land?"

"I did, and actually, I fired six shots total. His avicopter was behind where the officers and I were stationed. I missed the first two shots as he came out of the hole. He saw us between him and his avi and ran."

She patted his shoulder. "You did well, even if you did scare me with that extra shot."

"The explosions with the two of you inside didn't do much for my nerves, either." His breathing was still heavy, but not quite as labored.

After clearing an ID card, money, and a slip of crumpled white paper from his pockets, Amaya turned the suspect over. Silver collar tabs with the dark blue comm crystals glittered on his shirt.

"Another one?" She reached under his collar, released the clasp, and slid the tabs into her hand. Amaya flipped the tabs over and noted the number on the back. She reached up to her own collar, pressed one dark blue crystal, and tapped Pavwin's code on another.

"Pavwin."

The sound of a well-tuned avicopter's engine droned in the background.

"Amaya. I've found comm set two of five. Can you contact me when you're settled?"

"I will, but it might be late."

"Understood. Message received." She prayed God kept him safe whatever he was doing.

A click signaled the break in the connection.

Amaya pried open the scrap of paper. Analog clock, welding equipment, wire, tape, a list of chemicals, pipes with given dimensions. What was all this about? She fished a notepad from her kit and copied the list before putting all the thief's personal affects in a plastic bag to be turned over to the court.

"I'll get him secured and come back for you." She rested her hand on Vadin's shoulder.

He nodded.

She picked the suspect up and carried him to the avicopter.

## Ω

At the *kiat's* headquarters, Teviya drew the front curtains over the window while Emyrin ordered the windows to darken on his way down the hall to the rear door. The blue and green swirls of light reflected off the walls and ceiling a moment later. The communication system in her desk continued to beep as she hustled back and fished her key out of the pencil holder.

Teviya glowered. "Yeah, yeah, I'm working on it." She opened the large drawer and used the key to trigger the magnetic lock on the rear section.

She plunked the speaker on the desk and the communication module next to it. The two didn't look like they should go together. The speaker was state of the art with a wireless connection to the module housing the controller and mic. The module had started out with the most recent tech, but Emyrin had modified it to broadcast only to their hoodlum hirelings with the repurposed collar tabs. His tinkering had turned it into a do-it-yourself, cobbled-together mess.

As soon as the rear door lock clicked, she tapped the blue crystal on the top to acknowledge the incoming call.

"What is it?" she asked.

"Took you long enough." The leader's baritone brought up the mental image of the man.

He was dark-haired, pale-skinned, and heavier than average. Not quite supermodel material, but more than pleasant to look at. His personality, on the other hand, could evaporate the hydrogen out of any star.

She glared at the speaker. "You're supposed to wait for us to call you. It's too risky to contact us directly."

"Well, this is important. He was caught."

"Repeat?" Teviya asked.

"I said, 'He was caught.'"

He? He who? One of the riff-raff Emyrin had recruited, certainly, but which one? Some they could do without. Others were more critical.

She sat straighter. "Caught?"

"He tried to acquire some of our missing supplies. Police arrived then the *kiandarai*. A *kiala* took him down."

Teviya rolled her eyes and shook her head. She still didn't have enough clues to figure out who they'd lost, but if they kept doing dopey things like trying to get their supplies from stores during business hours, there wouldn't be enough of them to matter any more. "And why were you trying that acquisition while the store was open?"

"Not my idea. I told him to wait, and we'd go after dark. He took one of the avis and went on his own. I got there in time to see the *kiala* shoot him down." He growled and his voice dropped to a threatening whisper. "I told you he was a reactor on meltdown. Maybe next time you'll hear me."

Oh, that one. Emyrin hadn't hired him for his intellect. No big loss, but more troubling that he'd put the group at risk. There had been too many failures lately. Emyrin's insistence on using the worst Eshuvani society had to offer might backfire. Sure, they were expendable, but they kept making major errors like getting caught.

Emyrin joined her and set a paper on her desk.

She picked it up and scanned through it. The *tura*'s schedule should help them make the arrangements. "You have to get the supplies. Have to. You're running out of time to do it."

"Got it handled." His tone was a little too nonchalant. "You have the schedule for me yet?"

If Emyrin had just gotten the equipment for them in the first place, this little plan might go more smoothly, but if Amaya and Pavwin figured out what was happening in the end, Emyrin would have to explain why he had purchased the kind of supplies the hoodlums needed. No, their hired help was going to have to fend for themselves. They were certainly getting paid enough to do it.

"We'll leave the schedule in the usual place." But it wouldn't do them much good if they didn't come up with the gear they needed.

"I'll pick it up tonight. Stop worrying. We got it handled, but we will need someone to cover the open position now."

Of course, they would, but that wasn't going to be her problem. Emyrin insisted on handling the recruiting himself. That suited her fine.

A click signaled the end of the connection. She jabbed the blue crystal on the module.

"You better have it handled," Teviya grumbled. After glaring at the speaker and communication module for a few more seconds, she returned the equipment to the hidden compartment in her desk.

Ω

Amaya waited for Vadin to get inside the door of Hawk's Nest before she lifted off. Wearying himself by chasing down the thief turned out to be advantageous. Her next stop was the training center to look into the "training center administrative block" Pavwin had discovered in both the bogus personnel records and the records of those who had lost their collar tabs. If any of Amaya's poking around drew fire, she'd rather be the lone target.

The Buffer Zone grassland gave way to the edges of Woran Oldue. Buildings were scattered in any open area with rock gardens or a more traditional assortment of flowers and trees around a fountain. With all the time she spent flying over Las Palomas, the lack of streets in Woran Oldue was disconcerting, but the addresses marked on the tops of the buildings kept her oriented. Less than a few dozen strides from Emyrin's headquarters, the training center campus sprawled across several acres, contained in one low, windowless building made from heavy, reinforced plastic in a dull gray-blue.

She couldn't recall seeing a less visually appealing training center. The school where she'd trained had lacked all the modern amenities, but it was infinitely nicer than this corrugated box. Was

Woran Oldue's plastic structure another direct result of Emyrin's fund redirection? Likely, but where was it all going? The décor in his office was expensive, but the budget missing from her own station would cover it. Was he stashing the excess in a personal account or supporting some other person, group, or organization?

Amaya circled around to the parking area and settled the avicopter on the landing struts. She hopped out and grabbed her backpack. After securing the door, she slid her arm through one of the straps of her kit and headed for the center's main doors. Blistering heat reflected up from the pavement. She stepped into the training center and reveled in the cooler air.

Inside, the floors were polished concrete stained a dark blue. The walls were the same reinforced plastic as the exterior. The lighting overhead was a series of long fluorescent tubes, unshielded in their sockets and humming at a low but loud pitch. A small wooden plaque inside the door marked the construction date as only fifteen years ago. Neatly printed paper signage in a frame on the wall directed her to the right for the administration office.

As she walked down the hallway, other rooms split off to her left. Pristine paper signs identified the rooms by number and primary function. The hall ended in a closed door marked "Administration." Another paper sign advised her to turn the doorknob to open the door.

Human technology in an Eshuvani training center?

She shouldn't be surprised. The low tech was easier on the pocketbook.

The door handle turned without a catch. Amaya entered and pushed the door closed behind her. Across from the door Amaya had come through was another door marked "Private." A long, hip-high counter made of the same plastic as the walls spanned the space. A few computers, much more recent than the big clunker at her own dispatch desk, were evenly spaced down the length of the table. The unmatched chairs at each one were polished wood. Some day, Hawk's Nest might be blessed with equipment somewhat resembling modern. Amaya smiled. Here she was lamenting the "outdated" computer in her station, but human computers were still the size of the whole room with punch card interfaces. She should be happy Emyrin hadn't acquired one of those for her.

The *kiandara* at the center computer was a tall but pudgy fellow with brown hair stopping short of his collar. The silver tabs had the specialization swirls surrounding the lavender crystal for a data analyst.

He looked up from the computer and smiled. "Grace be unto you."

"And peace from God, the Father of our Lord." She walked over and set her backpack at her feet. "I need some information about one of my staff members."

He turned to the computer and started typing. "Who is it?"

"Orinyay Midorin. She—" Amaya cut herself short. Until they knew what was happening, she would do best to reveal as little as possible. "She's a *kiandara* under my command at *Uloniya Varoosht*."

"Here. I have the file." He turned the screen toward her.

She leaned around to see it and pointed to the coded blue box covering part of the list of her service record, exactly as Pavwin had described. "I am told by a specialist this block was placed by the training center. This is apparently a past duty. What was it?"

He turned the screen away from her and tapped a few keys before he pressed and held four keys at the same time. "Excuse me, please. I need to check another resource."

"Of course." She straightened up.

The *kiandara* rose and slipped through the back door.

Amaya leaned around to look at the screen. A solid blue screen had replaced Orinyay's personnel file. So, was this "other resource" an actual data source or was he contacting a superior to find out how to send her away diplomatically? As if she needed to truly wonder.

Leaving her backpack on the concrete floor, she padded down the length of the counter until she was directly across from the marked door. After glancing both ways to confirm the room was otherwise unoccupied, she leaned across the counter and strained to hear the muffled voices coming through the closed door. She made out little more than the pitch and cadence. One was the data analyst she'd been speaking to, and the other sounded familiar. The distance and the door in the way ruined any chance for an identification, but if she were closer, she might hear something.

Radio protocol could be useful. The usual sign-off phrases would give her enough time to get back to the right side of the counter. Amaya planted her hand on the counter and bent her knees.

The voices stopped. Amaya hustled back to where she'd left her backpack as the door opened. The muscles in her chest tightened, but she willed the sensation away. She'd done nothing wrong.

The data analyst resumed his seat at the computer. "I appreciate your patience, *Kiand*. The block is apparently some manner of computer error. I will file the appropriate form for you and have that cleared. Be advised that clearing the block may take a few weeks."

Did he think she had arrived on Earth just this morning? He or his superior was likely hoping that in a few weeks, she'd forget all about this or maybe become too busy with other matters. He'd have to get used to disappointment.

Amaya raised an eyebrow. "Really? What caused this error?"

"Sometimes things like this happen, *Kiand*." With a flourish, he turned one hand toward the ceiling. "I appreciate your diligence in tracking that anomaly down. As soon as a programmer is available, the problem will be dealt with, I assure you." He tapped several keys and pivoted the monitor toward her. "You can see here there's no gap in her service record. It's a simple error. Nothing unheard of."

If this were routine, he wouldn't have needed to consult a higher authority. "I see. I appreciate your diligence."

"Serve with diligence, *Kiand*."

Amaya slid her trauma kit over one shoulder and walked out. Like trying to contact Ianolin Simiala, the current owner of Orinyay's former collar tabs, dealing with the training center raised more questions than it answered. She wasn't naïve enough to believe the routine error story. Someone had set the blocks in place, but who and why?

And what about Orinyay? Was she involved or someone's pawn or completely innocent? Was the whole plan meant to breed distrust? Could Orinyay be trusted with the security information surrounding the human governors and His Transcendence? Amaya hardly had enough people to arrange security now. Losing her only full *kiandara* would severely hamper the effort. Well, someone would have to handle the regular calls, and that might as well be Orinyay.

A firm hand on her arm pulled her to a stop. Amaya jerked loose and spun. Her hand dropped to her pistol.

Nurinyan stood there, showing both his hands empty. "Peace!"

She blew out a breath. "Forgive me. I was startled."

"You didn't hear me call you?" He lowered his hands.

She clasped his right arm and hugged him. "I'm trying to work out some of the security details for Monday." A flash of silver on his shirt collar drew her attention. "Congratulations, *Kiandara*."

He beamed. "I'm official now!"

If only changing the color of his collar tabs included a change in his impulsiveness.

"You are indeed. Well done." She smiled, recalling when she'd first gotten her silver tabs. She'd been just younger than Vadin, full of hope and aspirations and grand dreams, some of which had come true. The others? Well, there still time.

"And, um–" He looked at the ground. "I, um, I've considered your warnings." He peeked up at her. "I will try to do better."

She gripped his arm. "Good. It would grieve me greatly to lose you, especially to imprudence."

They walked out together and boarded the avicopter. At least she was certain about his loyalty, if perhaps not his common sense. If Orinyay did have to be involved in the security details, putting a combat specialist with her might deter any plans for treachery, but Nurinyan would have to be put on his guard without outright accusing Orinyay on insufficient data. Doing that with the correct amount of tact and diplomacy would be tricky.

Ω

While waiting for Ishe to take her turn at Stellari, Vadin sipped his glass of water. He winced. It was still just a little colder than he liked, so he swished it around his mouth a few times before he swallowed. Ishe was the one assigned to dispatch duty, but after a nap to recuperate from chasing down the shoplifter, he'd decided to keep her company for a bit. Sitting here waiting for something to happen was a lot like watching ice melt on a cold day.

She drew a breath through her teeth. "This is a hard round."

He smiled. Stellari was one of those deceptively complicated games. The rules were easy enough even little kids could learn the basics after a few teaching rounds. The strategy part of the game, though, that's where the tough part came in.

Vadin studied the coins laid out on the table and saw the game from Ishe's perspective. There were a couple obvious plays for her, but only one that didn't set up a fantastic round for him. Either way, he had enough points to win. Surely, she had to see that.

When the hangar door rumbled up, Vadin twitched and looked toward the hangar. He couldn't see down the hall without standing up, though. A few moments later, the hangar door came back down.

Ishe watched him instead of either scooting over to the computer or looking down the hall. Normally, he'd get up and take a peek, but not in the middle of the game. To win the current game, all she'd have to do is flip the nebula coin to give herself a spectacular play at his expense, an illegal move. Although he had no reason to question her honesty, he'd lost enough games to his younger brother by not keeping an eye on the coins. At the risk of being paranoid, his curiosity would keep.

Before turning to the dispatch computer, Ishe heaved a terrific sigh. "That would have to be Amaya. We're just missing Nurinyan."

"—And Jevon will alternate going out with Orinyay to gain some more experience until we have a third avicopter," Amaya said from down the hall.

"Then we can function like a real station?" Nurinyan asked.

"Exactly."

Ishe turned to the dispatch computer and clicked the icon for Nurinyan. "That's all of us."

Vadin tapped out a pattern on the desktop with his fingers. He looked at Ishe, then at the coins, and then at his opponent again. Was she going to finish the game any time this millennium?

The rear door squeaked open and banged closed. That could only be Jevon. Orinyay always came in through the hangar because of where her house was. Heavy footfalls echoed in the back hallway. Jevon entered, wiping his dirty hands on a stained towel.

Vadin waved without taking his attention from the game. "Ishe, are you going to play?"

Ishe drummed her fingers on the cheek. "I'm thinking."

Amaya set her kit down next to the dispatch desk and looked over Ishe's shoulder. "Umhm. Difficult hand, but you really only have one move that doesn't give him a terrific score."

"I know, but it doesn't give me much." Ishe sighed.

Nurinyan leaned on the desk. "Either a few points for you or many points for him. Either way, you have no chance to pull ahead at this point."

Vadin nodded. The only question was how many points he'd win by. Since they didn't keep cumulative scores from one game to the next, what difference did it make, anyway?

"I suppose." Ishe picked up the star's coin and flipped over the supernova's coin. "Two points for me. Such a huge amount."

Vadin jotted the score on the notepad. He'd seen bigger point spreads but not by much. If he hadn't passed up some big plays earlier in the game, he might have beat his own best score, but she would've felt awful.

Jevon looked at the score sheet and snickered. "Close game."

Nice. Vadin flipped the page. Games shouldn't always be about destroying your opponent. He'd won. That was good enough.

"Don't push my face in it, or I'll tell everyone the score from the last game we played." Ishe glared and mimed thwacking Jevon's ear.

"Oooo." Jevon stood straighter and turned to Amaya. "The system from Wolf's Teeth works fine. It'll just be a matter of figuring out where to put the sensors."

That meant that soon, very soon since the conference was starting on Monday, they'd be spending some quality time on pre-hologram protocols. They were necessary, and he often looked forward to what Amaya would teach them, but he'd recently come up with a new idea for a painting. His hobby would have to wait. Vadin slouched, but only for a moment. He rubbed his ear and hoped no one else noticed his slack posture.

"Excellent. Setting up the perimeter needs to be a priority task. I'd like at least a couple days to test the system out before our august visitors arrive." Amaya retrieved her backpack and fished a notepad out.

Jevon groaned and shook his head. "Can the installation wait until it's less hot out there? You can get heat prostration walking from the back door to my house."

"Take care of it at the hour of your choosing any time within the next twelve hours." She glanced at her watch. "I would, however, suggest that you get your plans sorted out now so installation will go faster. If I can get to the bottom of my own task list, I'll help, but the responsibility for setting up and testing the perimeter alarm is yours and Nurinyan's. Do you need anything from me?"

Jevon nodded. "Training on pre-hologram protocols."

"I'll arrange it."

Vadin offered Jevon and Nurinyan a half-smile. Lucky them. He'd rather sort out menus and arrange the rooms.

She set her notepad on the table. "A list of these supplies was on the suspect Vadin chased down earlier. Any guess what our suspect might be shopping for?"

Vadin's brow furrowed as he scanned through the list of nails, wires, foam, pipes of various dimensions, bathroom cleaner, a clock of some kind, garden fertilizer, and other strange things. He hadn't taken his practical chemistry class yet, so what could all that be good for? Was it all for the same purpose, or were there multiple goals in mind? The only thing he knew for sure was that it wouldn't make lunch. He leaned back to let everyone else have a better look.

Jevon turned the list to look at it right-side-up. "With this stuff, he could make a truly impressive bomb or two." Jevon tapped the notepad as he listed things off. "He's got a timer, detonator, explosive, a way to keep it confined to build up the pressure. Everything he needs. This could cause considerable grief if placed in the right location."

Nurinyan blew out a breath. "So, we have to scan everything before the delegations arrive at the site."

"It's not that easy. If he does it right, the usual detection protocols wouldn't pick this stuff up." Jevon scratched his cheek. "All he'd have to do is clean up after himself real well and put this in or next to something metal. We'd never know the difference."

Vadin's eyes widened and the tension in his neck tightened. Even if they were as diligent as they could be, they might miss it. If they did ...

He shuddered.

Ishe rolled her eyes. "Then what good are the bomb detection protocols if they still miss problems?"

"Mortals make errors." Amaya put her notepad back in her pack. "If there's even a slim possibility of finding a bomb with the protocol, it's useful. It's just not guaranteed to succeed. We must keep our eyes open for anything unusual. That's why we are all going to tour the locations in detail before the meetings begin."

When the computer chimed, Vadin twitched. His ears warmed, and he rubbed his right one. The inbound call alert was hardly anything to get jittery about.

Ishe turned toward the computer and smacked a button on the keyboard. "Hawk's Nest."

"Dispatch. Las Palomas relay. Suspicious persons reported at abandoned furniture factory. Witness reports Eshuvani among them. West Division, Thirty-fifth Street at San Saba. Las Palomas dispatching a unit. Assist."

"Message Received." Ishe looked up at Amaya. "Another abandoned place?"

"That does seem to be the theme with these recent invasions into Las Palomas." Amaya shouldered her backpack. "Vadin, you're with me. Everyone else, start working on that perimeter alarm, even if it's just a map of where you think the sensors could go. I want to see your best three ideas with the rationale of their strengths and weaknesses."

Better them than him.

Vadin pushed away from the desk and jogged with her to the courier. His guts went all queasy. That would go away, wouldn't it? As he got more experience, that would go away. He hoped. Vadin went around to the passenger side and climbed in while Amaya took the pilot's seat and powered up. Vadin leaned over and triggered the remote for the hangar doors. By the time the courier was ready for service, the door was up. Once they were out of the hangar, he triggered the remote again.

She glanced at him and flew toward Las Palomas. "We may have to split up and search the building."

His neck muscles tensed. "Is it prudent to go alone in such a situation?"

"No, which is why I'll try to arrange for you to go with the senior partner of the Las Palomas officers, and I'll go with the junior partner." She made a course adjustment.

What if he did the wrong thing? What if he wasn't fast enough? He rubbed the back of his neck. "I understand."

She flashed him a tight smile. "You'll do fine, Vadin. Follow your partner's lead. The humans are skilled at the correct protocols. They just lack the strength and speed to match the opposition. They're learning how to use what abilities they do have, and quickly, but the majority of them aren't ready yet, and we haven't had a chance to improve their equipment to compensate."

He nodded and stretched his neck through the range of motion. He could do this. He'd scored high on his training and coursework.

She reached over and gripped his shoulder. "If I didn't think you could handle this, I would have brought Nurinyan or Jevon."

Someday, he'd be worthy of her confidence.

The city zoomed by below them. The blinking red lights reflecting off the structures were visible before the car was. The black and white patrol car was in the parking lot of a huge box of a building that had rows of windows, some of them broken. A massive sign advertised some construction company and promised a new shopping center by the end of the year. Two police officers stood on the side of the car furthest from the building.

Amaya landed the courier in the vacant lot across the street. While she shut down the systems, Vadin hopped out and waited. He followed her to the humans and introduced himself.

The shorter, blond-haired officer wearing dark glasses shook Vadin's hand. "Officer Gerald Henderson, and this is my partner Officer Conner Florentine."

Conner, the younger of the two, was almost a hand width taller than Gerald and had dark hair and dark eyes.

"Witness says three people entered." Gerald pointed to the factory with his thumb. "Claims one was too tall and too gaunt t'be a human."

"That would be a twist, wouldn't it?" Conner grinned like a child with a new toy and leaned closer. "How often are they in mixed bands of humans and Twigs?"

Vadin's eyes narrowed. He'd thought the police, at least, had accepted them.

Gerald smacked his younger partner on the back of the head. "Mind your manners, son."

Conner rubbed the back of his head. "What did–? Oh. Sorry. Eshuvani. Yeesh. You knew what I meant."

"Yeah, and words matter." Gerald looked at his younger partner over the top of his dark glasses.

Amaya nodded. "Gerald, I suggest we split up. You take Vadin, and Conner will come with me."

Gerald took off his hat and ran his fingers through his hair before putting his hat back on. "Sure. Cover more ground that way. We'll start on the north, y'all take the south, and we'll all work toward the center. Let's go."

Conner slapped Vadin's shoulder and ran for the front of the building.

Gerald reached for him and missed. "Florentine! Hold up, son."

The younger officer slowed to a quick walk but continued on to the building.

Vadin drew his pistol and powered it up. He walked around the car and turned toward where he expected Amaya to be, but she wasn't there. He looked back over his shoulder. Amaya and Gerald were still on the other side of the patrol car. They leaned close to each other, having a conversation too quiet to hear. Were they talking about him? His lack of experience? Vadin tried once again to rub the tension out of the back of his neck.

"Got it." Gerald nodded. "My boy's got plenty of enthusiasm, if ya take my meanin'."

So, was enthusiasm a bad thing? Some idiom he was missing? Maybe Amaya would give him a clue in her response.

Amaya smiled and led Gerald around the front of the car. "I've got one a little like that back at the station. Plenty of good intentions, but very little forethought."

That could only be Nurinyan. His impulsiveness had earned him two rejections from previous *kiandai*. Vadin blew out a breath. Maybe they hadn't been talking about him. Conner, then? He did act a little like Nurinyan.

Amaya twitched her head toward the police car. "Perhaps we need someone to mind the exits?"

"Might be best, if ya don't mind either taggin' along with us or goin' solo." Gerald rushed to catch up with his younger partner.

Amaya speed-walked around the car.

Vadin fell in step with her and spoke English. "Everyt'ing is all right?"

"You're fine, Vadin. Help Gerald, follow his lead, and be aware of the surroundings." Amaya charged on ahead and caught up to Conner.

Vadin kept her pace and drifted toward Gerald.

Amaya had no sooner reached Conner than he yanked the door open. His knees bent and he leaned forward, ready to spring in. Gerald reached for him and missed again. To stay well out of the way, Vadin took a step back.

She caught Conner by the belt. His shoes slipped on the asphalt, and he turned a scowl on Amaya before looking at his partner.

Gerald held his open hand up. "Don't look at me like that, son. Someone's gotta mind the exit, and you drew the short stick."

Conner huffed. "You don't think you'll need help in there?"

Amaya straightened. "With three suspects and two teams, one will likely slip past us. This is the obvious way out. Keep watch on it."

"I don't believe this!" Conner pointed at Vadin. "Make him watch the exit."

"They got a rule in the *kiandarai* that says he's too young to be flyin' solo. We don't have that rule, so get." Gerald gave his partner a push on the shoulder. "Sit on the radio and watch for anyone trying to rabbit outta here."

Vadin felt his ears getting hot again. They really did think he wasn't able to handle this.

Conner shoved his gun back into his holster. "Yes, sir." He trudged back to the car, kicking at loose rocks along the way.

That kind of behavior was what humans thought was ready for duty? Vadin's younger siblings were more mature than that. By comparison, Nurinyan was an even-tempered professional. Going alone into this situation might not be prudent, but at least Amaya wasn't going to have to put up with Conner's foolishness.

Gerald rolled his eyes and muttered. "That kid's gonna wear me out. How he ever made it out of the academy, I'll never know." He clapped his hand on Vadin's shoulder. "No offense intended, Vadin. Had to tell 'im somethin'."

"Be careful." Amaya entered and turned left.

Gerald unsnapped the strap on his gun and drew it. "We're going to do this by the numbers. Nothin' fancy. No hero stuff."

By the numbers? That had to mean the same as within the protocol. "Understood."

"Let's go."

Vadin followed Gerald in and crouched behind a reception counter made of old wood paneling like the walls at Hawk's Nest.

Gerald crept to the end and peeked through a door. "All right, son, stay on my tail and keep your eyes open."

Tail? What tail? Was that an idiom or did humans really have a tail? He'd have to ask Amaya later. For now, he knew where the tail would be if humans really had one.

Vadin followed Gerald through the door. They entered a short, narrow hallway adorned with a dense layer of dust and a few crumbled wads of paper. Broken glass crunched under Vadin's shoes.

Their movements raised thin clouds of heavy dust, which tickled Vadin's nose. He rose and trailed Gerald to the door at the end of the hall. Gerald paused and stifled a sneeze.

The human eased the door open and took a quick look. He bolted through. Vadin slipped the door open and found Gerald crouched behind a large metal frame that could have handled a massive piece of machinery. When the human sped toward the next bit of cover, Vadin took his place at the metal frame. The room itself was huge, an easy fifty strides on a side and ten strides straight up. Machinery had been stripped out, but the frames and workbenches bolted to the concrete floor remained. Vadin didn't see Amaya, but the forest of metal support structures obscured the far side of the room.

Gerald sprinted to the next workbench. Vadin raced into the vacated position.

Movement drew Vadin's attention left. He spun, keeping his gun aligned with his eyes. A man, half-hidden by equipment, aimed a revolver at Gerald. Vadin took aim and fired three quick shots, catching the man in the finger, the shoulder, and the cheek. The man's hand shook. He dropped the gun and collapsed.

Gerald whirled around and blew out a breath. "Good job. Cover me, and I'll get this guy secured."

Vadin nodded. "Go." He tapped Amaya's code on his comm crystals.

"Amaya."

"Vadin. One suspect down. Human."

"Good, but that doesn't preclude one of the others being Eshuvani." A soft thud came across the comm. "Let's keep the line open."

"Message received."

Gerald handcuffed the human suspect to the nearest piece of equipment and relieved him of weaponry before rejoining Vadin. "How long do those tranquilizers last?"

"Half an hour for most people." Vadin scanned the room. A blue and white figure flitted among the machine stations. "Dere. Amaya, Dere's anot'er one headed sout'."

"Message received."

Gerald pointed to the blue comm crystals. "You can leave those things armed?"

"Yes, it helps us coordinate."

"Huh. Handy." Gerald pointed. "There's number three."

Vadin followed Gerald's hand. An Eshuvani man stood on a second level balcony gathering indiscernible objects into a satchel.

"Amaya, number t'ree is on de balcony in de front of de factory." Vadin glanced down at his comm crystals.

"Understood. You two have that one. I'll take care of the one headed my way."

Gerald put his hand on Vadin's shoulder. "All right, son, while I figure out where the stairs are, you holler at him to drop that bag and put his hands up."

Vadin drew a deep breath and mentally switched to his native language. "You on the balcony. This is the *kiandarai*. Drop the bag and keep your hands in plain sight."

The man bolted for the front of the building. Vadin aimed and fired, missing all three shots. Glass shattered.

"Come on!" Gerald ran back the way they came and out the front door.

Vadin followed. Conner was nowhere in sight. The man from the balcony was already at the southern edge of the factory's parking lot. He paused and threw something dark.

A small cubical object hit the ground in front of them. Vadin scooped it up and pitched it into a stand of brush to the north then pushed Gerald back inside. A loud pop preceded a collection of hard pings on the outside of the building. Gerald pulled Vadin down. Some of the glass on the building broke and thuds hit the far wall on both sides of them. Blackened bits of metal stuck in the walls.

Five

Vadin hurried back outside and looked around. The place was deserted.

Gerald ran out the door and came up short. "For a minute there, I thought you were going to take off after the guy."

"I planned to, but his diversion worked too well." Vadin frowned and walked further into the parking lot. "Where did Conner go?"

Through the comm system, three shots from a dart pistol preceded the loud bang of a human pistol.

Gerald slapped Vadin's shoulder. "Come on. Sounds like trouble."

"Vadin, I'm hit." Amaya's voice came through her teeth. The strain had a tinny quality through the open comm. "It's not bad, but I need you. Remaining suspect is down."

Vadin's breath caught, but only for a moment before his training took over. "On our way."

He jogged back into the building but headed south from the entrance. The short hallway on this side was a less dusty mirror image of the one on the north. He exited into the main room with all the metal framework and wove his way back.

"Put that gun away, foolish one," Amaya ordered.

Vadin squinted into the distance to try to spot them, but the assortment of old workbenches blocked his view.

"Look, you stepped into my way." Conner's voice echoed through the comm and from further into the factory.

"Have you no better sense than to try to shoot past someone?" Amaya's scolding tone sounded like the sternest drill master at the training center. "Did you tell me you were there? Did you warn me you were going to take the shot? Did you step aside for a clear field of fire? No, you did none of these. To top it all off, you missed your real target altogether. You show a severe lack of professional discipline. Get the suspect secured. Now."

"If you had let me—"

Gerald leaned closer to the comm on Vadin's collar. "Florentine, don't you compound one dumb choice with another. Do as you're told, son." He groaned and moved back. "The brass isn't going to like this one bit."

"Brass?" Vadin glanced back.

"Superior officers. He's going to have to explain why he wasn't where he was supposed to be, why he fired his gun, and how he injured a fellow officer in the process."

When they came around a huge support brace for some unknown piece of equipment, Vadin finally spotted Amaya and Conner. Conner tucked a human gun into his belt and pulled out a set of handcuffs. Amaya sat on the floor with her back to the outside wall. Vadin rushed on ahead. He disabled his comm and holstered his pistol as he approached.

Amaya, keeping an eye on Conner, had a solid grip on her right arm a handwidth above the elbow. Blood wept through the fingers of her left hand.

Vadin knelt beside her and waved his hands back and forth to clear the dust. "How bad is it?"

"I think it hurts worse than it is." She looked down at her arm. "Open the seam on that sleeve so we can have a better look."

He unbuttoned the cuff and unsnapped the sleeve up to her shoulder. She let go of her arm and pulled the sleeve out of the way. A long line as wide as his finger traced half the length of her upper arm, deeper nearest the shoulder and shallow closer to the elbow. He prodded the area near the injury. Amaya's arm was cool. Her right hand shook. Was that the beginning of shock, an effect of the adrenalin, or something worse?

Vadin winced and drew a breath through his teeth. "Okay, what do I do?"

"English around humans." She clamped her hand over the wound again. "Tell me."

He nodded and changed languages. "Um, you have regen—" He looked at her collar and the little swirl set above the main collar tabs. "No. You cannot use regenerative gel. You are allergic. Um, use a spray styptic to stop de bleeding and an antiseptic, clean it up, and bind it."

"Reverse the first two. Antiseptic before styptic." She closed her eyes and leaned her head back against the wall.

Gerald leaned over Vadin. "I'll be back after we get the two suspects under wraps."

"That's fine." Amaya looked up at Gerald. "As soon as we get this treated, we'll go take a look upstairs."

"If you're up for it. Else me and the kid here can handle that."

The two humans took the unconscious man out. Vadin watched them for a moment before returning his attention to Amaya.

She raised her arms a few inches. "It'll be easier to get the backpack off by unhooking the lower clips."

Vadin traced the straps down to where they connected to the back of her trauma kit and pinched the connection to release the clips. She leaned forward, and he lifted it off her back and set it aside.

Dredging through his memory of the proper way to pack a trauma kit, he came up with the location of the fist-sized spray cans of styptic and antiseptic in the main compartment of the backpack.

He put the two cans next to his knee and picked up the sprayer for the antiseptic. "Move your hand away, please."

She smiled as she complied with the request but as soon as he triggered the bottle, the smile turned into a grimace.

"I am sorry." He winced. The last time someone had used this stuff on him, he was about to jump to the moon.

She blew out a breath. "There's no way around that."

He applied the styptic next before returning both cans to their proper places. The blood congealed and crystalized to stop the bleeding. After using a packet of diluted peroxide and a piece of gauze to clean the blood from her arm and hand, he secured a bandage over the wound. Vadin collected all the trash into a small plastic bag and stuffed that into the top of the backpack. Amaya pulled her sleeve back down and started connecting the snaps. As soon as Vadin had the straps of her kit reconnected, he helped with her sleeve.

"Thank you." She tucked her feet under her.

Vadin stood and pulled her up by the left hand. "What happened?"

"I saw our target over there." She pointed to where the human had fallen. "Conner came up behind me. He fired a moment after I incapacitated the suspect."

"Such intelligence." Vadin mimed thwacking someone's ear.

"He's not long for this career." Amaya slid her backpack over her left shoulder.

"Do you want me to carry dis?" He kept hold of the other strap.

"That means you have to stay with me."

He took her backpack from her and shrugged it on. "I have no complaints."

Vadin followed Amaya through the maze of support structures to meet Gerald as he wove his way back through the equipment racks.

The human officer took off his hat and ran his fingers through his hair. "You all right, *Kiand*?"

Amaya nodded. "I'll be fine."

How could she remain so calm about this? That wasn't an expectation of the protocol, was it? He would never become a real *kiandara* if he had to maintain such stoicism after being shot.

"Not to be tellin' ya your business, but the brass will want a word with you about this." He resituated his hat. "If I were you, I wouldn't go easy on the kid. I'd tell it plain, no sugar. He's a loose cannon and either needs boltin' down or removal from the ship, if ya take my meanin'."

Vadin leaned closer and tried to figure out all the idioms.

Amaya glanced at him. "He's a hazard to be sure. When your leaders ask for my account, I'll bring the details into the open."

Vadin straightened up. Amaya's translation had cleared that up.

She scanned the front end of the building. "Let's find the ladder to that balcony."

Gerald turned and waved for them to follow. "Found stairs up this way."

Vadin followed them to the front wall of the large room. Stairs running parallel to the wall led up to the second-floor balcony. Amaya kept her injured arm pressed against her belly as she ascended. Vadin went up after her, keeping a close eye on her in case she'd lost more blood than they thought.

When Gerald stepped onto the balcony, he whistled. "Got himself a nice little apartment all made up." He moved further in.

Amaya joined him. "It looks like he's been here a while."

"Den why has he not been discovered sooner?" Vadin arrived at the top of the steps and walked to the center of the room.

"Prob'ly sneaks in and out in the dark or mebbe there's a back door, whether part of the original construction or not." Gerald shrugged.

The corner of the balcony had a camp cot and a small stove on an up-ended crate. A metal toolbox in the corner was open but empty. A wooden box not quite big enough to fill his hand sat upended on the cot. The place had been cleared of dust.

Gerald snorted. "He's a neat criminal, at least."

"It's good to be organized." Amaya knelt by the bed.

"Best not touch anything," Gerald said.

"Not with fingers anyway." She drew her knife and used the point to flip the box over.

Vadin joined her. A couple loose scraps of paper and a silver set of collar tabs set with the dark blue communication stones were sprawled across the bed.

Amaya picked up the collar tabs. "Set three of five."

Gerald leaned over them. "Three of five?"

"Five sets of collar tabs went missing." Amaya slid them into her shirt pocket where they clinked against something else metallic. "The numbers were reassigned to names that are the Eshuvani equivalent of 'John Smith.'"

John Smith? Was that a popular character name?

"Huh. Something to do with that big shindig next week?" Gerald asked.

Amaya nodded. "We're assuming so until proved wrong."

Vadin picked up the slips of paper. He opened one and found a list of human names. The second was a list of addresses after the human mode.

Gerald rested his palms on his knees. "What's it about?"

"Names and addresses. Dey appear to be human but written in Eshuvani." Vadin handed the papers up to him.

"Huh." He scratched his head and gave them back. "Y'all better hang onto it and see what you can do with it. I don't think one guy in fifty in the whole Las Palomas PD can read that."

Vadin refolded the papers and tucked them into his pocket. Exactly one in fifty could: Ed.

"You better go get that arm patched up." Gerald nodded toward their vehicles.

She looked at her arm. "It'll be okay."

"Yeah, but humor me and go get an official word from the doc, huh?" He nodded toward the window. "You can fly that bird, can't ya, son?"

Vadin nodded. Did he look that young? "Yes. Easily."

"Good, then you two get." Gerald offered Vadin his hand. "Y'did good. You keep doin' it like you did it, and you'll be fine."

Vadin accepted the help up. "T'ank you." As he approached the balcony rail, he stopped and found where he'd been on the floor when he'd taken his shots. He should have had the suspect. The target had been right where Vadin was standing.

Amaya stood next to him.

"I missed him, Amaya. Clear shot."

"Not so clear." Gerald slapped the railing. "You had this stuff in the way, and he was a bit further back than we are."

"You were right there, where the footprints end?" Amaya pointed.

"Dat was Gerald. I was a stride or two closer." He leaned forward onto the railing. "I should have had him."

Amaya nodded. "Maybe. What is your estimate for the lateral and vertical distance?"

Vadin grimaced and imagined pacing it out. "Ten strides lateral? Maybe fifteen? Six or seven vertical?"

"Strides?" Gerald scratched his head.

Amaya glanced at him. "A stride is a little over a yard."

Gerald squinted. "'Kay, so yeah, I'd make it about forty feet out and twenny up."

"My estimate is similar." Amaya tapped the gun in his holster. "And the power setting on your gun is?"

Could he have been that foolish? He pulled his gun and checked the power level then smacked his forehead with the side of his fist. "I was set for close range. De shots never even made it dis far."

Gerald smiled and pulled him into a one-armed embrace. "Rookie error, son. We all made 'em. Learn from it and do better next time."

"But I could have had him."

"Maybe." Amaya took a step back. "This angle would have been difficult, Vadin. Possible but not entirely likely. If you're concerned about your accuracy, we can work on improving it."

"If dere is time." He looked at the marksmanship instructor crystal in her collar tabs.

She smiled. "We'll find time."

Vadin gestured for Amaya to precede him down the stairs. Gerald followed them out of the building.

Both of the human suspects sat in the back seat of the patrol car. Conner sat in the front seat with both doors open. He popped out and ran to meet them.

"I tol' you to stay with the car!" Gerald hustled forward and tried to get his arm across Conner's shoulder. "We got suspects to watch over."

"You stay with the car." Conner twisted away and came ahead.

Vadin interposed himself between Amaya and the human. Gerald glared and went to guard the suspects.

Conner walked backwards in front of them. "*Kiand*, I'm-I'm sorry about what happened. You were right. I should've stayed on the radio, but I thought I could help."

"It will be up to your commanding officers to determine the consequence for your lack of professionalism." Amaya stopped.

"At least it wasn't a bad injury. I mean, you'll be okay in no time."

Her eyes narrowed, and she approximated the stance she would have been in while aiming her gun. Her right hand still shook too much. "Look where the injury is."

"Yeah, it's on the back of your arm."

"You're missing the target I want you to see." She blew out a sigh.

Vadin walked around to her right. He couldn't fault Conner. He didn't see what Amaya meant, either.

Leaving her right arm in position, she lined her left fingertips with the injury and her palm near her chest. "Less than a hand-length to the left, and Vadin would have had much worse than a graze across my arm to deal with."

Vadin's jaw dropped and his brow furrowed. He hadn't thought about how close that had come to hitting her in the back. "He would have–You would be–"

"A full hand-length over is very nearly a kill-shot on an Eshuvani, Conner, but a human wouldn't be in good shape, either." She lowered her arm.

Conner made an abrupt gesture toward the trauma kit Vadin carried. "It would've hit that backpack."

"There isn't much in my trauma kit that could stop a bullet. Darts, yes. A bullet, no." She tucked her right arm tight against her belly. "You were reckless."

"And that's what you'll tell the brass?" Conner frowned.

Amaya's jaw tensed, and she blew out a breath. "If they call for me, I will answer their questions with the facts without embellishment. You should expect neither more nor less."

Conner scuffed the ground with his shoe and walked back to the patrol car.

Was that really how humans apologized? What a farce!

Amaya shook her head and continued to the avi. She spoke in their native language. "Let's go before I lose my composure and say what I'm thinking."

Vadin followed her to the passenger side and opened the door. He stayed near at hand in case she needed help getting situated. "Maybe you should."

"It wouldn't do any good." She climbed in. "He has disengaged his ears."

"At least he apologized." He closed the door and ran around to climb in the other side. Vadin set Amaya's backpack next to her. "That was an apology, wasn't it?"

"Only in form. Truly? No, it has suddenly occurred to him I can cost him his career, depending on what I say to his superiors." She leaned back against the headrest and closed her eyes.

Vadin pushed the ignition. "Then that was an effort to get you to feel more amicable toward him?"

"Exactly."

"Incredible. I'm glad they're not all like that." Vadin glared at the human for a moment and lifted off. "Do you need a hospital?"

Amaya shook her head. "Not for something this minor. Head for home."

He got his bearings off the sun and aimed the avi toward Hawk's Nest.

Six

Ed Osborn sang along to "Eight Days a Week" on the radio while the road between Las Palomas and Hawk's Nest threatened to rattle the car apart. At the rate the work was progressing on paving this road, he'd have a smooth ride by next year's summer. Maybe. He would never have guessed that paving five miles of road would take so long.

The bouncing ride ended with one last bump as he drove onto the avicopter landing pad in front of Hawk's Nest. There were no stripes on this parking lot, so he invented a space at the end to leave enough room for a couple avis. Pushing both the brake and the clutch to the floor, he shifted into park and turned the key. Ed stepped out of the car and slid the keys into his pocket. Staying in the shade of the building, he scooted along to the main entrance. The door slid open as he approached, and he stepped inside.

Little had changed in here since Consecration Day nearly a month ago. The ragged chairs, the battered wood paneling on the walls, and the makeshift dispatch desk hadn't been replaced. But then, Amaya hadn't had time to do more than breathe. Improving the aesthetics of the station would keep.

Ishe pushed off from the desk and rushed over. "Ed! So good to see you!" She threw her arms around him in a hug that would do a grizzly bear proud.

Ed wormed an arm free and patted her back. "It's good to be seen."

She pushed away from him and scurried back to the desk. Her dark hair was in a ponytail that kept it off her collar, barely. Any longer, and she'd have to wear the ponytail off the top of her head like a fountain.

"Is Amaya here?" Ed strode over to the half-wall and leaned against it.

The chair legs squeaked on the floor as Ishe slid across to the computer. "She and Vadin are on the way back from a call in Western Division. She should be back soon."

So, at average speed, assuming no technical malfunctions, they'd be here in ten minutes or fewer. He nodded once. "Great. How are things?"

"Oh, she's fine now." Ishe planted her elbow on the desk and her chin on her curled fingers.

He'd meant in general, but what did Ishe mean? Amaya hadn't been injured since he'd seen her last, had she?

Ed's brow furrowed. "Now?"

"Well, yeah, after we found out about the stuff up north, Nurinyan became her guide and—" Ishe's eyes widened and she clamped her hand over her mouth.

"Her guide?" Ed leaned closer.

There was only one thing Nurinyan would have to become her guide for. Who else had died?

"Nothing. Nothing. He was, um, really helpful. Yeah." Ishe grinned and batted her eyes.

Ed didn't buy that. Was she talking about Essien's recent death in the mine shaft or was there someone else? Either way, Ishe shouldn't have been talking about it. Talking about the dead was strictly taboo in Eshuvani society. Ed straightened. "She's blessed to have such helpful folk around."

"Yeah, for real, so, are you here on official business?" Ishe picked at her long, thin nails.

"No, actually. Esther and the kids are visiting at her sister's for a couple days. When I got off duty, I decided to come visit. With all this mess about the grand meeting, I really haven't had time to just chat with my *urushalon*."

The hanger door rumbled.

Ishe looked off toward the hangar. "So, do you think that's Amaya and Vadin or Orinyay and Nurinyan?"

Ed glanced toward the hangar. "They've switched partners around?"

"Nurinyan is a *kiandara* now, so Amaya's teaching Vadin." Ishe frowned.

"You'll get your turn." He reached across the table and jiggled her shoulder.

"Someday." She rolled her eyes. "I hope."

Ed walked around the desk and looked down the hall. Vadin climbed out of the pilot seat and grabbed Amaya's trauma kit. He slid it over one shoulder with enough gusto to throw himself off-balance slightly. Amaya came around from the other side, somewhat slump-shouldered by comparison. Her right sleeve wasn't hanging right, and she kept her arm tucked to her side. Ed's guts unsettled.

He glanced back at Ishe. "It's Amaya and Vadin, and she's hurt." He jogged down the hallway. "Amaya?"

She offered a smile that didn't make it to her eyes. "Hi, Ed. Just the guy I needed to see."

"What happened?" He looked at her sleeve.

There was a hole about halfway down her upper arm and another closer to her elbow. A white bandage was visible through the holes. Bullet hole? Sharp stick? He mentally tried out a series of possible causes and came no closer to an answer.

Amaya glanced at her arm. "Friendly fire incident."

A sympathetic pain tightened in his chest. Those happened sometimes, but it was never good news, not for the person who got shot and not for the person who did the shooting.

Vadin nodded, relaxing into his native language since Ed was fluent. "Someone was supposed to stay with the radio and watch the exits. He followed her in instead — I was with the other officer on the other side of the building — and then the idiot tried to aim past her. He didn't even hit what he was aiming for."

Worse yet. She'd been injured by someone's carelessness. Not even a reason he could understand or sympathize with. The shooter was going to have some major explaining to do. There was no excuse. Now Amaya was hurt because an officer hadn't exercised proper control.

Ishe leaned around the corner, jaw hanging open. "You're awfully calm for having been shot."

"I still have my professional mask on." Amaya managed a grin that looked no more convincing than the earlier smile. "Once safely back in my quarters, I may remove it."

"So, do you need a replacement?" Ishe asked.

"Not a bad idea." Ed gripped Amaya's shoulder. If her current partner had been someone with more experience than Vadin — hard to think of Nurinyan as fitting that category — she might be able to go out on another call, but with hole in her arm and an inexperienced *kiala*? An impending disaster in the works.

She shook her head. "Not necessary. If there's a call before Orinyay and Nurinyan get back, I'll take it. Once they're back, Nurinyan goes with Jevon. Orinyay goes with Vadin, and I'll be resting until tomorrow morning."

Ed shook his head but kept his comments to himself. He couldn't contradict Amaya in front of the *kialai*, but if the call came when it was just the two of them, she'd be hearing his opinion on that for sure.

"How can y—" Ishe's eyes narrowed for a moment and she smiled. "Right, we do actually have three full *kiandarai*."

"Umhm. Four, soon."

Once they reached the foyer, Ishe picked up a note. "Oh, um, while you were out, the secretary for His Transcendence was by. He wanted to be introduced to the facility. Funny, though, I thought the secretary was a really old guy. This one, he was old, but not that old, like your age, Amaya."

Ed chuckled behind his hand. She'd never been particularly sensitive about her age, but did Ishe know that?

"It is not wise to speak ill of the one who makes your schedule." Amaya leaned on the half-wall behind the dispatch desk.

Ishe pressed her fist to her forehead. "That's not what I meant. I mean, he's old, but not real old, like you're not real old, but you're kinda old, I mean—" She cringed and her ears flushed bright red. "Vadin! Help me out!"

"Why? You're doing so well," Ed said through a chuckle.

Ishe groaned.

Vadin smiled. "Halyuwin is old enough to be my grandfather. He would not send another in his place. His right and duty are to see to the arrangements for His Transcendence, and he takes it seriously. I've seen him go out to take care of things while he was ill or exhausted. And anyway, he was introduced to the station earlier this week."

"How much did you show him?" Amaya walked over to the desk and looked at the note in Ishe's hand.

"Nothing. Well, I mean, he could see the foyer and the signs, of course, but that's it." She winced and looked down. "I, uh, kinda made him mad. I thought something was weird. I mean, he didn't arrive in an official-looking avicopter, and I thought Vadin had said the secretary was an old guy, I mean a really old guy. So, anyway, something smelled funny about the whole thing, so I told him I couldn't leave the dispatch area and everyone was out, so he'd have to come back later. I didn't tell him Jevon was in his house working on the plans for the perimeter alarm. He got pretty mad."

Ed blew out a breath. At least this "secretary" hadn't gotten more than a good look at the foyer.

"Someone official would understand your duties." Amaya glanced out the front windows. "Did you get the tail numbers on the avi?"

"That was another weird part. There weren't any. That means it's stolen, right?"

Oh, lovely. In addition to Orinyay's old collar tabs in the wrong hands and someone equipping criminals with old *kiandarai* technology, some nut had redecorated an avi to look like the *tura's* on a quick look? And no chance they could switch the meeting to another venue.

Amaya nodded. "Most likely stolen. You did the correct thing, Ishe."

Ishe blew out a breath and slumped on the desk. "Oh good. I was sure I'd blown up the reactor by not showing him around."

"Did you try to identify the man?" Amaya asked.

Ishe shrugged. "Looked at pictures of the *tura's* staff in the database for a while. Nothing. I'll keep looking, though."

"Good. I'll be in my house."

"You might want to try looking at the pictures of known criminals, too." Ed took Amaya's backpack from Vadin. "If this nut wasn't really on the *tura's* staff, good chance he's experienced in creating trouble."

Amaya nodded. "That would be prudent if the search through the *tura's* personnel is not successful."

Without waiting for Ishe's response, Amaya headed down the back hall.

Ed walked alongside her. "You know I'll want the details about that friendly fire incident."

"That's why I was going to contact you once I got settled." Her hands shook.

Getting shot was bad enough, but something else was going on. "I'm glad I'm here, then." He opened the back door and held it for her.

The half-circle of almost identical stucco houses stretched around to both sides. Different plants and banners decorated some of the porches. Amaya had hung up the silly wind chimes he'd made for her in his high school metal-working class. Little metal Vs meant to be birds hung from strings at various heights around the scalloped ring representing a cloud.

He smiled. She still had that atrocious thing and hung it up?

The windows on Amaya's house were dark.

She stopped and turned toward him. "I did not leave the windows darkened."

He knew better than to ask if she were sure. "Let's make a circuit of the place and look for signs of entry."

Whoever was responsible was probably long gone, but better safe than dead.

She nodded.

Ed let her lead, trusting her better observation and tracking skills. Around the back of the house, they found an open window. Cool air from the air conditioner flowed out, billowing a lightweight, blue and gray curtain.

"I know you wouldn't have left it like that no matter what kind of hurry you were in." Ed pulled her back out of sight of the window and set her backpack down. "But how could he have defeated the locks?"

"That's a weakness of the magnetic system. If you can manage a strong enough magnet or current, you're in. I keep meaning to rig a physical backup." She crept closer to the window and drew her dart pistol left-handed. Most people would be incompetent off-handed but getting the marksman crystal on her collar meant she had to qualify ambidextrous.

"Let me go in and check it out." Ed drew his pistol from his off-duty holster.

"Ed—"

No, he would not let her argue him out of this. "Amaya, you're injured, and there are actually things that would hurt you worse than it'd hurt me. If somebody was here and set up this trap thinking to get you, I might stand a better chance."

"I can get Jevon or Vadin to go with you."

"They're kids. I got it, and if I see anything hinky, I'm back here in a flash." Ed checked the floor under the window and ducked through into Amaya's bedroom.

He'd seen the room only once when she'd shown him around, but as near as he could tell, there was nothing unusual. There was nothing in or under the hammock and the other furniture was built into the walls.

From across the room, he said, "Closet door, open."

The door slid open without a hitch. The closet held several copies of Amaya's uniform but very little else.

"Bedroom's clear." Ed returned to the window. "I'm moving on to the bathroom."

"Understood," Amaya said.

Ed crossed through a short corridor and found the bathroom in good order. Keeping Amaya informed, he checked the second bedroom and kitchen. He stood flat against the wall next to the storage room and ordered the door to open. He peeked inside. Boxes were scattered and their contents were strewn around the small room.

"Amaya! Whoever was here was hunting for something. He wasn't very neat about it, I'm afraid." He holstered his gun.

She walked out of the bedroom. "He was quite neat about searching through my pockets and drawers. Two people, perhaps?"

"Or one who ended up not having as much time as he expected? I'll just bet whoever was playing the *tura's* fake secretary was a decoy to keep your people away from the houses, and when Ishe didn't fall for it, they had to split." He stepped aside to let her look. "What do you think he was looking for?"

Amaya pulled some metallic things from her pocket. She showed him three sets of collar tabs like the ones they'd found among Wylin's things. "I'm guessing, but maybe these."

"Three of them?"

"The extras came from two other criminals we've apprehended today." She pocketed all three sets again.

"One was weird enough, but three?"

"Pavwin is helping me look into it." She looked into the storage room and groaned. "I did not need to deal with this today. There are too many things on my plate."

"Well, I'll help you look for evidence and clean it up. We can visit while we work." He pulled her into a one-armed embrace, careful to avoid contact with her injured arm. "Whatever I can do to help, I'm here."

She quivered. "I intend to take you up on that this time, but you may wish you hadn't offered."

As if he'd ever grudge his *urushalon* anything of his, including time. "Yeah, well, I've had a feeling something was wrong since you stepped out of the avicopter, and I've got a feeling it's more than that friendly fire incident. Ishe spilled the beans about part of why you're in Texas now, so I'm wondering if that has much to do with it."

Amaya stepped away from him and leaned her forehead on the wall. "What am I going to do with that girl?"

He rubbed her back. "Don't tell her anything you don't want the entire state of Texas knowing."

"At least it was you she told. We've already talked about it, and you, I can trust with anything."

"Yet you chose Nurinyan for your guide." As soon as he said it, he winced. That pushed the edge of petulant. If she chose someone else as a guide, she had a reason.

She went back to her room and returned with her backpack. "There was no choice. I had reached a point of crisis, so the Rite had to done immediately."

That was strange by itself. She was typically well ahead of deadlines. "Why did you let it get that far?"

"There was so much going on with trying to track down Wylin that I lost track of the days and dismissed the early symptoms as exhaustion." She sighed. "In any case, I would have probably asked Nurinyan to be my guide even if it weren't at crisis level. He's a combat specialist. He still had a bigger task than he'd bargained for."

He arched an eyebrow. "Come again? Why would Nurinyan's specialization matter?"

"I fought him as hard as I could." She opened a side pocket of her backpack and pulled out a small camera. "Fortunately, he's skilled at defense, so no harm done."

What was he missing? He took the camera and went to the storage room. "Y'know, you and I have done full-speed sparring before."

"This is different, dear one. During the Rite, I'm in no mental state to be controlling the force of my attack. I'm afraid I'd hurt you."

He snapped the pictures they needed and turned around. "Huh? Why would you—"

She held up her hand to pause him. "Forgive me. I assumed you knew what you seem to know nothing about. My fault. Eshuvani are rather private about funeral customs, and I think Essien is the only one I've lost since meeting you." She pulled out a fingerprint scanner. Her posture shifted as she squared her shoulders and settled into instructor mode. "When confronted with the reality of grief, some Eshuvani react poorly. They become so entrenched in their false assumptions about why they're grieving, or they blame themselves so heavily for the death, that when the guide presses the truth, the grieving one reacts violently. I am not in control when that happens. I actually have injured a guide before."

"So, now you always go with a combat specialist because although you're competent with hand-to-hand combat, you're not as skilled as one of them." He took the scanner from her. "Makes sense."

Amaya nodded. "Yes. Less chance of hurting someone that way."

Ed flipped the little switch for the scanner and ran the light coming out the end over the door frame. "But when I was a kid and pestered you about your bracelet, you sort of went into a seizure of some kind and slept for a while, but you didn't take a swing at me."

"That wasn't a Rite of Final Memorial. That was just relating an already resolved story that I hadn't fully dealt with."

"Oh." That incident had been bad enough. He picked his way through the debris in the storage room and scanned the plastic boxes. Asking more about the specifics of that old situation would be rude, and clearly, something bigger was going on now. There would be another time. "Can you tell me about this friendly fire incident?"

"Finish the official work first."

Always taking care of business before caring for herself. That would never change. "Right. You rest. I'll do the work."

She reclined on the park bench and pillows serving as her couch and closed her eyes. "I'll let you."

To give in that easily, she really had to be feeling rotten. He frowned and kept running the scanner over all the flat surfaces the intruder might have touched.

He finished before the end of a half-hour and found not one print that didn't match his, Amaya's, or one of her *kiandarai*'s on the scanner's file.

Ed got a clean shirt for Amaya from her closet before returning to the living room. "He wore gloves."

"That's about what I expected." She sat up and unbuttoned her damaged shirt, revealing the black tank top she always wore underneath.

He helped her out of the ruined shirt and inspected the holes in the right sleeve before he set it aside. The bandage covered a long stripe on half of her upper arm. She'd called it a friendly fire incident, and those holes hadn't come from a dart pistol. That meant one of the human officers. From Vadin's description, Ed had assumed someone had gotten careless, but was it really that? Could it be bad judgment? Surely, it wouldn't be deliberate.

The *kiandarai* were helping them. Everyone in the department knew that, right? They were all smart enough to set prejudice aside, weren't they?

Then again, maybe not. Parrish had transferred to Ed's watch last year when some of the guys in his previous assignment had raised a ruckus about his skin color. Nevermind that Parrish was good at the job and an upstanding citizen by all accounts.

The bigger concern was her frame of mind. The physical injury would heal. Even without regenerative gel, she'd healed from worse just within the last month. Emotionally, though. Nothing good ever came from an Eshuvani stuffing their emotions.

"Take off the professional mask and tell me how this incident went down." He held the new shirt open behind her while she slid her arms into the sleeves.

She buttoned up the front. Her jaw clenched and her left hand formed a tight fist. "Oh, if that kid stays on active duty much longer, he'll kill someone."

He parked on one of the stools fashioned from a few cinder blocks, a board, and some cushions and listened while she recounted the caper that ended with the new injury. He clenched his teeth while she described Conner Florentine's recklessness. Personally, he wanted to be assigned to the review team so he could have some of the responsibility for getting him out of the uniform, but professionally, he would have to decline if asked, or a halfway savvy lawyer would claim a conflict of interest had existed.

When she finished, he leaned his elbows on his knees. "Well, he discharged his gun, so he'll be on desk duty until the case is reviewed. He's a probationer, and I can't even think of a valid explanation for what he did, so I think it's pretty much a done deal that he's out. How are you holding up?" He already knew the answer to that, but he had to get her talking about it.

She rubbed her eyes with her trembling hand. "Not so well."

He moved over to the couch next to her and rubbed her back. "Anyone would be rattled by what happened, Amaya. Anyone."

She nodded. "I know, but it's not just this event. I've been hurt in the line of duty before. I've even been hit by friendly fire before."

"What's making this one different?"

Amaya fiddled with the cuff of her right sleeve, where her wedding bracelet used to be. "This isn't the first time I've been hit across the back of the arm. Last time, two people died."

Ed thought back through the time he'd known Amaya, trying to remember when she'd received an injury like the one she had now. His eyes widened. Years ago, when he'd pestered her about the bracelet she wore, she'd finally told him about the human with a deadly grudge and bad aim. He'd tried to shoot her and managed a glancing shot across her arm. Although he'd missed his target, he'd killed her husband and their baby.

He pulled her into a hug. She was a little cooler than normal, but not even close to the glacial chill he'd expected. A good sign.

"Would it help you to speak through it again, or is it enough to know I recall which incident you refer to, and I know why it hit you so hard?"

"It is enough." The tremor in her hands faded. "I had wondered if maybe I was still overreacting to the event."

"Hardly. A guy you should've been able to rely on shot you from behind while trying to do something stupid and then tried to make excuses? Anybody I know would be unsettled even without a previous event for a reminder. I was more worried when you seemed to have no reaction to it at all. You need to bring these things into the open for your own health and sanity."

She held onto him for several minutes. Her body temperature rose again before she pulled away. "I am greatly blessed you adopted me so many years ago."

"Not that many years ago. You're the old one, after all." He smiled and looked sidelong at her.

"Be careful about giving me a hard time about my age." Amaya chuckled and tucked her shirt tails into the waistband of her pants. "I may not make your schedule, but I will suggest some changes to your superiors."

He smiled. "As long as it involves coughing up the money to buy the equipment we need, fine by me."

"They're still thinking about it?"

"Umhm."

She shook her head. "They'd better think about it faster. Next week is coming quickly."

Ed snorted. "They're concerned about how it'll look for the men to have 'jewelry' on their collars."

Specifically, the captain had expressed concerns that the men wouldn't be taken seriously if they had "feminine shirts." There might be something to that. Two of the fellas on his watch would object to the "jewelry" no matter how useful it was.

"They're concerned about fashion sense?" She rubbed her forehead. "That shouldn't surprise me.

There's a way around the concern. Use the black apprenticeship collar tabs and attach the crystals on the underside of the collar. The black will blend in with your uniform and the back side of the comm crystals looks like a black dot. The apprenticeship tabs are not reflective, so I would guess most people wouldn't even notice them. Since they wouldn't be visible, you wouldn't need to be concerned about one on each side of the collar. Only half as many will be needed, so it's less expensive. Crisis averted."

Apprenticeship tabs. Of course! The LPPD officers didn't need collar tabs to distinguish rank and training like the Eshuvani did. They just needed the collar tabs to hold the comm crystals. Who cared what color they were?

"I hadn't even thought about the black tabs. I'll suggest that. I was trying to do a direct rank translation."

"The black will look less garish than the silver, so they may be more willing. If I'm called to report Conner's actions to the review board, I'll see if your captain has time for a quick meeting." She walked over to the storeroom. "Hmm. A pity my unauthorized visitor wasn't as tidy with his search in here as he was in the other rooms."

Ed pushed off from the makeshift couch and joined her. "Any chance he might have found information about the meetings?"

"Anything related to that is either in our brains or in the safe room." She crouched and picked up the cracked lid from one of the plastic boxes. She sighed. "I'm not convinced that's protected enough."

He rested a hand on her shoulder. The muscles there were broad steel cables pulled taut. He'd be glad when this conference was over. Amaya had been running nonstop since her arrival here a month ago. The tension in her shoulders testified to how much she needed a break. "There is no foolproof way."

"No, especially with so many interesting new ways to interrogate someone. We can only do our best job and leave the rest to God." She dropped the broken lid and stood. "I think we're going to need to clear everything out of here before we actually start cleaning up."

"That's what I was thinking. I'll haul." He pointed to the park-bench-turned-couch. "You sort."

She drew a breath and turned toward him.

"No arguments." He stepped past her and grabbed the first half-filled box. "You're hurt, and there's only so much spray styptic that can be used in one day."

Amaya shook her head. "I'm a long way from hitting that limit, even if I do tear the injury open again."

He nodded. "And I'm not going to let you get any closer. Go sit down over there, and I'll bring the stuff to you." He gave her a light push. "Go on."

Her smile turned more genuine as she found a spot to sit. "All right."

He set the first box next to her on the floor and went to get the next load.

Ω

Amaya took her leave of the captain of the Las Palomas department and nodded a farewell to the receptionist seated outside the door. She checked her watch. A lot had been accomplished in the few hours she'd been here this morning. The sun had barely crested the horizon when she'd begun her testimony about the friendly fire incident yesterday. In spite of Ed's assurances that she wasn't exaggerating the severity of what had happened, she'd been relieved when the committee had expressed a reasonable degree of professionally moderated shock and dismay when she related the events. They weren't going to simply give the boy a warning.

Whether he would be relieved of duty for good or sent back to the academy for more training, she couldn't say. Amaya would have sent him back for more training and left a suggestion in his file that his first few years be scheduled in remote places where his excess of enthusiasm would be less likely to injure someone. A few years of maturity might be all the boy needed to level him out. Whatever the decision, it was out of her control.

Her testimony had finished by mere moments when she'd sat down with the captain to suggest using black apprenticeship tabs installed upside down to get past the complaints of the fashion-conscious. Allaying his concerns and pointing out that the black tabs were less expensive than the metallic ones resulted in the pay voucher in her pocket earmarked for enough collar tabs and Eshuvani handcuffs to equip the senior officer in each pair. A stop at the bank to exchange the funds to the right currency and another at the requisitions office would take care of getting the equipment purchased for Las Palomas.

She wove her way through the small room packed with dispatchers, records clerks, and officers stuck on desk duty and jogged down the stairs.

"Hey, wait up!" Conner Florentine called.

She turned. The tall, dark-haired, dark-eyed cause of yesterday's trouble strode toward her. The ache in the back of her arm reminded her of both the recent injury and the similar one from years ago.

Amaya glared at him hard enough to drill a hole through his lead-filled skull. "I have many things to do today. What did you need?"

He glanced at the stairs. "Are you here to give your testimony?"

"Among other things, and with those chores completed, I must be going." She schooled her harsh look. No matter how justified, her ire would solve nothing.

"So, what did you tell them?" He shifted one foot backward and his eyes narrowed.

From that position, he was well-prepared for aggression. Surely, he wouldn't do something that foolish in the midst of so many people.

"Exactly what I told you I would." She took a half-step away from him to prepare to meet an attack if one came. "I answered their questions without embellishment. What they decide next is their own will."

"So, you couldn't even cut me a break?" His jaw clenched.

The room quieted as if controlled by a switch. A few of the men rose and crept closer. Apparently, they'd caught the same body language she had. Good of them. If Conner tried anything, he'd have more than her to deal with.

"I was not going to lie for you, no, but neither did I make any effort to deliberately influence their decision." Her hand drifted closer to the butt of her dart pistol. "I simply told them what happened and answered the questions they had. If the truth is distasteful to you, you should make a greater effort to make the truth palatable."

After a look around the room, he crossed his arms over his chest and brought his feet together. "Did they tell you what they were going to do?"

That simple move might be a good sign, but she stayed ready. "It would have been horribly unprofessional if they had."

One of the clerks from the upper floor took the stairs halfway to the ground floor and stopped. She leaned over the rail. "Florentine, Cap'n wants you."

Conner huffed. "Thanks for nothing."

"And thank you for the injury to my arm and the reminder of a much deadlier sniper," she muttered.

He disappeared up the stairs with the clerk. Once he was out of sight, she waved an acknowledgment to the other officers before she turned and left the station.

At mid-morning, heat mirages were already rising from the parking lot's black pavement. Amaya walked to the back corner where the light cargo hauler sat. Doing most of the work with her left hand, she opened the door and pulled herself inside then set the trauma kit next to the seat. The inside of the cargo hauler could've been used for an oven.

She flicked the switches to power up the systems and hit the ignition. Pulling up on the collective lever in her left hand, she got underway.

When her collar chimed, she pressed a blue crystal. "Amaya."

"Jevon. The perimeter alarm is installed. When you return, I can scatter everyone throughout the station to watch for the lights to change while someone trips one of the sensors."

Good. She hadn't wanted to be unpleasant about getting that set up, Texas heat or not. She'd done too much growling lately. "I'm on my way back now. Get everyone in position."

"What's your estimated travel time?"

She smiled. "I'm not going to tell you that or which way I'll be coming in. It will be up to you to find me. Follow the protocol."

The intruders they were watching for would not do them the courtesy of calling ahead. Their practice and tests should reflect that reality.

He groaned. "Message received."

The connection clicked off.

Now where could she set down where the avi wouldn't be easily visible? She would have to be flying the cargo hauler.

As the city sped by below her, she recalled the terrain around the station. There was a large, low-hanging oak a quarter mile southeast of Hawk's Nest. It wasn't large enough to hide the entire avi, but if she set down behind the tree, the camouflage might be sufficient.

She adjusted her course to circle around and come in from the southeast. She flew in low enough to brush the top of the grasses in case someone tried to be clever and watch for her. After setting down with the oak between her and the station, Amaya powered down, grabbed her kit and hopped out. After easing the avi's door closed until the latch clicked, she shouldered her backpack and walked toward the station. There was no protocol for where to set the sensors. Otherwise, a creative criminal only had to learn the protocol and set down inside the perimeter. After verifying that their best three plans were all suitable, she'd left the installation details to the whim of Jevon and Nurinyan, which was just as well. She didn't know any more about the placement of the sensors than any potential attackers did.

What cover there was out here amounted to a few stands of scrawny yaupons, spindly oaks, or shrubby junipers. After sprinting from the cover of one short, fat juniper, she got halfway to the next cluster of yaupons when her people erupted from the station. Nurinyan and Vadin headed off to the north. Orinyay came south by herself. Jevon and Ishe were not yet visible. They had probably gone out the back.

Amaya crouched among the gray-barked yaupons. The juniper she'd left and another three strides away were better cover but moving now would increase her chances of being spotted. She stayed where she was and watched Orinyay while keeping an eye out for the other two.

Orinyay kept her gaze at ground level and moved too fast. A real threat could easily get around her or worse. Amaya shook her head. Orinyay was just old enough to have been trained in the pre-hologram protocol. She should know better. Amaya picked up a pebble and waited for the analyst to get within range then tossed the pebble at her. When it hit her in the leg, Orinyay startled and drew her pistol.

Amaya stepped out of the cluster of yaupons. "You could easily be dead. I prefer you alive."

She returned her pistol to the holster and sighed. "You startled me."

"Mmhm. What did you do incorrectly?" Amaya jogged over to her analyst.

Orinyay studied the dirt at her feet and bit her lip. "Kept my eyes on the ground watching for snakes and came too quickly. It's been a long time since I reviewed this particular protocol."

Amaya clapped her hand on Orinyay's shoulder. At least she'd recognized the error. That was the first step to correcting it. "Let's amend that. Help me bring the avi in and we'll get everyone together for a review and more practice. First, though, you need to report your find."

While Orinyay contacted the others, Amaya led her back to the avi. She prayed for a light call volume. If her most experienced staff member had erred on such a basic level, the *kialai* were likewise going to need practice with this low-tech solution.

Seven

After several practice sessions in the ridiculous heat and impossible humidity, Amaya sat in the briefing room sipping her water. Most of her people were reasonably competent on responding to the proximity alarm. Ishe had caught on to the new protocols faster than anyone else, including Orinyay, which gave Amaya hope for the *kiala's* future. There would be more practice later in the week at a cooler hour for those who were not ready.

Her collar chimed the pitch reserved for dispatch. She sat up straighter and tapped one of the blue crystals. "Amaya Ulonya *Kiand.*"

"Dispatch. The *kiat* requests your presence at his office immediately."

Yes, because she could always drop everything and come running. She scowled and rolled her eyes.

After requesting pickup at her location, Amaya signed off and groaned. She discarded her half-finished water in the kitchen before grabbing her trauma kit from its spot behind the dispatch desk.

"Going somewhere?" Ishe twirled her hair around her fingers and managed to get it tangled.

Amaya nodded once. "Instant meeting with the *kiat*. I'll be back as soon as I can. For calls, send Nurinyan with Jevon and Orinyay with Vadin."

"You got it!" Ishe freed her hand and jotted a note on a scrap of paper.

The avi landed in the parking lot. Amaya darted out and climbed into the passenger side. The pilot was Sotril, the same elderly, gray-haired *kiand* she'd met soon after arriving in Woran Oldue. Deep scars marked his left hand, and a hinged, metal brace supported his right knee. His life of protecting the far frontiers of inhabited land hadn't treated him well, but even at his advanced age, Sotril was still in active service, a worthy goal Amaya hoped to attain some day.

Sotril leaned across and embraced her. "Well, how's it going on your own frontier?"

She smiled. "Oh, inventive engineering has been the way for certain."

"Yeah?" His eyes lit up. "Well, let me hear it!"

She recounted some of the engineering projects she or others at her station had used to get things running, everything from her furniture assembly projects to Jevon's efforts to keep the two cobbled-together avis in the air.

The old pilot reached over and gripped her shoulder. "That's the way to show that ol' piranha." He landed the courier in the *kiat*'s parking lot. "You keep at it, *Kiand*." He grew serious. "And watch yourself on these meetings come Monday. I don't know anything definite, but if the piranha wants to start something with the humans, killing three governors and the *tura* would sure get it done."

So, even Sotril, with his decades of experience, was expecting trouble. Maybe she and Pavwin weren't unnecessarily paranoid after all.

"Thank you. Pavwin and I are using every resource we can."

He nodded. "And inventing a few?"

"As necessary." Everything from creatively organized meeting spaces to hastily rebuilt, low-tech proximity alarms.

He winked. "You'll do fine. If I get wind of anything definite, I'll let you know."

"I do appreciate it." Amaya thanked the pilot of the courier and stepped out. She backed away and waited for him to take off.

Simply standing outside Emyrin's office prickled her skin. She'd have to stay alert.

She walked into the undersea-themed waiting room. As if the previous decorations hadn't been garish enough, ceramic fish now hung from the ceiling on pieces of transparent wire. Most were above head height, and the ones that weren't were in the corners or near walls.

Teviya sat at her desk. Yellow lip gloss and blush colored her lower face. Dark eyeshadow trailed all the way back to her hairline. Her hair had been dyed the same dark gray as the eyeshadow, and the form-fitting dress she wore today was predominantly white with semicircles of material attached in an overlapping pattern. Wide sleeves drawn tight at the wrists hung from her arms. Her fingernails and the webbing between her fingers had been painted brilliant yellow.

How did humans describe seagulls? A useless bird that flies in, squawks, makes a mess, and leaves? How terribly appropriate! Amaya pressed her lips together to avoid laughing.

"Grace be unto you." Teviya recited the greeting with all the emotion of a machine.

Amaya came nearer and smiled. "And peace, from God, the Father of our Lord."

"Once Pavwin arrives, I'll show you both in." She waved somewhere in the general direction of the chairs.

The door behind Amaya opened. Pavwin entered. A heavy bruise on the side of his neck disappeared under his shirt. Had he not used regenerative to heal the damage? Perhaps he couldn't. She looked at his collar tab and noted he was missing the swirl that would mark him as allergic. He'd exhausted his permitted daily dose of regenerative, and the injury still looked like that? How badly had he been hurt? He should be resting at home.

She clasped his right arm and embraced him with the lightest touch. "Are you well?" she whispered in his ear.

"Later." He stepped away from her.

Teviya rose. "This way."

Her typical stiletto heels had fanned out extensions in the front that looked a little like duck feet. At the door of Emyrin's office, she waved a hand over the sensor before returning to her desk.

Pavwin preceded Amaya into the room. Just crossing the threshold sent a chill through Amaya. Somehow, Emyrin had to be involved in the threats. Nothing else made sense. Who else would have the authority to reassign collar tabs and block training records? Proof, though. Her hunches, no matter how logical, wouldn't matter to the judge. He was far too cagey to let the wrong words slip, but she'd watch him anyway.

"Sit." Emyrin flipped a notepad closed and tossed his pen down.

Amaya squashed an urge to rebel and remain standing. Her personal irritations with this man would not keep the incoming delegations safer. She parked herself in one of the two chairs as Pavwin eased himself into the other.

Emyrin leaned back and crossed his arms. "You wanted this meeting, Pavwin. What are you bothering me for?"

"You blocked an effort of ours to locate a potential threat to His Transcendence." Pavwin rested his elbows on the arms of the chair and steepled his fingers.

"You mean that request you made to use the tracking circuits to locate several *kiandarai* with 'suspicious names?'" He brushed the idea away with an abrupt motion of his hand. "Of course, I did. It was ridiculous request."

Pavwin shouldn't have brought her into this. He might have made some useful ground on his own. Emyrin was likely to reject any suggestions, no matter how logical or necessary, just to spite her.

Amaya shook her head. Since she was here, she had to back Pavwin's play as well as she could. It would change nothing, but she couldn't leave him hanging. "There is cause. Three collar tabs with communication crystals were found on three apparently unrelated criminals. Each has identification numbers belonging to someone who reported the set missing before the numbers were then reassigned to a set belonging to Ianolin Simiala, Ianolin Yharu, and Ianolin Welyans. You must admit that's a rather intriguing pattern. There are two more collar tabs fitting that pattern, but the dispatcher won't connect us through to the individuals."

Emyrin leaned forward. "They are more likely to be undercover officers and your activation of the tracking system might very well expose the *kiandarai* to unnecessary risk. No. Your request is denied." He turned to his computer and powered up the system. "His Transcendence will arrive on Tuesday. Be ready."

Yes, and if something did go awry regarding these other two collar tabs, he would insist they were foolish not to seek out their source.

"Serve with diligence." Amaya stood.

She maintained silence and a neutral expression until she was outside and well out of sight of the front windows. Pavwin followed her.

"The closer we get to the meeting, the less comfortable I am about having them at Hawk's Nest." Amaya turned toward Pavwin. "If someone wanted to eliminate all cooperation between humans and Eshuvani, a tragic event during the meeting would be one way to do it."

"Yes, our concerns are shared by others. We'll have to be careful." He stumbled.

Amaya caught him, but not knowing the extent of his injuries, she prayed she didn't hurt him further. She guided him to a nearby cluster of thin oak trees and helped him sit in the shade, supporting much of his weight. "You should be resting."

"As soon as I get home, I will." He patted her hand. "I had to try to get approval to activate the circuits on the other two tabs. My request for this meeting didn't include you, but I guess Emyrin wanted a bigger excuse to decline. I should have predicted that this would fail terribly and just stayed home to rest."

Perhaps, but with the peace between humans and Eshuvani in possible jeopardy, they had to try everything they could to predict problems and circumvent as many as they could. He knew that as well as she did.

"What happened, Pavwin?" She twisted to face him directly.

"Your warning about the invasion into your house in your absence was timely." He leaned back against one of the trees. "I arrived at home last night after a call. My partner had come with me to check the house after we found some of my front windows dark. I only darken the bedroom one and then only at night. No windows were compromised, and I spotted an unusual box half-hidden by one of my curtains, so we tried to enter through the front door. When I opened a door, an explosion blew me halfway to the station. I was quite a mess. My partner was behind the wall, and that protected him to some degree. It was a much nearer thing to loss than I ever want it to be, but with additional regenerative treatment tonight and tomorrow and rest until our review lesson tomorrow evening, I'll recover before I'm needed."

If he pushed the allowable outside limits of regenerative, maybe. Her chest ached in sympathy as she recalled some of her own major job-related injuries, the most recent a mere few weeks ago. "We're now doing frequent patrols and house checks."

"Prudent. I'll order the same." He closed his eyes and leaned back against the tree behind him. "Your perimeter alarm? Did you get yours to work, or is Wolf's Teeth's old one serving?"

"My old one reacts to squirrels, so we're using the one from Wolf's Teeth. It's up and functioning.

We put it through a thorough test earlier while I retrained my group on pre-hologram protocols."

Pavwin chuckled and winced. "You do have some young kids. The training centers focus too much on technology and not enough of what to do when the technology fails."

"Agreed, but even my analyst had forgotten the procedures. We'll be as ready as we can." Enough planning for now. She needed him to be well, and that wouldn't happen without rest. Amaya offered Pavwin her arm. "You need to sleep. Let's get you home."

She pressed and held her comm crystals.

Ω

Sergeant Ed Osborn finished Monday morning's roll call for his watch and passed out the dull black collar tabs to Nigel Parrish, Mark Hollis, Harry Gale, and Mike Stevens.

He picked up his own. "Okay, you're going to clip them to the point of your right collar but upside down so the crystals are on the bottom side." He demonstrated before checking the senior officer of each pair. "Good. Now ours are not programmed on the same system as the *kiandarai*. We have our own system, and Hawk's Nest is linked into it by a special access number. Your code is your car number in Morse code."

Hollis glanced up from his notepad. "Just the number?"

"Just the number." He picked up a stack of small notecards and handed them out. "Here's a quick reference card for all the guys in our division and the folks at Hawk's Nest. To contact the dispatcher, press and hold both crystals until someone answers. To key in someone's code, press and hold one crystal and tap the code on the other. It doesn't matter which you hold and which you tap. The system will take it either way. If someone contacts you, the tabs will chime. Tap one of the crystals to answer. Tap it again to end the transmission."

Parrish tucked the card in his pocket. "Can we reach Hawk's Nest dispatch directly, or do we still call our own dispatch for a relay?"

Hollis leaned closer to him and pointed to the bottom of the card. "Here. They're H-one through seven."

"Seven? There's only six–" Parrish squinted at the card. "Oh, I see. Seven's their dispatch. Thanks."

Osborn tapped his collar. "Use these to contact the *kiandarai* as needed and coordinate during a call. If you need backup, contact the dispatcher first, and she'll arrange it. Do not contact each other directly for backup, or we'll lose track of where everyone is. These do not have the tracking circuit because an apprentice is expected to stay glued to the training officer when doing field work. Questions?"

Kirby raised his hand shoulder high. "Will we all get one eventually?"

"As soon as money can be found in the budget. Anything else?" Osborn waited only a few seconds then clapped his hands once and rubbed them together. They needed to get on the way, and if he didn't curtail the question and answer session, the governors would land before he could get his people in position. "All right. Amaya already has four of her people in place at the airport watching for snipers and other problems. She reports there is a small band of human picketers protesting the meeting. So far everything's peaceful."

Tucker frowned. "If there are protesters, should *kiandarai* be there? Won't that rile things up?"

"The *kiandarai* are not in plain sight." He checked his watch. The plan called for all police and *kiandarai* to be in place sixty minutes ahead of the first plane. If they left right now, they'd get there in time. Barely. Time to roll out. Questions could be handled on the fly. "We have about an hour before the first plane arrives, so Hollis, Kirby, Parrish, and Tucker, you're with me at the airport. The rest of you will be handling our usual calls. I'll call you in if you're needed. Let's go."

Osborn led the way out and walked through the heat mirages to his patrol car. A headache hovered at the edge of his brain, and he rubbed the tight muscles across his forehead.

They were going to be fine. Between his crew and Amaya's, they'd have nine people there plus whatever security the airport assigned. They just had to land the three private planes and get the governors and their families to their hotel. Easy. Theoretically.

When he arrived at the airport, he drove around to a back gate that would let him in close to the hangars where the governors would disembark. Airport security had set up check points to turn back other traffic at both ends of the street. A half-dozen picketers walked a long but narrow loop at the edge of the airport's property. Their signs read useful things like "Go home, Twigs!" and "Earth is for Humans." So far, the group appeared to be content with their signs.

Nice sentiment. The Eshuvani would've gone home three hundred fifty-odd years ago if they could've. Wasn't an option with their damaged ship. Still wasn't an option now, and really, having them here wasn't so bad. For the most part, their hands-off policy meant humans could continue to develop their own culture and technology without being force-fed Eshuvani norms. The ones who did cross the line into humanity's sphere were usually benign, helpful even. Osborn couldn't imagine growing up without his *urushalon*.

An airport security officer slid the gate open. Osborn drove through and parked on the far side of one of the hangars, leaving the space by the gate open for the vehicles that would carry the governors to The Mansion, a swanky, tourist trap hotel on the west side of Las Palomas. Parrish and Hollis parked on either side of him, and all of them got out. More than anywhere else in the city, the air here lost its oceanic qualities and smelled more like a congested, big city street with its chemical tang, a cross somewhere between car exhaust and burnt dirt. A few minutes of this and Osborn could truly appreciate the coastal environment further from the airport.

There were a few buildings scattered around the parking area with one wide-open space big enough to taxi a small plane through without risking the paint job. A few of the buildings were massive box-like structures, big enough for two stories, but, he supposed, they probably just had high-ceilings. A few of the other buildings looked like metal barrels cut in half down the long axis, still lidded on both ends, with the open face stuck in the concrete.

His collar beeped at him. He pressed one of the crystals. "Osborn."

"Amaya. Good morning."

Osborn smiled. "Good morning." He looked around, but there wasn't an Eshuvani in sight. "Where are you?"

"From your current position, Vadin is in the hangar to your right with our avicopter. The rest of us are on roofs. Nurinyan is at three o'clock. Jevon is at six o'clock. I'm at—"

"Nine o'clock?"

She chuckled. "Eight o'clock. There isn't a building at nine."

He glanced to the wide-open area on his left. "True. Anything interesting?"

"Just the sign-carriers. They seem to think we landed here on purpose."

He took a few steps toward the picketers, a bunch of college-age kids in tie-dye, heavily worn jeans, and sneakers with one older, balding fellow. "Well, I, for one, am glad your people did. It's unfortunate they didn't make it to where they were going, but here's not so bad."

"No, I find here to be very favorable."

His hand hovered next to the crystals. "We're going to do a perimeter and building check."

"Good. Have everyone key in my comm code so we can keep an open line. Otherwise we're going to wear our fingers out tapping codes."

"Message received."

Parrish and Hollis were already tapping the code in.

"*Hay tres limusinas negras a su izquierdo,*" Jevon reported. Yes, Spanish was a handy language in this part of the world, but Osborn reflected that the kid had to start learning English. Only a handful of officers spoke both, fortunately Kirby was one of them, compliments of his Mexican mother.

Kirby pointed. "There."

Osborn followed his hand. The three black limos came toward them. If everyone had done their jobs, the previous watch had already thoroughly inspected the site and the limos and cleared them for this event.

Tucker grinned toward the nearest rooftop. "Pretty handy having them up that high."

Hollis tipped his head toward his collar. "We see them."

"All right. Parrish, you and Tucker inspect vehicles. Hollis, you and Kirby check out the buildings. I'm going to walk the perimeter. Keep your eyes open." Sure, he trusted the guys on the last watch, but another quick check couldn't hurt. Osborn checked his watch. The first plane is due in thirty minutes."

He made a circuit of the area, checking for crates, boxes, barrels, or disturbed dirt — anywhere a hazard might be hidden. He checked around all the corrugated metal buildings. The place was clean and well-groomed. No scraps of paper, pop bottles, or cigarette butts. Not even plant life grew up through the cracks in the concrete. The place was almost too immaculate.

No, he was not going to get paranoid about whether someone was hiding something under all the perfection. He would simply be happy that nothing was here, and he'd keep reminding himself of that until it stuck.

His headache threatened to get worse as he headed back toward the gate.

Maybe one more check. He went back to a tight spot between the buildings where someone with a rifle might get a bead on someone coming out of the aircraft. Finding nothing nefarious, he went to the gate and checked for sign of a bomb. Normal concrete and chain link fencing were all he could find. If there were a bomb like the one that had blown Pavwin halfway across the yard, the device was well-concealed.

"Sergeant, incoming plane. Looks like a Cessna Skylane," Tucker said.

Osborn returned to Tucker. A little red and white prop job rolled off the landing strip and came right for them.

"Pretty sure that's not Governor Zeldin." Osborn shielded his eyes with his hand. "No way you could get two adults, the pilot, and two kids in there."

As the plane taxied into sight of the road, the picketers started chanting and waving their signs. "Send them home!"

Yeah? With what? There were several million of them now, and humans hadn't gotten one guy to the moon yet, let alone a whole race to the far side of the galaxy, and Earth didn't have the raw materials for Eshuvani space flight. That was why they'd gotten stuck here in the first place.

The plane stopped. A heavy-set, balding man getting up toward retirement age disembarked followed by a mature lady with a shorter but still heavy build and black hair too solid to have been a natural color for her.

Osborn met the couple at the plane. "Governor and Mrs. Ginsberg?"

The couple looked up at him.

"We have a car for you over here."

Trusting lookout duties to the Eshuvani, Osborn had his people shield the governor and his wife all the way to the rear door of the first limo.

Once they were inside, he closed the door. The plane taxied away.

Jevon rattled something off in Spanish.

"No," Kirby said before he continued in Spanish.

Jevon answered.

Kirby whirled toward the fence.

Parrish leaned closer. "Did he say 'bomb?'"

"Yeah." Kirby jogged over to Osborn. "Jevon says there's a fence pole near where he's hiding that has scratch marks near the top like someone pried the cap off. It may be nothing, but he wants to check to see if someone slid an explosive charge into the pole."

"Ed, some of the equipment lists we've found on suspects would make efficient pipe bombs." Amaya spoke quickly but clearly. "I suggest Vadin contact the tower to hold the remaining two aircraft at altitude. Get Governor Ginsberg to a safe distance. Back the protesters off. Jevon can check the fence out. When it's clear, we can bring the other two aircraft in."

"Right. Let's go ahead with that. I'll get the limos out of here." He pointed over his shoulder with his thumb. "The rest of you back off the protesters and get the airport security out of the way, too."

"Jevon, wait until the protesters are out of range before you start, or we may end up with a mini-riot," Amaya said in Eshuvani.

Jevon snickered. "Very mini. There are, what, six of them?"

Osborn squinted in the direction of the *kiala's* hiding place. "All it would take is one with a makeshift weapon and an attitude." He opened the rear door of the limo and ducked to look in.

Governor and Mrs. Ginsberg were angled away from each other on opposite sides of the car. All was not happy on the home front.

The governor turned his head but not his body toward Osborn. "Are we getting under way soon, Sergeant?"

"Not quite, sir." He glanced back over his shoulder at the fence. "We've found something suspicious-looking. It may be nothing, but we want to check it out. Until we have that settled, sir, we're going to back the limousines away from the fence."

Mrs. Ginsberg leaned forward. "What did you find?"

"We're not sure. I'll advise you further when we know more." He closed the door before they could press him for more information and opened the driver's door. "Fifty yards back from the fence, please." He closed the door and jogged to the other limos to deliver the same instructions.

"De tower had already landed de second plane," Vadin said in English, hard-ending consonants carried over from his usual speech. "Dey are keeping it at de far end of de runway. De t'ird is in a holding pattern and apparently not too happy."

"They'll get over it." Osborn squinted toward the protesters still hollering and waving their signs. Naturally, they couldn't do as asked. He hurried over there.

Five of them were college-aged kids. The last was an older fellow with heavy, plastic glasses and a receded hairline.

The older fellow wagged his finger in Hollis's face. "We have every right to be here."

Osborn stepped forward and restrained the urge to match the older fellow's belligerent tone. "No one's saying you don't. We found something suspicious that we want our specialist to check out. Until we confirm that all is safe, we're just asking you to move your protest fifty yards away. We'll let you know when it's clear so you can resume your current place if you'd like. Please, just–"

A blond-haired student pointed. "Hey, man, where are the limos going?"

Hollis glanced back over his shoulder. "We're backing everyone away except the specialist."

A girl with long, dark hair lowered her sign. "So, you're not putting us on?"

"No, we're very serious." Osborn waved them back. "Please. Just go fifty steps that direction while we check this out." He stayed put while his men and the airport personnel escorted the group back then switched to Eshuvani. "Okay, Jevon. Go."

Jevon jumped down from the roof of the building he was on and ran to the gate. He climbed up the chain link until he was high enough to reach the top of the pole easily.

"Hey! What's that thing doing here? If there is a problem, I'll bet he started it," one of the protesters hollered.

Osborn glanced back. His people had the crowd blocked with Kirby standing in the road to direct traffic if any bothered to come this way. With the airport people helping herd the protesters, someone needed to stop incoming traffic from the other direction. Osborn ran down the street away from the others and set up at a safe distance to turn back cars from that direction. Osborn looked for the other Eshuvani. "Amaya, are you pulling your people back?"

"We've already retreated per the protocol. Jevon, do you need other hands with you?"

"Let me try to do this preliminary look alone. No unnecessary risk." He looked all around the edge of the cap and slid it up a quarter inch. "It's loose. Is that normal?"

"I'll check." Nurinyan ran out of cover close to where Osborn stood, climbed the wire fence, and tugged on a pole's metal dome cap. "Nope, this one's snug." He tried the next two with the same result. "Apparently, these are supposed to fit tightly."

"Then that's weird to start."

Osborn kept his eyes on the road but stole peeks at Nurinyan as he darted back behind the building he'd come from. "I can call the bomb squad."

"No unnecessary risk. I can check this by myself." Jevon spoke through his teeth. "Okay, the lid's off. Nothing attached. The pipe is hollow. Going to peek down the hole. If the sun were directly overhead, this sure would work better. Yeah. I see something. It looks like a cl–" He gasped. Chainlink fence rattled over the comm. "Take cover!"

Amaya repeated the warning in English.

Osborn dove into the ditch furthest from the airport property and prayed he found nothing with fangs or a stinger. He hit the ground and covered his head with his arms. His heart beat hard and fast. Nothing happened for several seconds.

## Eight

Two explosions within moments of each other blew shock waves past Ed Osborn. He scrunched down and waited for a third.

"Declare your status when called," Amaya said in Eshuvani, sounding far calmer than Osborn thought he could manage. "Jevon."

The kid coughed hard. "Safe and uninjured. Just a lot of smoke and dust. Moving to cleaner air."

"Declare your status when called." She'd switched to English. "Nurinyan."

"Safe and uninjured."

"Vadin."

"Safe and uninjured."

"Ed."

Osborn lifted his head and sat up. "Safe and uninjured."

She continued through the check-in while Osborn listened to his own men respond. No one reported an injury or sounded more keyed up than he expected. Only Tucker's voice read any discernible tension, but he was like that. He'd keep it together. Hollis reported no injuries for the protesters or security folks.

Osborn blew out a breath and walked back to the street. The gate was a cloud of dust around a couple good-sized potholes. The fence for ten feet in both directions was mangled wire and bent poles. The hangar nearest the gate had a debris-pockmarked side caved in.

Osborn whistled. "Oh, wow. What a mess."

Amaya snickered. "Truly. Do you think it's safe to proceed?"

"Let's check for other loose posts first." He walked back to the fence. "You keep your people up high and watch for trouble. If we find something, we'll sing out."

"Understood. Once we get the other planes in, we'll handle the follow-up here while your people get the governors to their hotel."

That alone was a terrific blessing. Paperwork was the bane of his existence.

"Okay." He looked down the road and waved at his men. "Let's get to it."

Ω

After yesterday's attempt at the airport, Vadin expected more trouble with the *tura*'s arrival. Everyone, especially Amaya, was more wary. Six weeks ago, Vadin would have said Amaya looked calm as they walked away from the group of Eshuvani protesters lined up in two equal rows on the sides of the dirt road, but he knew her better now. There were subtle differences in the way she carried herself when she was relaxed. She didn't stand so straight nor square her shoulders so perfectly. If he hadn't known better, he'd swear she came from the same social rank he did. That was probably just as well. Although the reputation was ill-deserved — especially in this case — many people related intelligence to social class. Her less relaxed posture would give a better first impression with the *tura*.

Like yesterday, protesters were ready to express their unhappiness. These protesters, Eshuvani who didn't trust the humans, stood with their backs to the dirt road leading to Las Palomas, refusing to countenance even the idea of a stronger alliance with the humans. Each of the dozen men and women wore red and black meant to show the hatred in their blood.

Amaya fidgeted with the cuff of her right sleeve. "If they do what they say they're going to do and stay on the other side of the perimeter sensors, we should be fine."

"They really don't seem like much of a threat." Vadin shrugged. "None of them were armed."

"There is no lack of rocks and sticks to be had, Vadin." She glanced back toward the group. "Further, we did not find a weapon, which is not the same as there were none to find."

"What can we do about it?" He wiped the sweat from his face.

She stopped in the shade of a large juniper and scooted over to make space for him. "Watch and pray we haven't missed something critical. We were fortunate at the airport. If Jevon hadn't noticed the scratches when he did, one or more of the limousines and their passengers would have been destroyed in the blast." She huffed and shook her head. "I fret over possibilities too much. We should take the events as they occur."

A cloud of dust approached along the dirt road.

Vadin pointed. "That must be them."

Amaya nodded. "I hope so. The sooner they arrive, the sooner we can go inside."

The procession drew close enough to make out individual vehicles. One police car led the group and another trailed, sandwiching two limousines between them. There had been three limousines yesterday. Had one of the governors left before the meetings even began?

Vadin glanced at Amaya. "We're missing one?"

She shook her head. "Unlikely. These coordination meetings are as important to them as they are to us. More probable is that one limousine carries the one larger family and the other has the two couples."

He pressed his fist to his forehead. Why hadn't he thought of that instead of jumping to the worst conclusion? The lead car reached the group of protesters and slowed a little. As promised, the protest lines on either side of the road stuck to their peaceful dissent. When the last car crossed the boundary into Hawk's Nest, one of the protesters scooped up a rock near his foot.

Amaya drew her gun and primed it. It whined through startup as she took aim. Vadin tried to follow her lead but fumbled when he drew his. The man nearest the one with a rock spun and struck his companion's wrist. The rock hit the ground while the second man had an intense but inaudible conversation with the potential rock-thrower. Abrupt movements on both sides threatened potential hostilities within their ranks.

Vadin finally got his pistol clear of the holster and aimed. His ears warmed, and if he hadn't had a job to do, he'd go to his room and practice drawing his pistol one hundred sixty-four times, or until he could do it without looking like an undisciplined idiot.

After nearly a minute of fussing, the group herded off together toward the collection of avicopters parked nearby. Once they were in the air and out of range, Amaya gestured toward the main building. "Let's not keep them waiting."

Vadin followed her. "Humans do seem to get impatient now and again."

"They can be intense and often become resentful of things they feel are slowing their progress." She shut her gun off and returned it to her holster. "They do better when they know the purpose of the delay."

The engines of multiple avicopters droned in the distance.

Vadin scanned the sky for them. That had better not be the protesters returning. They'd promised to leave as soon as the humans had arrived.

Without looking, Amaya pointed toward one of the more affluent sectors of Woran Oldue while she continued toward the station. "They're coming from that way."

Vadin turned and spotted a trio of blue and gold avicopters in the distance. "How do you do that?"

She smiled. "I've been in this profession longer than you've breathed air, Vadin. I've had a little practice."

He looked again and gauged their speed. If they didn't hurry, the *tura* would arrive at the station before they did. "We need to be back in the station prior to the avicopters's landing, or it'll be perceived as an insult." He tapped her on the arm and moved faster.

She caught up with him. "An insult because they have to wait a handful of seconds for us to come in from making sure we're safe? Now who's impatient?"

"It's just—"

"Protocol. I understand. I think it's silly, but I understand."

Did she really? Growing up poor, she hadn't learned the protocols for dealing with nobility.

Vadin entered the station ahead of Amaya. The rest of Hawk's Nest was standing behind or sitting at the dispatch desk. Officer Gerald Henderson and three other policemen Vadin didn't recognize stood around the foyer while the three families parked on various chairs around the room. He knew them from the pictures Amaya had passed around.

New Mexico's governor Bill Ginsberg and his wife Yvonne sat closest to the dispatch desk but angled away from each other. That suggested some conflict between them, but Vadin prayed that the cause wouldn't interfere with the conference.

The Texas governor, Patrick Farrell, and his wife Jackie occupied the next two chairs. He was a tall, thin fellow who might have almost passed for Eshuvani on a quick glance. Both of them wore a tan sports coat with a white shirt and a tie made of a leather cord bound by a brooch. She was turned toward him with an amiable smile.

The last family was Governor Sam Zeldin of Oklahoma and his wife Isabella. They were much younger than the other two couples. Vadin estimated their ages at late thirties or early forties, human calendar. Their son sat next to Isabella and fidgeted with the buttons on his bright green shirt. Their daughter perched on her father's lap and stroked the hair of a doll dressed in a gauzy yellow dress like the girl's.

The kids were young. Too young. Having them here put a whole new layer of tension across the back of Vadin's neck. This was a leadership conference not a family vacation. There were better times to provide an example of humans and Eshuvani working and playing together.

The door closed behind Amaya seconds before the three avicopters landed outside.

He leaned closer to her and whispered. "That was close."

"I'm sure everyone would have survived if we had been a few seconds late." She smiled.

Survived, yes. Avoided a major social gaffe, no. He suppressed a sigh.

The door opened and Halyuwin entered. Vadin caught his eye and nodded. Everything was as ready as it would ever get without another year or two to do some remodeling. After a glance around the room, Halyuwin backed out. His Transcendence Rinulyn Tolu *Tura* walked in with his wife, Leniya. Their two children trailed behind. Both the *tura* and his wife were dressed in white. His pants and jacket had blue and gold piping and the hem of her floor length dress was decorated with swirls of blue and gold.

His Transcendence stopped in the middle of the foyer and turned toward the governors. "May the light of God illuminate your path."

Amaya tipped her head downward and turned her empty palms toward the *tura*. "Walk only on the path He provides."

Governor Patrick Farrell of Texas stood and offered his hand. "Howdy!"

Rinulyn's brow furrowed.

Amaya started forward, but Vadin caught her forearm and held her back.

Rinulyn mimicked the Texan.

Amaya's jaw clenched. Apparently, that wasn't the right response, but was it offensive?

Patrick grinned, clasped Rinulyn's hand in both of his, and shook hands. "Put 'er there. Patrick Farrell." He gestured to his wife. "This is Jackie, my beautiful bride."

Vadin smiled. Apparently not, at least not for the human.

The Texas governor continued and introduced all the governors and their families in turn.

Vadin leaned closer to Amaya and whispered, "I'm sorry, but if you had interfered–"

She held up her hand to stop him. "Keep correcting me when I misstep, but I do find it amusing that I deal more effectively with humans than with our own upper echelons."

He nodded. "It's a different skill set."

Once Patrick had finished introducing everyone, Amaya took over and introduced all the *kiandarai* and police officers.

She gestured down the hall toward medical. "If you'll come this way, I'll introduce you to the station."

Vadin bit his lip. She hadn't phrased the offer as a question. At least she hadn't stated it as a command. He leaned forward and whispered, "Always use a question."

She nodded once.

Bill from New Mexico bounded to his feet. "Can we skip all this preliminary nonsense and get to the purpose for this meeting?"

"Aw, simmer down there, Bill." Patrick offered his wife a hand up. "I figger the nickel tour won't take ten minutes. We got plenty o' time to get to the business. I been wantin' t' see what one o' these stations looks like anyhow."

Bill rolled his eyes and slapped the nail-scarred wall paneling behind him. "A wreck, that's what."

Sam set his daughter down and stood. "Oh, I don't know. It's not the prettiest décor I've ever seen, but sometimes you have to do with what God gave. Besides, the kids would like to see the place, I think. Rinulyn?"

"The introduction is customary." Rinulyn turned to Amaya. "*Kiand*, if you would, please."

"Thank you for the opportunity to serve." Amaya walked backwards down the hall toward medical. "This way, please."

Vadin started to follow the group, but Amaya waved him off. She was right. The introduction to the station was the privilege of the senior officer. He would have been horribly presumptuous to tag along, but what if she needed him? His imagination conjured up all kinds of protocol errors she might make. He rubbed the back of his neck. She would manage. She'd have to.

Once they were all in medical behind the closed door, Gerald ran his fingers through his hair. "Boy, that Governor Ginsberg is sure in a snit about something."

Ishe sat behind the dispatch computer. "Yes. He and his wife are disagreeing about somet'ing to do wit' de dog, at least dat is what I t'ink she said."

Nurinyan squinted and leaned closer. "What? She did not say anyt'ing about a dog."

"Did, too." She pointed to the computer screen. "I looked up dat last word. See? Female dog used for bre–"

The human officers chuckled. When had there been any exchange between the governor and his wife? Vadin thought back through the *tura's* arrival and the introductions. He'd been so focused on the *tura*, the others could have talked genocide, and he'd've missed it.

Orinyay clamped her hand over Ishe's mouth. "Not in de open. Dese walls are not soundproof. Dat word has a different connotation. Try de idiomatic dictionary."

Vadin spoke just louder than a whisper. "I really do not t'ink dis is appropriate to discuss."

Ishe shrugged away from Orinyay and clicked a few icons. Her eyes widened. "Oh, so she is saying her husband has a—"

"Yep. That's what she's saying all right, whether it's true or not is a whole 'nother ball o' wax." Gerald perched on the edge of the dispatch desk.

The medical door opened down the hall. Vadin stepped forward to get a good look down the hall. No one in the tour looked back, but that didn't mean they hadn't heard.

Orinyay frowned. "Discuss somet'ing else, people."

"Before we create an interspecies incident," Vadin muttered.

Gerald slapped Vadin's arm. "Say, how's Amaya's arm holdin' up?"

He tried out a smile that felt a little tight. At least that had nothing to do with the governor's domestic trouble. "It is improving. I helped her change de bandage on it dis morning. It does not look as bad as de day it happened."

Ishe planted her elbow on the desk and her chin on her curled fingers. "So, whatever happened to dat guy who shot her?"

"Florentine? Oh, he was invited to find another career. Better for everyone that way. That wasn't his first flub, but it was his worst." He twisted around toward Ishe. "So, the schedule for this conference is to drop 'em off here at eight and get 'em at one?"

"Uh, yes, I t'ink." Ishe looked up at Vadin. "Right?" She turned to the computer.

Vadin nodded. "Right. Dey will start at eight and stop for lunch at noon."

"Yeah, dat is it." Ishe tapped the computer screen. "Den dey go play tourist."

"Awright. We'll be back about one. Come on, fellas. Calls were stackin' up when we picked up the governors." Gerald led the human officers out.

The tour came back through the kitchen and went on down to the hangar. Halyuwin stepped away from the group.

Vadin clasped Halyuwin's arm and embraced him. "It is good to see you again."

"Likewise. Are you well?" Halyuwin spoke in Eshuvani.

"I'm fine," Vadin answered in like manner. "My parents send their regards. They'll return from their travels next week."

"Splendid. They've been missed." Halyuwin glanced down the hall. "May I see the meeting room?"

Vadin led the way down the hall to the storeroom. Inside, he passed his hand over a panel on the back wall then moved a crate aside and found the X. When he tapped the code five centimeters above it, the hidden door slid open.

Halyuwin walked into the safe room. "Oh, excellent. Much improved."

The room had been outfitted with the four most comfortable of the station's chairs and a long, thin table constructed of plastic storage bins and a well-sanded board with smaller pieces of wood forming brackets around the top of the storage bins to keep the wood from sliding. Four pitchers of water and some glasses were arrayed in the middle of the table along with some raw fruits and vegetables. Each seat had a notepad and a few pencils and pens.

Vadin joined Halyuwin and winced. "It's still a little makeshift."

"It will serve." He jiggled the table. The top rattled a bit, but it stayed in place. "And lunch?"

"Aunt Arrellia was hired to cater."

"We should do well." Halyuwin guided Vadin from the safe room. "I noticed your *kiand* has improved in some areas of protocol but not others. Did she give you any trouble about allowing you to make arrangements?"

The door slid closed behind them.

"Amaya?" Vadin turned toward Halyuwin. "She's not that sort. She acknowledges she's more familiar with humans than with nobility and gave me control of those things I know more about. I had to run everything past her before I finalized it, but even that was more a matter of keeping her informed and making sure the arrangements were agreeable with human preferences, too."

Halyuwin cocked an eyebrow. "Truly? I was told by the *kiat*'s office your *kiand* was—"

The storeroom door opened and the Amaya came in, glanced around, then backed out. The *tura* led the others in.

Vadin smiled. She'd gotten that part of the protocol right.

"And this is the storeroom where we keep extra supplies of all sorts," Amaya said in English.

Patrick, the Texas governor, took several steps into the room. "Huh. So, where's the meetin' room?"

Amaya smiled. "We're actually very close, Governor. Vadin, if you'd trip the panel at that end please."

He walked back and ran his hand over the sensor. Amaya tapped the code on the wall at the other end. The door opened.

Patrick took his hat off. "Well, ain't that somethin'?"

"This is our safe room." Amaya stepped into the small room then backed out and gestured for the dignitaries to precede her. "This room can be secured against intrusion and should provide minimal distractions for your meeting. If you need anything, someone is always manning the dispatch desk in the foyer, and I will be here at the station unless an emergency call requires my attention. Ladies, would you like to see the briefing room?"

Vadin followed Halyuwin, the women, and the children back out to the hallway.

The Oklahoma governor's little girl tugged on her mother's skirt. "Mommy, can I go play outside? I promise I won't get dirty."

Isabella reached for Amaya's arm. "*Kiand*, is it safe for them outside?"

"If they stay inside the perimeter, yes." Amaya nodded.

If these kids were anything like his younger siblings, they needed hard, practical boundaries. "Between the houses and the station maybe?" Vadin pointed toward the back door.

Isabella crouched next to her children. "Okay, you can go out. Stay between the buildings. No wandering off, all right?"

The *tura*'s wife Leniya turned to Halyuwin. "I would prefer someone watch the children."

With the meetings officially underway, Amaya wouldn't need him for a while. Vadin caught Amaya's eye and waited for her smile. "Would you like for me to take care of that, Your Transcendence?"

"Thank you, *Kiala*."

The four kids ran screaming for the back door. Vadin followed.

Ω

Amaya watched the children run out. She'd never gotten to know her own child at that age, but she had found the joy of watching Ed grow up through those exciting times. She smiled and conducted the ladies down the hall to the briefing room, which had been stocked with cards, drawing materials, a few books in English, and some random board games. The makeshift table near the wall had pitchers of water and a platter of fresh fruit and vegetables.

Yvonne, the permanently grouchy wife of the New Mexican governor, looked into the room and scowled. "Is there somewhere I can lie down? I'm feeling jet-lagged."

New Mexico was only one time zone off, so she couldn't possibly be that far off her schedule. Amaya smiled and led her down the back hallway. "My guest room has a hammock you can use. I can darken the windows to make it nearly night-like."

She rolled her eyes. "Oh please, no. All that swinging back and forth will make me sick."

"I understand. My couch is about as makeshift as most of the furniture here, but the pillows are comfortable, and you're welcome to lie down there, if you'd like." Amaya opened the door.

The kids, joined by Orinyay's children, were chasing each other around the yard while Vadin and Orinyay's husband watched over them from the shade of Vadin's porch.

Yvonne huffed. "I suppose I'll hear these screaming brats from inside, too."

"There is noise-canceling technology in the walls. I'll engage it for you. It won't give you complete silence, but it will moderate the children's exuberance considerably." Perhaps there was more she'd like to complain about. Amaya dodged kids and stepped up onto her porch. She mentally switched to Eshuvani. "Door, open." Inside the living room, Amaya moved the pillows from the two chairs to the park bench-turned-couch and retrieved the ones out of the guest room and her own bedroom. "Noise canceling on. Windows dark."

The windows went black and the sound of the kids outside deadened to barely audible.

"Will that serve?" Amaya asked.

Yvonne stretched out on the couch and grumbled. "I suppose it'll do."

Amaya smiled. "If you need anything, the dispatch desk is always manned, and I will be around the station if I'm not on an emergency call. From the inside, you can open the door by pushing it to the left. The sensors in the wall will discern your intention and slide it open for you."

She left before the grouchy woman could find some other source of lamentation.

**Ω**

Emyrin stood within the shade of a large oak tree. The dart pistol in his holster was already switched on and set to rapid fire. If these humans tried to get feisty with him, they would not be walking away from the meeting.

An older model pickup truck bounced across the terrain, kicking up a cloud of dust. Only one silhouette sat in the cab. That had to be Conner Florentine finally putting in his appearance. There were supposed to be others. Just as well. The fewer of these backwater locals he had to work with, the happier he'd be.

He checked his watch and muttered. "Twenty minutes late. Fortunately, you're not wanted for anything timely."

The very idea of working with a human left an acrid taste in his throat, but the word was that Florentine had cause to hate Amaya. In the end, Emyrin would need a human to blame for the disaster. That should drive a wide rift between the Eshuvani and the humans. If his people answered the call for eradication of humans, Eshuvani would be free to advance as a culture again instead of stagnating while the humans caught up. His children and his grandchildren deserved better than sharing space and resources with these glorified apes.

The truck slowed as it drew near and stopped well away from the tree. Without turning off the engine, the tall, dark-haired driver stepped out and tucked something into the back of his pants.

Oh honestly. Did that stupid boy really think he could draw a weapon faster than an Eshuvani?

Emyrin bared his teeth. "You are late."

"Yeah, what of it?" Conner asked.

"If I cannot trust you, Florentine, I will seek someone who wants de work."

Conner propped his hands on his hips. "What's the job?"

"Dere are two for you or whoever else you wish to take part." And with the ignorance of the human species, he would either get himself killed and remove another nuisance from the world or become Emyrin's target for blame.

"What does it pay?" Conner plucked a dry grass from the ground and chewed on the end of it.

"What do you want?"

He shrugged. "A few thousand should do. Plenty for me and some for whoever wants to join me."

Emyrin looked away from Conner and squinted as if seriously considering the offer. Conner was a dead fool anyway. "Fine. You will meet me back here for your payment when all is finished. Listen closely. I will not explain twice."

That the boy didn't take out a notepad and pen didn't bode well.

Nine

After weaving her way back through the game of tag, Amaya re-entered the station and went to the dispatch desk.

Ishe muttered, "She's midnight-on-a-sunny-day."

Amaya thwacked Ishe's ear. "Not in the open as long as we have guests. I heard you all talking about Governor and Mrs. Ginsberg's potential problem while I was giving the tour. Fortunately, I don't think anyone else heard. If they had, that would be a bigger social gaffe than walking in after the arrival of His Transcendence."

Ishe paled. "Oh."

"Umhm. Huge insult."

Ishe twisted around in her seat. "Why did she say something out loud?"

"To embarrass her hus–"

The back door opened.

"Amaya!" Vadin's heavy footfalls ran down the hallway.

She whirled toward the sound.

He entered the foyer carrying the little human girl in his arms. Her breathing came in tight wheezes. She clung to him as tears streamed down her face.

Amaya grabbed her trauma kit from behind the dispatch desk. "Set her down on the floor. What happened?"

"That juniper between my house and Ishe's, she tripped into it." Vadin knelt and set the child down. She kept a solid grip on his hand. "There's a wasp nest. They stung her several times before I got there and pulled her away."

Amaya opened the front pocket of her backpack and pulled out the anaphylaxis kit. "Ishe, get her mother."

"That's Governess Isabella?" Ishe hurried toward the briefing room.

"Mrs. Zeldin."

She struck her forehead with the side of her fist. "Right, right. Last name, last name."

Amaya brushed the child's hair away from her face. "My name is Amaya. I'm going to take care of you. You'll be okay." She took the child's pulse and checked her over. "Were you stung, Vadin?"

He nodded. "Yes. Four times. Twice on my left hand, once on my right, and once on de side of my neck."

"Are you allergic?" She glanced up at him.

"I have no idea. I have never been attacked by a wasp."

"If you have any problems breathing at all, tell me immediately." Amaya counted three stings on the girl's legs, another three on her arms, and one on her forehead.

Isabella Zeldin ran out of the briefing room and knelt next to them. "Vera! What happened?"

Vera turned loose of Vadin's hand and reached for her mother's.

"Wasps were in one of de junipers outside," Vadin said.

Isabella grabbed Amaya's arm. "She's allergic. Terribly."

Obviously.

Amaya opened the anaphylaxis kit. "I'm trained in human medicine. With your permission, I can begin treatment."

"Yes, yes, please." Isabella held her child's hand in both of hers.

She took out a pre-loaded epinephrine syringe. "Is she allergic to medications?"

"Penicillin."

Penicillin wasn't part of the protocol, so they should be fine there.

She tore open the foil wrapper and injected the epinephrine into the girl's leg. "Ishe, take Vadin to medical and administer first aid. He is not to be alone at all for the next hour. Watch for an allergic reaction. Get Orinyay if there is one."

"Yep." She tugged Vadin up. "Come on, you."

What was the rest of the protocol for a child this little? This hole in her knowledge only confirmed her plan of putting a Human Pediatrics class into one of her remaining slots for her attempt at promotion to *kiat*. Amaya pressed and held two comm crystals on her collar and mentally changed gears to her own language.

"Dispatch."

"Amaya Ulonya *Kiand*. Connect me to a physician knowledgeable of human pediatrics. Life-threatening emergency."

"I'm sorry, Kiand, we have no such specialist."

That delay wasn't even long enough to bring up the database. This was not the time for political games! "Message received." She ended the transmission.

The girl's breathing eased.

Isabella stroked the child's hair. "Oh, thank God."

"I'm afraid the epinephrine is only temporary, Mrs. Zeldin." Amaya stuffed the anaphylaxis kit back into her pack, shouldered it, and tapped out Nurinyan's code on the blue crystals.

"Nurinyan."

"Amaya. Medical emergency. Meet me at the courier."

"Message received."

She picked up Vera. "Come with me, please, Mrs. Zeldin."

"Where are we going?" Isabella hurried to keep up.

"I couldn't reach a specialist to give me the rest of the protocol for a child this small. I know which medications to use, but I don't have the dosages, and I don't want to try to extrapolate." Amaya shifted her hold on the child. "We'll fly her into the hospital at Las Palomas."

Nurinyan ran past them. "I will get it started up."

Isabella's brow furrowed and tears filled her eyes. "Vera can breathe now. She'll be okay, won't she?

Amaya had lost her own child, but with God's help, this one would live. "The epinephrine wears off quickly. She was stung seven times that I saw, and I haven't looked through her hair or under her clothing or on the back of her legs. I will do everything I can for her."

The courier's engine started to spin up but wound back down. Nurinyan tried again, but it stubbornly waited for the third try to start. The hangar door rolled upward. The back door of the courier already sat open.

Amaya climbed into the back while Nurinyan leaned across to give Isabella a hand into the front seat. Amaya set Vera on the floor, reached out to push the front passenger door closed, and tugged the rear door into place. She crouched into the tight space between the child and the door.

Nurinyan lifted off and left the hangar. "Daughters of Mercy?"

"Yes, with all speed." Amaya checked the girl's pulse and counted her breaths.

She pulled a stethoscope from her backpack and listened to Vera's lungs. Almost clear for the moment, perhaps a touch of wheezing. She went on to check the child more thoroughly and found two more stings on her back above the collar of her dress.

Isabella twisted around. "Where did she get into wasps?"

Amaya kept her attention on the child. "Vadin tells me she tripped into a juniper bush, and they swarmed."

Nurinyan glanced back. "De one between Vadin's and Ishe's houses?"

"That one."

He nodded once. "I have insect poison in my house. I will take care of it when we get back, with caution, so none of de odder children run into trouble wit' dem."

"Good. Thank you." Amaya listened to the child's lungs again. The wheezing was getting worse. "Nurinyan, where are we?"

"We are coming up on a half mile from Las Palom–"

The avicopter lurched forward. The engine wound down. The wings snapped into the extended position and locked in place with a loud pop. Isabella shrieked.

Amaya crashed into the back of the passenger seat. Her forehead and shoulder smarted. She pressed her hand to her forehead and looked at her fingers. No blood. She picked herself up and checked on the girl.

The corrugated floor had kept her from sliding more than a handwidth, but her wheezing continued to worsen and could be heard without the stethoscope.

"We lost de generator." Nurinyan said. A thunk came from his side of the avi.

"Battery?" Amaya blinked hard.

"Enough to land."

"Bring us down. Contact Las Palomas dispatch and have a car meet me at the end of the nearest street."

"You are going to run dat distance?" Nurinyan looked back at her with a raised eyebrow.

"You have a faster way?"

"Let me do it. I am younger, and I actually have an anaphylaxis kit now." He reached behind the seat and patted his new trauma kit.

"No. You can fix this thing. I can't." She switched to Eshuvani. "If this was a deliberate bit of sabotage, you might need to protect Isabella against multiple attackers. You're better trained for that than I."

His jaw clenched, and he nodded while he tapped on his comm crystals.

She reverted to English. "Mrs. Zeldin, Nurinyan will bring you along as soon as the avi can be repaired or when someone can meet you here with our other avi. I will do everything I can to protect your child."

Isabella brushed tears from her eyes and nodded. "Vera, you go with the nice policewoman, and she'll take you to the doctor so he can help you breathe better again. I'll follow as soon as I can. I love you, honey."

When Vera twisted around to see her mother, her sobs worsened.

Nurinyan set down in the knee-high grass.

"This will help with that wheezing again until we can get you to a doctor. Okay?" Amaya got another epinephrine syringe from her pack and gave Vera another injection. She slid her backpack across both shoulders, threw open the door, and stepped out under the extended wing, keeping her head down. Amaya lifted Vera out and hunched over until she could get out from under the wing.

Vera hung onto her.

Nurinyan leaned out of the avicopter's rear door. "Mark and Robert are on de way to meet you. I will brief Mark on de specifics."

"Thank you."

Amaya turned and ramped up from speed walking to jogging to running flat out. The distance to the edge of Las Palomas looked like miles. The longest distance she'd ever run without stopping was a quarter mile. The distance she had to go was twice that, and she was a lot older now.

Ω

Nurinyan finished with Mark and Robert then closed the connection and tapped out Jevon's code.

"Jevon."

"Nurinyan." He spoke Eshuvani. "The courier came apart at the welds. We lost the generator. We're down, almost a half mile from Las Palomas. Amaya is continuing on foot, but I am here with-with-" What did he call the governor's wife? First name only was wrong. He thought back through Amaya's lesson on addressing humans. "With Mrs. Zeldin, and-"

Isabella reached over and grabbed his arm. She pointed.

He followed her hand. Indistinct forms moved through the tall grass.

"And?" Jevon asked.

An adrenalin surge unsteadied Nurinyan's hands. "There is movement coming toward us. I can't see the cause clearly. I'll step out, lock up, and take care of it."

"No. Stay inside the courier." Orinyay's voice echoed weirdly through Jevon's collar tabs. "You don't know how many there are, and if one gets past you, she's dead. Stay there."

"What she said." Jevon's hard footsteps came through the comm. "Secure it as well as you can, and move back toward the engine compartment. The metal plating is stronger there, especially if you fold the wings back down. I'm on the way."

"'I?'" Nurinyan secured the doors and spoke English. "Move toward de back. I will join you soon."

His passenger nodded and complied.

A police siren grew closer. That would be Mark and Robert meeting Amaya.

"Someone with a medical kit has to stay here for Vadin. We don't know if he's allergic yet."

The rumble of the hangar door came over the connection.

"Oh." Nurinyan hit the switch to bring the wings down. "Keep the line open."

"Right."

The cargo hauler's deep rumble started up.

Nurinyan thumbed the on switch for his pistol as he joined Isabella at the back of the courier. She had scrunched herself between the rear wall and the back seat. The wings locked down, blocking the part of the side window aft of the door.

He crouched in between Isabella and the side door and kept his pistol in hand. "Help is coming. De metal shielding is better back here near de engine."

The police siren faded away. There had been no human gunshots, so whoever was out there, they must not have bothered Amaya. None of the tension faded from his muscles, but he had some confidence she and the child would be fine.

When a dart pinged off the side window, Isabella squeaked.

Nurinyan brought his pistol to bear. "Peace. De glass is reinforced wit' a sheet of heavy plastic. Dey must have a very strong gun to get t'rough."

"Who is it?" she asked.

He scanned the entire range he could see from his position but saw no one. "I do not know, but I t'ink it is probably de same men Amaya and Pavwin have been trying to track down."

The temperature inside the avi climbed without the air cooler to offset the harsh sun.

Several rapid pings hit the side of the avi. Nurinyan swallowed. Automatic fire. They had at least a Model Six pistol. He hoped it wasn't more than that, or the minor armor on this old crate wouldn't hold.

The baritone rumble of the cargo hauler drew closer. He prayed that was Jevon, and not friends of their attackers. If someone had weapons sturdier than a pistol, the courier's armor wouldn't protect them for much longer.

"I'm almost there," Jevon reported, sounding far calmer than Nurinyan felt. "I see them. Two Eshuvani males. They would blend in with the grass if not for their hair. Nothing wrong with your eyesight."

"Mrs. Zeldon saw them first. For some reason, I didn't think they could see that well." He twisted to block the governor's wife as another burst of darts struck the side window. "Where are they?" Nurinyan rose up slightly.

Several shots struck the window at the level of his head again, and he ducked back down.

"Ten, fifteen strides at the most. Oh, they've seen me, and they're retreating."

Sweat beaded on Nurinyan's forehead. He blew out a breath and tried to will his tense muscles to relax. "We'll stay put until the cargo hauler is in the way."

"You do that."

Nurinyan glanced back at Isabella and spoke English again. "Help is here. We will stay until he is in position to shield us."

She nodded.

The deep rumble shook the courier and rattled a few loose deck plates as the cargo hauler settled. Nurinyan left his pistol powered up but holstered it and threw the rear door open. He offered Isabella his hand and helped her out.

Jevon hopped out of the larger avicopter and headed immediately for the engine compartment of the courier.

"Stay here wit' Jevon. He does not speak English, but he will protect you." Nurinyan turned away.

She caught his arm. Her brow was furrowed, and her eyes were wide. "Where are you going?"

He covered her hand with his and pointed upward. "To de roof of de larger avicopter. I want to be sure de men who attacked us are gone."

Isabella nodded and let him go then took a few steps closer to Jevon.

Nurinyan jumped and caught the edge of the cargo hauler's retracted wing. He hauled himself up and scanned the horizon. A blue and yellow avicopter lifted off from behind a dense stand of junipers. If the courier were operational, they might have caught up to the escaping avi. The cargo hauler would never keep up.

Turning toward Las Palomas, he found no sign of Amaya. Did that mean she made the rendezvous safely or had she been intercepted? She had to have met up with Mark and Robert. He'd distinctly heard the sirens grow closer and retreat. No gunfire, and certainly Mark and Robert would have put up a fight if the adversary had gone after Amaya and the child.

He frowned and sighed then jumped back down.

Jevon was head and shoulders in the courier's engine compartment. Something inside snapped.

He took a step back and closed the compartment. "Sabotage."

"Sabotage?" Nurinyan joined him.

"Someone swapped a low amp breaker into the generator's slot." He pointed at the avi with his thumb.

"Okay, but sabotage? How–"

Jevon frowned. "I know what I put in there, pal."

Nurinyan showed both hands empty. "Not what I mean. How did someone get into the hangar? The sensors didn't trip once. Is the system broken again?"

"Who said they they got into the hangar? When we go on calls, do we leave someone to guard the avi?"

"Nope." Nurinyan smacked his forehead with his fist. "All fixed now?"

"Should be, but I want to take it back home and check it out thoroughly. I was just working on the cargo hauler this morning, and it hasn't been out since, so I know that one's safe." He nodded toward Mrs. Zeldin. "Take her in that one. I'll take this beast home." He slapped the courier with his palm.

"Thanks."

Jevon nodded and headed around the avi.

Nurinyan escorted Isabella to the passenger side of the cargo hauler and spoke to her in English. "He is taking dat one home to check it out. I will take you to de hospital in dis one. We know dis one is functioning." For the moment. He could only hope it'd stay in working order long enough to get there and back again.

She nodded and climbed into the passenger seat.

Ω

At a little over a quarter of the way to the nearest street in Las Palomas, Amaya's breathing came harder. Her vision blurred at the edges. Her muscles burned, but the child in her arms was not going to die because Eshuvani endurance was too low. She pushed herself and continued at top speed, resolving to pay the price for such persistence later.

Police car sirens grew louder. A Las Palomas patrol car turned the last corner and screeched to a halt at the end of the road. She was perhaps twenty strides from them. Robert bailed out of the passenger side and sprinted out to Amaya. The blurriness of her vision occluded all but a narrow, central field of vision. She slowed and handed Vera to Robert. They hurried the remaining distance. Mark yanked the back door of the patrol car open. Robert slid in with the child.

Amaya staggered and fell to her knees as everything whirled to the left.

Mark hauled her to her feet, helped her into the front passenger seat, and closed the door. He ran around and sat behind the wheel. "Daughters of Mercy has been alerted, and they're waiting for us."

Amaya nodded but couldn't get enough air to talk.

Lights and sirens blaring, Mark drove. "You'd better eat something."

He was right. She had over-exertion syndrome, and it wouldn't get any better until she had food, rest, and water, in that order. Working by feel, she unclipped the straps of her backpack and leaned forward to slide it off. Sweat drenched her shirt, which glued itself to her. When she tried to open the side flap on her backpack, her fingers slipped off the edge. Mark reached over and snapped it open. She pulled out one of the nutrition bars but couldn't see enough to tell which she had. That didn't matter, really. Both kinds would serve the purpose her body required. The only difference was flavor, and she was too weary to be picky.

She tore it open and took a bite. There was more sugar than salt. She'd gotten the right kind. Once she'd finished it, she tucked the wrapper back in her pack and fished out another one. The twirling sensation faded, but as hard as she'd pushed herself, it'd be back shortly.

"Robert." She croaked his name out, cleared her throat, and tried again. "Robert, how is she?"

"She's still breathing fine, a little raspy maybe."

Amaya squinted and tried looking out the windshield, but her blurred sight wouldn't get past the dashboard.

"We're almost there," Mark said.

The car bounced up a shallow driveway.

Mark flipped the switch to disable the sirens and pulled to a stop next to a tall building. "Wait here, Amaya. I'll be back for you as soon as the kid's in."

"Go." Amaya closed her eyes and leaned back against the headrest.

The car door opened. Had any time passed at all? That couldn't have been long enough to get the child inside and come back for her. She looked and made out a black uniform and dark hair. That could be either Mark or Robert.

"Okay, you're next." Mark lifted her backpack out and gave her a hand. "I've got a wheelchair for you."

She swung her legs out of the door. "I don't think I'm quite that pathetic."

"You were a few minutes ago. You've driven yourself hard enough today."

"On that, I'll have to agree with you." She came to her feet and everything spun leftward again.

Mark caught her by the left arm. "See? I know what I'm doing." He planted her in the wheelchair and set her backpack in her lap. "Let's go. The doc needs some information." He wheeled her inside and backed through a swinging door. "I've got her here, Doc."

Her vision was too unclear to make out more than a tall, dark human, another mostly in a strange shade of green, and a shorter one in all white. The room itself was a pale tan color with plenty of silver metal.

"*Kiand*, I'm Dr. Javier Alvarez. Officer Kirby told me about the wasp attack. What treatments have you used?"

"Two injections of point-one-five milligrams epinephrine intramuscular. I wasn't sure of the dosage of diphenhydramine for such a small child and couldn't reach a pediatrics specialist, so none was administered." A wave of dizziness slammed into her.

He turned to the shorter human next to him and issued orders she didn't hear correctly. Someone jostled her shoulder. "*Kiand*, are you okay?"

"Over-exertion syndrome. I'm already taking corrective measures." Amaya tore open the second nutrition bar's wrapper and took a bite. Salty. Wrong one. She grimaced. Not fatal, but not her favorite.

"She ran most of half a mile carrying the kid when their avicopter went down." Mark leaned against the wall next to her.

"Is that where that abrasion on your forehead came from?" Javier asked.

"Abrasion?" She ran her fingers across her forehead and winced with the sharp sting above her right eye. "Yes. When we lost power. The avi jerked, and I hit the seat in front of me."

The doctor leaned forward and pressed his fingers on Amaya's forehead. "You're sure the dizziness and blurred sight are over-exertion syndrome?"

She'd probably been a practitioner longer than he'd been a doctor and knew far more about Eshuvani medicine than he did, and he was second-guessing her diagnosis? Amaya squashed her annoyance, most likely another result of over-exertion syndrome. His questions were logical, and her irritation would help nothing. "Yes. A typical reaction to the kind of activity I was doing. I spent the last several decades in Michigan and have not yet adapted to this climate. That exacerbates the situation. There's no headache, but if it doesn't clear up with the proper protocols, I'll have one of my *kiandarai* take me to the hospital or send for a courier to bring me in. I really don't think I hit the seat that hard."

"Hmm. That might be adrenalin talking. Let me just take a quick look. Look right here."

She couldn't see where he was pointing, but the process for checking for a concussion was familiar. She stared toward his head while he flashed a small light in each of her eyes a few times. Then he aimed an otoscope in her ears and up her nose. She tolerated the completely useless exam patiently.

"You check out, but if it doesn't clear, get to your physician. Pronto." The doctor straightened.

"I will, thank you for your diligence." Well, the exam had been useless, but at least the confirmation was nice to have.

"Gentlemen." He left.

Mark crouched next to her. "You might as well get some rest, Ann Packer."

"Ann Packer?" She glanced at him, making out little more than an indistinct black uniform.

He laughed. "Olympic gold medalist last year, eight-hundred-meter."

She nodded. "About a half-mile."

"Uh-huh. I'll have some water waiting for you when you wake up."

Amaya propped her elbow on the arm of the wheelchair and her chin on her hand and dozed off. Sometime later, the wheelchair moved, and she jolted awake. Her vision had cleared through the middle, but it was still blurred around the edges.

"Just me." Nurinyan offered her a cup. "Here's some water for you. I'll take you back home where you can rest."

"Isabella?" She sipped the water. It was a little cool but not enough to cramp muscles.

He backed her out through the door. "Here and safe. We were attacked by two men, but they bolted when Jevon brought the cargo hauler in and landed between us. The courier has a couple new personality dings, but Jevon's low-tech armor on the window did great."

"Good." Best of all, he'd resisted the impulse to leave Isabella unguarded and try to find the attackers alone. She downed the rest of the water. "Do you know anything about the child?"

"Here for observation at least until tomorrow."

"And possibly the day after that. Thanks to you, she's safe."

He helped her into the cargo hauler's front seat and left to take the wheelchair back.

## Ten

Ed Osborn hung up the phone and tapped his pen on the desk. He rubbed his ear. "If I have to make one more phone call today, I'm going to have that thing growing out of my ear." His collar tabs chimed. He huffed and tapped one of the crystals. "Osborn."

"Howdy Ed. It is Ishe. Did I get dat right?" She spoke English.

He smiled and shook his head and answered in her language. "Not exactly comm protocol, but it'll do. What do you need?"

"Pavwin checked out that beach you suggested, you know, the one to replace the original destination because the courier got sabotaged with the wrong breaker and went down and they were attacked by those two guys but Nurinyan couldn't chase after them without leaving Isabella and—"

He leaned his forehead on his palm and his elbow on the desk. Yes, Amaya had said this kid had potential, but come on! "Right, right, I know which you mean and why. What does Pavwin say about the beach?"

"It's great! He says it'll be just fine. He wants to know how the aquarium replacement is coming.

Apparently, the kids are very excited about going to an aquarium for one of the tourist visits."

"Tell him one option would be the aquarium in Woran Kishay if enough larger avicopters can be secured."

"Falcon's Wing has two cargo haulers, and there's ours, so that's eighteen seats." She counted softly.

"There are thirteen dignitaries, so that leaves five seats for *kiandarai*. It would work fine." Osborn smiled.

"Thirteen! There are thirteen, so that leaves five spots for *kiandarai*. No problem!"

That sounded awfully like what he'd said. "I'm still working on a replacement for the museum. No one wants to open up at the last minute on a Sunday. I'd suggest either moving the date or canceling altogether."

"Oh, no. Vadin suggested canceling, and Halyuwin didn't like that at all. He's sure we'll be safe enough inside."

One thing they didn't need was one of the dignitaries issuing orders.

He sighed and rubbed his forehead. "I'll keep trying. How's Amaya?"

"Up and around again. Out on another call, actually."

"Ask her to call me when she gets in."

"Yep! Message received."

A loud click signaled the end of the connection.

Osborn arched his back to stretch out the stiffness and returned to his list for the next place to call.

## Ω

Vadin flexed his left hand as he entered the station. The stiffness from yesterday's wasp adventure had relaxed, but the back of his hands and the side of his neck were still sore. In the foyer, Amaya was conducting the ladies and children to the briefing room. Isabella Zeldin and little Vera weren't among them.

When the briefing room door closed, Amaya's rod-straight posture relaxed ever so slightly. She turned to him. "Good morning, Vadin. Are you well?"

He flexed both hands comparing the difference in movement. He frowned at the slower, more restricted movement of his left hand. That would go away, and he knew that, but for now it demanded his attention like a dripping faucet. "A little stiff and sore, maybe, but fine. Vera?"

"The hospital will hang onto her for another day." She glanced toward Las Palomas. "The severity of the reaction and the number of stings are concerns for such a little one."

He frowned and pressed his fist to his forehead. "It never occurred to me to check the junipers for wasp nests." If he had, he would've spotted the one in that shrub and used the proper chemistry to evict the wasps. The child would not have been in danger, and he probably wouldn't have been stung.

Amaya pulled him into a one-armed embrace. "This is no fault of yours, Vadin. Not all things can be anticipated. You recognized the problem quickly, rescued her from the danger, and got her to medical help immediately. You have no cause for shame."

"Thank you." But next time he'd check for such things. "How was the aquarium yesterday afternoon?"

"Nurinyan tells me all went well. Are you still up for the beach this afternoon?"

"I'm looking forward to it." He smiled. He hadn't been to a beach since his last visit to his grandparents' home. There would be no sand tunnel projects this time, but still amusing.

"Too much sand for me but enjoy yourself."

How could anyone not enjoy a lovely afternoon on the beach? The sound of crashing waves and the smell of the salty air could chase even the worst stress out of his mind, and the seagulls were funny to watch, especially when he tossed snacks to them.

The overhead lights went out and the lone blue bulb came on. Vadin keyed Amaya's code into his comm crystals. Her collar tabs chimed three times.

He waited for the other two, but they didn't happen.

Ishe hit the reset switch on her desk for the lights, and everything returned to normal.

Amaya tapped the blue crystal. "Jevon and Orinyay are on a call. The rest of you, do it by the protocol. Go."

Not good. The low-tech protocol was tricky enough with all five of them here. Two people short? Someone could get past them. If that happened, Amaya would have to take care of it.

Vadin rushed out the back door. "No one in the yard. Proceeding southeast." He drew his pistol and primed it.

"No one in the parking lot. Proceeding southwest," Ishe reported.

"No one outside the hangar. Proceeding north," Nurinyan said.

Vadin walked between the houses and headed toward Woran Oldue. He kept his pace slow enough to be able to observe everything and constantly scanned the area.

"I've got them! I've got them!" Ishe's broad smile sounded in her voice. "A bunch of dumb kids almost straight west of the station."

"I see them." Nurinyan blew out a breath. "They can't be more than fifteen years old, human calendar."

Amaya sighed. "You two turn them back. They might be a decoy. Vadin, find cover and stay alert."

Ishe snickered. "Wasp-free cover."

The back of his neck tensed. "Right." He found a dense stand of skinny oaks and yaupons and crouched among the gray trunks.

"What are you kids doing here?" Nurinyan asked in English.

"We, uh, we got lost. Yeah, that's it. We were wandering around out here and got lost, and so we saw your building and made for it." The kid's voice slurred.

"Yeah. Lost. Can you help us, Mr. Alien Pig?" Another kid chimed in.

The kids laughed. Vadin picked out five distinct voices. Lost? Right. Apparently, those kids thought the Eshuvani were newly arrived on the planet.

Ishe groaned. "Turn around and go dat way. You can see Las Palomas from here."

"That way? You sure? Can't we come in and call our mommies?" a girl asked.

"Get moving before I put you under arrest for trespassing." The hard edge in Nurinyan's voice brought on a collective giggle from the kids.

"Come on. This scene is nowhere. Goodbye, Mr. and Mrs. Alien Pig," one of the boys slurred.

Ishe huffed. "Okay, they're going. Mr. and Mrs. Alien Pig? Seriously. What dope-heads."

"That might be truer than–" Amaya's footsteps on the hard floor preceded a click. "Another blue light. Fan out."

Vadin stayed in his hiding place and pivoted. Movement caught his eye about fifty strides away. There were three human men. Each carried a long-barreled weapon, but Vadin couldn't tell if they had rifles or shotguns.

He rubbed the back of his neck. "Amaya, I have three human males armed with rifles or shotguns. They're about fifty strides from my position and headed for the station using trees for cover."

"Can you hit them from your location?" she asked.

If only. His aim was pretty good when he had time to set up, but the recent failure at the abandoned factory proved how useless his skill could be in a crisis. "With my aim, not all of them, not fast enough."

"Understood." Amaya drew a deep breath. "Ishe, find cover and keep an eye on those kids. Make sure they keep heading toward Las Palomas. Nurinyan, make your way around toward Vadin. Vadin, make your way closer if you can, but do not reveal your location until Nurinyan is in position. Go."

That might work if he didn't step on something that made a lot of noise. Still, if he could keep the local flora between himself and the humans, he'd stand a good chance. Vadin darted to a juniper bush and crouched. Every slight crunch and clatter made his guts twist, but the humans gave no sign that they knew he was there. He made his way from one clump of brush to another until he was within his comfortable shooting distance.

Nurinyan approached from the south. "Vadin, I see you. You take the guy nearest you. I've got the other two. Go."

Vadin leaned out of cover and took aim on the one nearest him. Nurinyan fired three shots before Vadin fired the first of his three. His target turned and fired in a shot in Nurinyan's direction. Vadin tensed, but Nurinyan didn't cry out. Three more darts had the second human down before Vadin fired his third dart. He hit his target three times in the arm. The humans collapsed.

How did Nurinyan shoot that quickly?

"That was way too close." Nurinyan stood and holstered his weapon. "All three are down."

"Excellent. Are either of you hurt?" Amaya asked.

Vadin blew out a breath and shook the tension out of his arms. "Safe and uninjured."

"A rifle shot almost gave me a new haircut, but I'm safe and uninjured." Nurinyan said.

"Bring them in here and lock them up. Then patrol the perimeter." Amaya's voice had a smile in it. "As soon as Orinyay returns with the cargo hauler, we'll take them to the courthouse."

Vadin powered down his weapon and joined Nurinyan where the humans had fallen.

## Ω

Teviya checked the shine on her ruby red nails as she carried the matching dress into her apartment. The narrow skirt flared into the tail of a betta fish of Thailand. Other projections on her arms and down her back would simulate the other beautiful fins. So what if the more decorative fish were the males. She deserved to look beautiful, and Emyrin loved to see her dressed up. The happier she kept Emyrin, the more he would give her, and the happier she would be.

She hung up the dress in the closet and checked her hair and makeup in the mirror. Tomorrow would be perfection. The smile on Emyrin's face would be worth the two hours she'd spent getting her hair and nails decorated.

The electronic notebook in the other room chimed.

She huffed and strode into the other room. Just a few more days of this foolishness and she'd be done with playing shepherdess for Emyrin's band of useful idiots. She tapped the screen and thwacked the icon for the comm relay. "What?"

"They weren't there," the team leader said.

"Who wasn't?" She tapped the schedule icon on the screen and waited for the file to load.

"Who do you think?" he snapped.

The file faded into view. Teviya scrolled down to the current date. Aquarium. The team should've been ready to take care of the *tura* and the governors today and obliterate even the vague notion of peace with humans.

She flopped onto the couch and bounced most of a handwidth. "You sure you were at the right place?"

"Are you sure you gave me the correct aquarium?"

She glared at the notebook. "There's only one in Woran Oldue."

"There are other ones in range of an avicopter." He matched her snarky tone perfectly, which only made her want to rip his brains out through his left ear.

"That's twice." She pointed one glittering fingernail at the notebook, a useless gesture that made her feel a little better. "You can't make that mistake again on Sunday."

"That's why I'm calling. We're recovering our equipment and getting things set up tonight. Are you sure you sent us to the right place?" he asked.

Teviya glared. "As far as I know. They're apparently not communicating changes in the plan."

"Find out."

She stood and bared her teeth. "Oh, that won't be suspicious at all. They've already caught on to the collar tabs. They may be suspicious of everyone at this point and asking them will only make them that much more cautious. There are only three comparable museums in range. You have the materials from the other two sites. Rig all three, and maybe a couple smaller ones."

He gasped and laced his response with sarcasm. "What a brilliant idea. While we're at it, we can all be in five places at once!"

Teviya stormed over to the notebook, leaned close to the microphone in the corner, and yelled, "They'll be touring the place for hours! When they don't show at one, try the next! All five are close enough to get around to in less than two hours!" She sneered at the notebook and paced away. "Do you want me to chew your food for you, too, or do you think you can actually manage that on your own?"

"Watch it, girl, or you may find yourself taking care of this without us, and what's this about shoving an unknown isotope into our carefully tuned molecule."

Adding Conner and his pals to the group had been Emyrin's idea, so why didn't they ask him?

"You're down a few men. The leader's got a grudge against one of the targets. Stick him somewhere so he'll feel useful and won't interfere with the rest of the plan. Maybe he'll get lucky. If he doesn't make it out alive, all the better."

"Right."

The connection clicked and closed. Teviya growled and mimed thwacking someone's ear. Halfway through tapping in Emyrin's number, she stopped and canceled the call. Best if she calmed down some before talking to him. Anything that jeopardized her relationship with him was severely unwelcome. She stomped off to the kitchen to get a snack before the evening movie came on.

$$\Omega$$

Amaya sat at the dispatch desk, catching up on the ubiquitous paperwork. For the duration of the meetings, Emyrin wanted a daily report, no doubt so he could look for things that weren't done with incredible precision. He'd said nothing about Vera's wasp encounter, but maybe that wasn't too surprising. The harm to a human child wouldn't register on his list of important events.

The back door opened, and Ishe pirouetted into the room. Her long, dark hair stood straight out from her head as she twirled.

Amaya smiled. If only she could be that carefree again. "Excited?"

Ishe grabbed a chair and sat facing the desk. "These dumb talks end today! We can go back to our normal business, as if anything around here is ever normal, but you know what I mean, right?"

"I know what you mean." Amaya finished the report and sent it on to Emyrin.

Orinyay and Jevon came in from the hangar. Amaya marked them both as present at the station.

Jevon parked on the corner of the desk and twisted around to face Amaya. "Both avicopters check out. Everything should be ready to go at least until the next time we have a crisis and have to rely on the dumb things to get us somewhere."

"Thank you for looking into that." Amaya turned away from the dispatch computer. "Anything at the museum seem out of place?"

Jevon shrugged. "Found a bomb in a metal trash bin."

His nonchalance suggested they'd taken care of it.

Ishe's eyes widened, and she sat up straighter. "You say that with a very straight face."

"It wasn't very sophisticated." Orinyay set her pack down by the wall. "I could have disarmed that one."

"Well, that's good, right?" Ishe leaned back in her chair, which creaked in protest. "That means everything's nice and safe for this afternoon, right?"

Amaya turned toward their youngest member, trying to remember if she'd ever been quite so naïve. "No, that means we found one bomb. How many were there in all, do you think?"

"Uh, hard to say." She ran her hand partway through her long, dark hair and leaned her elbow on the desk. "There might be another one."

"Umhm."

"Well, we took the place apart and looked for anything that seemed incorrect, but nothing else was out of place. I'll be in my quarters if anyone needs me." Jevon left through the back door.

That couldn't be the end of this. Today would be the last day for Emyrin to try something that would affect both the governors and the *tura*. The plan called for the *tura* to leave immediately after the museum visit. Tomorrow's send off for the governors at the airport would be low-key, except for the inevitable protesters, but there'd been the bomb at the airport when the *tura* wasn't around. Maybe she was still exhibiting some of Ishe's hopeful naivete.

Orinyay came around to the front of the desk. "Ishe, will you excuse us?"

"Um, sure. I'll just go get a–a piece of fruit or two, maybe three." Ishe pushed off from the chair and darted into the kitchen.

A private meeting? Well, as private as they could get with the briefing room and safe room both occupied.

Amaya gestured Orinyay to the chair. "Something is disturbing you."

"Yes." Orinyay sat and fidgeted with her watch. "I seem to be excluded from service where it concerns our guests. Am I under suspicion for something? The issue with the collar tabs found on criminals, maybe?"

If that was bothering her, she shouldn't have waited until the end of the conference to bring it up. She had to know that this late in the game, no personnel changes would be happening.

"You were during the earliest phases of setting the plans. The collar tabs with the number of your lost ones were in the possession of Wylin Leonan. So, yes, Pavwin and I did discuss leaving you out of all matters regarding the visitors. Then, as we did more digging the more questionable things became, and the clearer it was that you were not at fault. At this point, I'm certain someone stole your tabs, waited for you to report them missing, and reassigned the number to a set given to the criminals. To my mind, the matter is no longer an issue of whether you're involved but rather why someone would try to implicate you. If I thought you were a danger to the dignitaries, I would have temporarily traded you to another station until I gathered proof. Tomorrow, I will resume the search for the information to clear you completely. My opinions are one thing. Proof is another."

Her brow furrowed, and she showed a bit of her teeth. "So why am I so systematically excluded and relegated to regular duties?"

Such an intense reaction for something so minor? Amaya had come to expect that sort of foolishness from Ishe. She'd expected Orinyay to know better. Again, her shortcomings were not in line with her years of experience. Perhaps she hadn't had a supervisor with an eye toward improving performance. Maturity should have made up the difference, but apparently not in this case.

With an effort, Amaya squelched that response. Educate. Don't berate. Amaya counted the crystals on Orinyay's collar. "You're seven classes away from being able to test for *kiand*. Step back from the situation, consider our available staff, and tell me how you would handle the allocation of personnel."

"If I were going to be fair—"

Amaya held up her hand. "You think duty assignments should be based on what's 'fair?' Do you think this is a child's classroom where we must concern ourselves with fairness?" She sat forward in her chair. "We have multiple dignitaries of two races in potentially hazardous situations with criminals on the loose who have been harassing us lately, even with incendiary devices. Add to that the current imbalance of fully trained personnel. Based on the situation, not some malleable concept like fairness, how would you assign personnel? If you assign the staff incorrectly, you increase the chances someone will suffer critical injury or die."

Orinyay frowned and stared at the corner of the room. "You're a specialist in interspecies relations, so you need to be on hand. Nurinyan is a combat specialist, which could be handy if an attack occurs, so he should be there. Jevon is a demolitions specialist with a subspecialty in mechanics, or will be when he finishes his training in the next couple weeks, so you need him. Vadin is familiar with dealing with the nobility, so you, being unfamiliar with that rank's protocol, need him around to advise you. Ishe is too immature and too short on her training, but someone needs to mind the dispatch desk anyway." She drew a deep breath and sighed. "That leaves me to handle the calls when everyone's out on the tourist parts of the day."

"Exactly." Amaya leaned back and steepled her long fingers. "There will be other missions in which your expertise will be invaluable and someone else will be taking the calls. This isn't that mission. You should know that at Falcon's Wing, their combat specialist and their social hierarchy specialist are going on these field trips when they're in the enclave. They also temporarily traded a *kiandara* with Wolf's Teeth to get a demolitions specialist along. Since they have no *kialai*, the other *kiandarai* and the *kiand* alternate who's going to take calls and who's going on the field trip. If we had that option, I'd've taken it, but we don't."

Orinyay pressed her fist to her forehead. "I apologize. I should not be so sensitive."

No, she shouldn't have, but she would learn. In the meantime, questions needed to be answered. "I don't mind honest questions, Orinyay, so next time, try not to let your concerns fester so long." She patted Orinyay's arm.

Ishe leaned out of the kitchen. "Is it safe yet? Arrellia says lunch is almost ready."

"It's safe. My business is concluded." Orinyay headed down the hall toward the hangar.

Ishe raced over and sat down with a chipped yellow bowl full of grapes. "So, what was that about?"

Amaya shook her head. Immaturity from Ishe was expected. Irritating sometimes, but expected. "If you were meant to know what Orinyay and I discussed, you would not have been asked to excuse yourself."

Ishe popped a couple grapes in her mouth. "Just curious. That's all."

The door down the hall opened, and Texas Governor Patrick Farrell's booming laughter came down the hall. "Seriously, though. Y'all oughta come out to my property this fall. There's some good deer huntin'. I'm tellin' ya, you ain't seen bucks so big."

Amaya had seen the local deer. Relative to the ones up north, the bucks here were lightweights. The briefing room door opened. Amaya turned.

Yvonne Ginsberg stormed up to her husband. Her pastel pink purse dangled from her arm and blended in with the solid, pastel pink dress. "Are you finally finished now?"

Governor Ginsberg flushed red in the face. "Our ride to the hotel won't be here until one, dear. We'll skip the museum if you want, but we might as well sit down with everyone for lunch."

The other gentlemen ducked into the briefing room.

She growled and stormed over to the dispatch desk then stabbed her finger at Amaya. "You. Contact Las Palomas PD and have them send a car."

"I'll try, but we haven't been as available to Las Palomas as usual because of the meetings going on here. On unusual calls, they've had to send multiple cars. They may not have anyone to come get you until the scheduled time."

Yvonne crossed her arms and glared.

Amaya tapped the Eastern Division's dispatcher code on her comm crystals.

"Las Palomas, Eastern Division."

"Amaya Ulonya *Kiand*. Governor and Mrs. Ginsberg would like to return to their hotel early. Do you have a car available?"

"I apologize, *Kiand*, but we have a terrific backlog of calls today. I may have someone in about forty-five minutes," the dispatcher reported.

"Cancel request. We'll find another way or wait for the scheduled pick-up."

"Ten-four, um, message received."

Amaya tapped the blue crystal again to end the connection.

Governor Ginsberg rested his hand on his wife's shoulder. "Dear, let's just–"

Yvonne shrugged away from him. "Don't you 'dear' me, William Ginsberg. Just you wait until we get home." She jabbed her finger at Amaya again. "Western Division. Try them."

"They're short-staffed on their morning shift for this week and next." Amaya stood and grabbed her backpack. "There's a helipad on your hotel. I'll fly you in."

"No!" She shook her head and brushed her hand back and forth. "No, no, no! I'm not flying in one of those rundown contraptions again. Call Western Division."

Amaya set her backpack on the chair. She'd never given in to Ed's temper tantrums when he was a toddler, either. "My mechanically inclined personnel tell me the avi has been properly repaired and succeeded in the test flight earlier. Either I will fly you back to your hotel, or you will wait for the scheduled pick-up. There are no other options available. It's a rather long walk to your hotel from here, and you aren't dressed for hiking in this weather, so I don't recommend it."

After growling again, Yvonne retreated to the briefing room, grumbling the whole way.

Governor Ginsberg rolled his eyes. "I apologize, ma'am. My wife's been listening to too much gossip again, and she won't be happy until we get home and I prove the gossip wrong."

"I understand, sir." Amaya moved her backpack to the floor and sat. "I regret I was unable to supply a satisfactory way to get you back to your hotel."

Arrellia came out of the kitchen. Vadin's aunt was a little overweight for her height, enough to make a modeling career feasible. "Lunch is prepared. Please find your places."

Amaya called the missing members of her staff to lunch and forwarded the dispatch calls to her own comm system.

Eleven

Hovering over the hotel, Vadin looked out the avi's window at the limos below. The New Mexican governor and his grouchy wife, recognizable by the pink dress and black hair, got out. Once the Las Palomas officers ushered them inside, the entourage of limousines, police cars, and avicopters continued to the museum. They all parked and landed in the almost-empty parking lot. The one car that didn't belong to them would have to belong to the curator, here to open the place on the usual day off and lock up again when they left.

As they disembarked, a smallish man wearing wire-rim spectacles opened the large glass door. "Good afternoon. I'm Jacob Templeton, the curator. You'll have the run of the place today. If you need anything, let me know. I'll be in the office down the hall from the restrooms." After looking at each of them, the curator scurried away.

Peculiar. Was he afraid to stay near at hand? Vadin watched until the curator was out of sight and turned to Amaya. She smiled but made no effort to retrieve the man.

"Where's he off to?" Patrick, the Texan, walked over to the museum map on the wall. "I was kinda lookin' fo'ward to a guided tour."

Ed pulled Amaya aside. "Your folks have been all over the inside of this place this week. You'd be more likely to spot problems than we would. How about I set my guys up watching the perimeter, and your folks can handle the inside?"

Vadin strained to hear their conversation.

"Perhaps you should take one of mine with you in case you find another well-equipped Eshuvani who doesn't have your good health in mind." She looked at each of them.

He prayed she didn't pick him. The heat out there was stifling, and there wasn't much of a breeze off the coast today.

"Probably needs to be Jevon. You'll need Vadin for protocol issues, and Nurinyan in case it comes to defending someone. I can keep Jevon with me or send him out with Kirby to bypass with the language issue."

"Agreed."

Ed collected Jevon and the human officers and headed out.

Blowing out a breath, Vadin drifted closer to the *tura* and Halyuwin.

Patrick tapped the map and looked back at the Oklahoma governor. "Sam, there's a kid area here up on the third floor. Might be the spot for you and the missus to go with the young'uns."

Nurinyan smiled. "Dere is some interesting stuff up dere. Dere is a big tree house and some dinosaur bones."

Both human kids spun toward their parents. "Can we go, Daddy? Please?"

Recalling his two youngest siblings, Vadin smiled.

Sam grinned. "All right, let's go."

The kids cheered.

"Go with them, Nurinyan," Amaya said.

"Right." He gestured toward the back of the museum. "De elevator is back dis way."

The five of them went off.

Patrick chuckled. "Hey, honey, they must've known we were comin'. Fourth floor's got an aviation display and a quilting display. How d'ya like that?"

Vadin turned to the *tura*. Where would he like to go?

His Transcendence straightened his gold trimmed blue jacket and drew a breath. "I t'ink I should prefer to start on de ground floor and work upward."

Amaya glanced at Vadin. "If you'd like, Your Transcendence, can I leave Vadin with you? I'll accompany Governor and Mrs. Farrell upstairs."

Good. She'd avoided making the suggestion sound like a command.

The *tura* clasped his hands behind his back. "Your suggestion is agreeable, *Kiand*. Execute your plan as described."

Vadin confined his reaction to a smile to avoid offending the Texas governor. If he were too obviously pleased about Amaya's assignment, Patrick might assume some offense. Really, though, the division of labor made sense. Vadin didn't have to worry that he'd have a misstep with the humans or that Amaya would misstep with the *tura*.

As Amaya led the humans toward the elevator, Vadin followed his group around to the first display on the left. After six visits to this museum in the last week, Vadin was sure he could recite the plaques without looking at them, but he had a different job this time.

Halyuwin drifted back and joined him. "Your *kiand* is a perpetual surprise, Vadin. A source I had considered reliable gave me to understand she didn't trust the rest of you."

Vadin's jaw clenched. Emyrin. That had to have been Emyrin giving false information about Amaya. He relaxed the tension in his jaw. "Your source is confused. She's been like a parent for all of us, and old enough to be a parent to most of us. She has blocked us if she didn't think we were ready for something. Otherwise, she lets us work at whatever we can handle. Sometimes she pushes us to go beyond what we'd prefer to do, but never without enough information and support."

"Does she perceive herself as a parent to you?" Halyuwin held his hand palm up uncurled four of his fingers. "Is that why she chose four *kialai*?"

Incomplete information led to the wrong conclusion. Emyrin, or whoever Halyuwin had been talking to, hadn't mentioned the origin of Hawk's Nest. Vadin shook his head. "We were hired prior to her arrival. When we got to the station that first night, she explained what we were up against and gave us each the option to stay or leave without prejudice."

Halyuwin looked at Vadin from the corner of his eye. "So, you don't feel like she's waiting for you to make a mistake?"

If that had been her goal, she wouldn't have needed to wait very long. "We have all made mistakes, and some were pretty impressive. She only pounced hard on one person, but that was more about unresolved grief." He turned toward Halyuwin.

Halyuwin leaned closer. "Since then?"

Vadin kept his shoulders squared as he shrugged. "More patient than half of my instructors. She did let a human officer know her mind clearly, but he'd shot her while trying to sneak a shot past her at a target."

Halyuwin's eyes widened. "That was not very wise."

"No, and he's no longer with the police." Vadin inclined his head toward Halyuwin and lowered his voice. "They've dismissed him."

"I did not know that was a choice." His brow furrowed.

Vadin nodded. "It is for the humans."

"So where did your station's budget go? Certainly not into equipment or facilities." Halyuwin pointed at Vadin's outdated but functional Model Five pistol.

Vadin's neck muscles tensed. Halyuwin wouldn't be doing all this data collecting without a reason. "What budget? I saw her allocating funds one morning and looked over her shoulder. Mother couldn't run the house on the budget we were allotted, and Amaya has to support the six of us and Orinyay's family. You saw the station—" He bit his lip. His defensiveness would come across as aggression, which would help no one. He took a breath and started again. "The station was built with multiple deficiencies and the budget she was given was inadequate. The protocol doesn't allow Amaya to get too creative with acquiring additional funds."

Halyuwin scratched his cheek. "This gets more curious all the time." He patted Vadin on the shoulder. "I've made you ill at ease, and I apologize for that. I commend you for resisting the urge to speak poorly of your superiors, and I assure you I have observed and heard what you didn't say as much as what you did. I shall see what I can do to amend the situation your station has been handed."

Oh terrific. If he'd just gotten Amaya fired or reassigned, he would've given Emyrin his greatest wish and likely condemned the humans all in one move. Maybe instead, Halyuwin had just figured out that Emyrin had the station in his crosshairs.

Vadin grimaced. "I don't understand wh–"

A loud pop like an outsized firecracker deafened him. Others echoed from a distance. Vadin pushed Halyuwin down next to one of the displays and covered the older man. A heavy mass smashed into Vadin's shoulder.

Ω

Sergeant Ed Osborn sat with Jevon on the patio of the restaurant across from the museum. The sun beating down on the pavement radiated stifling heat, but an ocean breeze had started up and the shade of the eatery's red and white awning kept him from baking while they kept an eye on the front door.

He looked at the coins on the table, picked up the pulsar coin and flipped over the supergiant coin. He tapped Jevon on the shoulder. "You're it." He scanned the area while Jevon considered his next move.

Jevon groaned. "You are far too good at this game."

"Have you played my teacher yet?" Osborn grinned.

"Amaya? No, but I've seen her score cards against some of the others. If she taught you, I guess I'm lucky to have a score at all." He picked up the nova coin and flipped the supergiant back over. "You win again." He drew a line across the notepad they kept score on.

"Rematch?" Osborn set the coins he'd collected on the table in a neat stack with the largest coins on the bottom.

Jevon collected all the coins and put them back in his pouch. "Give me a few minutes to repair my wounded pride. Here I thought I'd be able improve my win ratio against you."

Osborn chuckled. "At least I didn't skunk you this round."

"There's a bright spot for—"

An explosion of what sounded like firecrackers erupted across the street. Ears ringing, Jevon's solid grip on Osborn's arm yanked the man from his chair and shoved him to the ground. The concrete scraped the side of his hand. A loud rumble followed the explosions. Once the noise ended, Jevon let him up. Osborn's collar tabs chimed twice.

He tapped a crystal and spoke English. "Osborn. Report your status. Hollis."

"We're both fine, but those explosions collapsed enough of the façade to block the door."

"Parrish."

"Same story, here, Sarge."

Osborn squinted and tried to see through the cloud of dust. The decorative rockwork on the museum was piled up around the base of the building, leaving the cinderblock interior wall scarred and pockmarked, but relatively intact. "Yep. Front door looks the same."

Jevon tapped Osborn's shoulder. "I want to take a closer look and make sure we're not in for another round."

Osborn nodded. "Key into my comm and go."

The kid started tapping, and before he made it to the other side of the street, Osborn's collar beeped.

"Osborn."

"Jevon. I'll keep you updated."

"Do." Osborn walked to his car.

"Sarge!" Parrish yelled as a car door slammed. "Eshuvani male carryin' a bag and runnin' away from the museum. Tucker's in foot pursuit. I'm goin' to try to get ahead of him. Suspect's headed south on Mirabeau." Although he spoke at a rate that could be measured in words per second, each one was clear.

Osborn slid into the driver seat and started up his car. "Stay on him and don't let him rest."

"Kirby and I are on top of the bank building." Hollis reported in a monotone, a common feature in a tense situation. "We think we see the tail end of an avicopter. That'd be the parking lot of the furniture store where Mirabeau crosses Tenth."

"Good. Parrish, back up your partner. I'm going to try to get to his avicopter first." Osborn flipped the switches for lights and sirens.

"Ten-four," Parrish said.

Osborn picked a path through the streets. The sparse traffic pulled aside as he approached. He slowed at intersections to make sure he had a clear path before accelerating on through.

"The guy ditched the bag. Tucker's got it. I'm passing them now," Parrish reported.

Osborn reached Tenth Street and turned toward Mirabeau. A blue and yellow avicopter without tail numbers sat in the empty parking lot of the La Tienda Home Furnishings.

"He jumped over the car!" Parrish exclaimed.

"They'll do that, but that's okay." Osborn turned into the parking lot and parked between the oncoming Eshuvani and the avicopter. "Any extra effort you can make him expend will tire him out quicker. Remember, ambush predators. He doesn't have half your endurance. Use that."

"All right, I'll set up another hurdle for him."

Osborn bailed out. He took cover behind his car and unlatched his sidearm. "If this is his avicopter, I'm in position."

He looked down Mirabeau. About a block away, Parrish parked across the intersection. He hopped out of his car, took cover behind the fender, and aimed. He hollered something Osborn couldn't make out. His guts quivered as the Eshuvani kept running toward Parrish. Not that long ago, Parrish and Tucker had confronted a hostile Eshuvani, and they'd both landed in the hospital.

The Eshuvani skidded to a stop and turned to dodge around the car. He made it to the rear bumper by the time Tucker caught up and tackled him around the knees. The Eshuvani pushed Tucker off and backed away, keeping both officers in sight.

Osborn started around the car to go help them but stayed put. "Don't let him rest."

Parrish holstered his weapon and ran toward the suspect. Osborn tensed as Parrish ducked a punch and blocked a kick. The Eshuvani stepped back to regain his balance. He shook his head and blinked hard. Tucker got back up and stood in the way back down the road.

"He's showing over-exertion syndrome." Osborn nodded and smiled. "Keep him moving."

Parrish tackled the suspect like Jim Brown on game day. The Eshuvani dropped to the ground. Tucker moved in and helped Parrish pin the suspect.

"We got 'im, and he's pretty much outta gas." Parrish fished something out of his back pocket. "We'll get him secured and contact Hawk's Nest dispatch to see if someone can come get this guy. Meet you back at the museum?"

Osborn latched his gun and slid into the driver's seat. "I'll be with you in a moment. We need to keep a close eye on this one until the *kiandarai* take custody, and I want to ask him a question or two."

"Ten-four. Oh, and he's got silver collar tabs with blue crystals."

"Why am I not surprised?" Now maybe they'd get to the bottom of who was supplying these guys. He headed down the street to join Parrish and Tucker.

Ω

After the last rumble, Amaya stayed still for seconds that passed like eons. When she was certain the explosions were over, she picked herself up from the floor and offered her hand to Patrick Farrell. When she'd tried to push him down, he'd shrugged her off with some gusto and had instead protected his wife. Maybe he'd accept her help now.

He clasped her wrist and stood with her support before helping his wife to her feet. "Now 'Maya, I didn't mean t'push ya outta the way like that. I know you're a police officer an' all, but it's gonna take me a long time 'fore I accept a woman shieldin' me from harm. Supposed t'be the man's job."

"I understand it's contrary to your culture." She dusted herself off and looked over her charges. Neither showed any obvious bleeding, and their movements were stiff enough for their age but not so much that they seemed to be protecting a new injury. "I'll try to balance doing my duty and causing offense."

"Fair 'nough. Now what in blazes just happened?"

Jackie flexed her left hand and grimaced.

On second thought, Jackie may have injured her wrist, but if that was the worst of the damage, they'd gotten off lightly.

"It sounded like multiple explosions. Beyond that, I'm not sure." Amaya stepped toward the governor's wife. "Are you injured, Mrs. Farrell?"

"I think I landed wrong on my arm." Jackie gripped her left wrist with her right hand.

Amaya looked around and found a bench near one of the displays of an intricate quilt. "Let's sit over here, and I'll have a look."

"I'm sure it'll be fine."

Patrick led her to the bench. "Now, honey bunch, if I hafta let a woman pertect me, you gotta let her have a look at that hand."

Hopefully, Jackie would be more agreeable to accepting help than her husband had been. Amaya pulled out her transdermal viewer and tapped the switch to turn it on. "This is like a mini-X-ray device. It won't hurt you, and it'll let me see the tissues involved."

"Well, isn't that something?" Jackie rested her injured hand on the bench's armrest.

Once the device pinged to show it had passed the power-on self-test, Amaya brought the eyepiece up to her eye and scanned the joint. With each pass, she adjusted the dial on the side to change the viewing depth. The bones were intact, but small tears showed in the ligaments.

"You've sprained it." She powered the viewer down and put it away. "Fortunately, the damage isn't so bad. I can splint and wrap the joint for you, or we can do a quick blood test to see if you're able to use the regenerative salve in my kit to repair the injury."

"Oh, I don't think it's as bad as all that." Jackie shook her head. "Keep your salve for someone who might need it more. A wrap will do fine by me."

What a difference between this lady and the wife of New Mexico's governor. Amaya opened the main compartment of her backpack and dug out a stiff, gel-filled, foam wrist support and an elastic wrap. "If the pain becomes worse, I can give you an anti-inflammatory." She slapped the splint on the ground and shook it up. "Let me know if this becomes too cold. The foam is usually a good insulator, but some find they need more between them and the splint." She laid the support against Jackie's forearm and hand and wrapped the elastic around it to keep it in place.

Jackie inspected the splint. "Thank you, dear. I'm sure it'll be fine."

"Let me check in with the rest of my people." Amaya tapped Nurinyan's code.

When no answer returned, she tried Vadin, Jevon, and Dispatch.

"Problem?" Patrick asked.

"My comm system seems to be malfunctioning." She tapped Ed's code.

"Osborn."

"Amaya. My comm seems to be disabled on the Eshuvani frequency. I can't reach any of my own people, including Dispatch. What's happening?"

"All your doors out are blocked. Whoever placed those bombs knew their business. Blew the façade off the building, including the decorative stonework around the roof, while leaving the interior cinderblock wall mostly intact. We caught the bomber with a sack full of gear that looks handy for making incendiaries, but I'll run it past Jevon for confirmation. Naturally, the suspect won't say anything." He blew out a breath. "We've called for pickup, and Orinyay's on the way. Are you all right?"

Amaya glanced at her two charges. "We're okay. Mrs. Farrell has a sprained wrist, but no major injury. We're on the fourth floor and will try to find our way to ground level."

"Understood. Leave the line open, and we'll relay through me this time."

"Good. Can you try to reach Nurinyan and Vadin?"

"I'm on it."

She stood and shouldered her backpack. Something about this scenario wasn't sitting right. There was no reason to blow the decorative stonework off the building. Sure, that blocked the doors and may have injured a few people, but what difference would that make in the long term? She tapped her holster with her finger.

Patrick helped his wife up. "'Maya, yer chewin' on somethin'. Spit it out 'fore ya choke."

"I'm considering the purpose for the bombs," Amaya said.

"You mean why did they seal us in here instead of leveling the whole building?" Jackie gestured toward the ceiling and the nearest wall with her uninjured hand.

"Exactly." She looked for a window, but windows would let in sunlight and sunlight was ultimately destructive to most materials. Beyond the foyer, most museums she'd been in were windowless. This building didn't have roof access, so they would have to get to the ground floor to exit.

Patrick drew a breath through his teeth. "Now that ain't a comfortin' thought."

"No." She took a mental step back from the problem to see it from an attacker's perspective.

Trapping them in a building instead of dropping it on their heads could lend itself to a handful of scenarios. Either there would be another bomb, or they'd loosed someone or something dangerous in here and blocked the doors to prevent escape. Alternatively, could this turn into a hostage situation? Three leaders, their immediate families, and a handful of *kiandarai* might be worth something to someone.

Amaya rested her hand on her dart pistol. "Let's find a way down."

She recalled the layout of the building and led the way toward the elevator. There was a stairwell next to it. When they reached the entrance of the quilt exhibit, Amaya put her back to the wall and used the flat of her stainless-steel knife to peek around the corner.

A loud bang echoed through the chamber.

## Ω

Glass shattered. The rumbling faded out. In the silence that followed, Nurinyan stayed still. A child cried.

"Daddy!" a girl screamed.

Nurinyan pushed himself up and sat back on his heels. Governor Sam Zeldin and his wife looked uninjured.

"Kids." He bolted to his feet and whirled toward the playscape with its different textured surfaces and various physics demonstrations.

The ladders had broken away, leaving both kids stranded.

Vera stood at the edge of a platform. Where was the boy?

"Daddy, I want down." Vera reached for them.

Nurinyan looked back at the governor, who was helping his wife to her feet. "I will get dem."

He jogged over to the chin-high platform.

She backed up. "No. I want Daddy."

"Your dad is helping your mom over dere. You want down, right?" Nurinyan reached for her. "I am a policeman. I can help. Okay?"

She looked past him and came closer. "Okay."

"Sit down on de edge here, and I will lift you down."

As soon as she was seated with her legs hanging off the platform, he caught her around the chest and pulled her to him before setting her on the floor. "Where is your brodder?"

"David got hurt. He said I could go get Daddy." Vera ran to her parents.

The muscles in his neck tightened. He didn't have much practice with human pediatrics, but there was no one more experienced to pass the task on to. He could reach out to Amaya if he didn't know what to do.

Nurinyan grabbed the edge of the platform and hauled himself up. He followed the sound of the crying kid. David sat against the wall next to a pendulum set up to show how friction shortened each swing of the ball on the end. The movement of the weight was more erratic now. Gray-brown dust covered David's black pants and his blood-stained blue and green plaid shirt. A shard of glass half the length of Nurinyan's hand stuck out of the boy's arm about two finger-widths. His face was pale and damp with as much sweat as tears. He cradled his arm. Not likely a fatal injury but certainly something Nurinyan needed to address soon.

"Governor Zeldin, David is hurt. I can assess and start treatment if you wish." Swinging his backpack off his shoulder, Nurinyan rushed over to the kid and knelt.

"Go ahead. I'll be right up." Heavy footsteps came closer.

Nurinyan opened the front pouch of his backpack and pulled out the regenerative salve test kit. "I am going to do a quick blood test and have a look at how far into your arm dat glass is. Okay?" He pulled out a capillary tube and touched it to the blood. The blood was drawn up into the tube. Next, he pulled out his transdermal viewer and flipped the switch on.

A man grunted nearby.

Protocol demanded that Nurinyan stay with his patient unless another trained person could take over, so the governor would have to figure out how to get up here on his own.

The viewer chimed.

Nurinyan picked it up. "Dis is an x-ray machine, sort of." He held the scanner end up to his own hand and the eyepiece near David's eye. "I am going to look at your arm wit' dis."

David nodded.

Sam squatted next to him. "Hey, David. You're going to be fine."

Aiming the scanning port at the injury, Nurinyan adjusted the viewing depth. "De glass is all one piece and shallow. It missed de major arteries and veins. Even if he cannot use de regenerative salve, I can safely remove it." He shut the viewer off, put it away, and held the capillary tube up to the light. "No warning colors. Dis is good. I can remove de glass, treat de injury wit' de gel, and den bind up his arm and put it in a sling so he does not try to use it before tomorrow at dis time. Unfortunately, dis first part will hurt."

Sam pulled the boy into his lap and held onto him. "All right, son, you're going to have to be real brave for me, okay?"

Nurinyan opened the main section of his backpack and pulled out a pouch of regenerative. He pulled the shears off his belt and set them next to the pouch. He grabbed the piece of glass and pulled it loose. The boy cried out and clung to his father. Tossing the glass aside, Nurinyan swept up the pouch and shears. He cut a corner off and squeezed the gel into the wound. Over the next minute, the injury became shallower and filled in, leaving pink skin. That would fade over the next day or so and leave no scar behind.

Sam looked at David's arm and traced the remnant of the injury with his finger. "That's amazing."

"Yes, but, David, you cannot use dis arm until dis time tomorrow. De new muscle and skin is not as strong as it needs to be. If you try to use it too soon, it will tear open, and den I cannot use more gel to fix it." He fished a roll of gauze and a cloth sling out of his pack. "To help you remember, I am going to wrap your arm."

David nodded.

Nurinyan wrapped the boy's arm and slipped the sling over his head. He let Sam get it adjusted.

"Can you walk on your own, or do you want me to carry you?" Nurinyan shrugged his backpack on.

David sniffled. "I can walk."

Nurinyan pushed off from the floor. He hopped down off the platform and turned. After lifting David down, he stepped away to let Sam jump down. Nurinyan hung back while the family shared hugs all around. Watching them gave him a bittersweet counterpoint to recollections of his own family. That sort of affection would never have happened no matter what kind of crisis had occurred. In a culture that supposedly valued physical contact, he'd grown up never sharing a handshake, never mind a hug, with the people who lived under the same roof. Hardly any wonder he'd spent so little time there. The *kiandarai* had given him stability and normalcy his biological family never had.

Thinking of his *kiandarai* family, his collar tabs hadn't beeped yet. Odd. In general, Amaya was quick to do check-ins during an emergency. He tapped in her code. No answer. His brow furrowed. Was she busy treating injuries, or had she been hurt? He pressed and held two blue crystals. Dispatch didn't answer. Were his tabs broken? He reached into his pocket for the card that had the Las Palomas codes. His collar tabs chimed. Finally!

Nurinyan tapped a crystal. "Nurinyan."

"Ed. Amaya can't seem to reach anyone using Eshuvani codes, so we're using me for a relay. You okay? Where are you?"

If Amaya couldn't get a call out on the Eshuvani system, there had to be something more systemic than just a malfunction in his collar tabs.

Nurinyan puffed out his cheeks and blew out a breath. "We are on de t'ird floor, and we are all right. The governor's boy was injured but regenerative healed de injury. We were about to go find a way down."

"I wouldn't trust the elevator if I were you."

"No, no. Stairs for sure." Nurinyan frowned. What weird malfunction would allow his collar tabs to work only with the human system? It was all the same circuitry. "And, Ed, my comm is not working on the Eshuvani codes, eit'er. I could not reach Amaya or dispatch."

"Okay. Might be something with the whole network. Good thing we thought to link you guys into ours. Leave the line open."

Sam pointed toward the far corner. "Stairs were next to the elevator."

Nurinyan led the way. He passed a pond display made of a pit full of slime-colored plastic balls and labeled statues of animals and plants common to the ecosystem.

A dart pistol whined through start-up.

He spun trying to find the source. All he could see were the usual displays, but this kid-zone didn't lack for hiding places. The hairs on the back of his neck prickled.

Nurinyan pointed to the base of a large tree that kids could climb up to get to a display on rainforests. He wrapped his arm around the governor's shoulders and pushed him. "Go, go, go! Take cover at that tree." Nurinyan pulled his own pistol and started it up.

The muffled bang of a human gun fired overhead.

## Twelve

Vadin lay on the ground, shielding Halyuwin from the explosion. The shrieking pain in Vadin's shoulder convinced him to stay immobile long after the noise ended. The dust in the air tickled his nose, but he didn't dare move his arm.

"Stay here," Rinyulin Tolu *Tura* was muffled somewhat, as if he were facing away. Instructing his family, probably. Heavier steps came closer. "Halyuwin, Vadin, are you well?"

"I'm fine, a little shaken up maybe. I think Vadin was struck." Halyuwin started to slide out from under Vadin.

Shrieking pain radiated from Vadin's shoulder with even the slightest movement. He hissed and drew a breath between his teeth. "Something hit my shoulder. I think I've either broken or dislocated it."

"Stay still. I'll try not to aggravate it." Halyuwin pulled himself free. "What can we do?"

"Amaya and Nurinyan have medical kits. They'll be able to figure out what I did and treat it." Vadin gritted his teeth as he rolled onto his uninjured side and sat up. The flare of pain as he moved turned his stomach. He waited until the nausea backed off slightly before he spoke. "Is anyone else hurt?"

Halyuwin shook his head. "Past a bruise or two, no. You shielded me well."

His Transcendence glanced back at his wife and children. "My family was far enough inside and behind that half-wall over there."

At least he'd succeeded in protecting the others. That was the important part. He had done his duty, and as soon as someone with a kit reached them, he would be healed.

"Good. It could have been worse." Vadin tapped out Amaya's code on his crystals. When she didn't answer, he tried Nurinyan.

Halyuwin looked up at the ceiling. "You don't suppose they were hurt?"

Vadin tried Dispatch. No one answered. Was the comm net down?

There was an easy way around that. The police system was independent of the *kiandarai* system. Left-handed, he held his right shirt pocket open. No card.

Did he leave it in the shirt he'd worn yesterday? He frowned. "You wouldn't happen to know Morse Code?"

Halyuwin squinted. "What code?"

"My son might know. His *urushalon* has been working with him on some kind of communication code." His Transcendence turned toward his family. "Tacin, the code you and Donald are working on. Is it Morse Code?"

"No, Papa. It's the alphabet code. Alpha, Bravo, Charlie, Delta–"

"Very good, Tacin. Show me the rest later. Thank you."

"I guess I can start trying until I get one." Vadin sighed and tapped the access for Las Palomas followed by a single dot.

He added a dot with each try. When he got to the fifth attempt, he heard distant traffic and birds.

"Hollis."

Thank God! He mentally switched to English. "Vadin."

"You okay?"

He swallowed hard. "I am hurt, Mark. Broke or dislocated somet'ing in my shoulder. I cannot reach Amaya or Nurinyan. De *tura*'s family and Halyuwin are wit' me on de ground floor. Dey are okay. What happened?"

"Explosions blocked all the exits. Parrish, Tucker, and Osborn are chasing down the bomber." He drew a deep breath and hesitated. "Y'know, you might be able to sneak out the side door. I see an opening. It's not much but maybe big enough for you lanky sorts. Can you get there?"

"Yes." With Halyuwin's help, Vadin gritted his teeth and came to his feet, tucking his arm against his chest.

"Meet you there. If we keep the line open, will it relay you to Osborn if I'm linked to him?"

Vadin shook his head. "I do not t'ink it works dat way. I do not remember his code, and I do not have my code card, so I kept trying more dots until I reached you."

Mark chuckled. "On the fifth try?"

Halyuwin's eyebrows went up.

"Yes." Vadin managed a smile. "How did you know?"

"Morse Code for five is five dots. None of the other numbers line up like that."

"I am glad dat one did." He made a mental note to memorize the card later.

"I'll give you Ed's code."

Vadin gasped. "No! Wit' de comm net misbehaving, I do not want to risk losing contact."

"Fair enough."

Vadin led everyone around to the side door. Debris, including some large pieces of stone and concrete, clogged the opening, but one of the doors tilted inward off the hinges and daylight came through.

His Transcendence stepped closer. "Yes, de children and Leniya will certainly fit t'rough. Vadin, I t'ink you would also, but it would pain you terribly. Halyuwin and I are stuck on dis side until more of dis debris is cleared."

The *tura* was right. He'd fit through that opening, but he didn't look forward to the pain it'd cause to twist and squirm that much. Still, that would be temporary. He could get to a hospital and get treatment for his injury.

But what about the *tura* and Halyuwin? Whoever had set off the explosions could've brought the museum down on their heads. Blocking the doors implied there was more going on. His responsibility was to protect the dignitaries. Without another *kiandara* to pass the responsibility to, he couldn't leave.

"I am staying wit' you." He had training they didn't. Protocol left him no other option. "Mark and Robert can take care of your family, but somet'ing is odd about blocking de doors, like we were meant to be kept in here."

Mark looked in through the opening. "Hi there, folks. I think at least the women and kids can get out this way. Who's first?"

His Transcendence frowned and spoke in Eshuvani. "You trust these men, Vadin?"

"Very much," he answered in like manner. "They're good men. Mark is a father himself. He won't let harm come to them if he can have any effect in the situation."

Leniya crawled up the debris with her daughter. Some of the rocks slid. Vadin stepped forward, but Halyuwin got there first and steadied them. The daughter passed through to Mark first, then Leniya herself. Halyuwin helped Tacin up the rock pile and kept him steady until Mark could grab him and pull him through.

"We'll work on the rocks from this side." Mark poked his head through the narrow opening. "Think you can get anywhere from that side?"

Halyuwin tried lifting a stone. "We will try it."

Mark shifted a rock away and looked in. "Just don't overdo it. I don't have any of those granola bar things." He retreated from the opening.

"Granola bar?" Halyuwin asked.

"Nutrition bars." Vadin patted his left breast pocket.

"Which you should eat yourself, young man." Halyuwin wagged his finger at Vadin. "Your skin tone has a great deal in common wit' unused paper."

Vadin shook his head. "Dat is just de injury. I am okay."

Halyuwin nodded toward the nearest bench. "You should sit and eat something."

A bang like gunfire echoed from somewhere far above. Vadin drew his dart pistol off-handed and flipped the switch to prime it.

Mark reappeared in the opening. "I don't know what's going on, but you guys better find somewhere to hide. *Tura*, we'll get your wife and kids out of range. Go on."

Vadin nodded and started for the narrow corridor in the corner. "The janitor's closet is next to de restroom."

More shots echoed from above.

When he reached the janitor's closet, the knob wouldn't turn. Vadin led them into the men's room and pointed them toward the gap in the wall that separated the door from the stalls. He turned the volume way down on his collar tabs.

"–take care of that curator?" an Eshuvani woman's voice asked from the hallway.

Why was that voice familiar? The cadence of her speech marked her as familiar with nobility, but something about her pronunciation was off. He'd have to listen harder to find out what.

"Yes, he's very dead, but I don't like this search and destroy nonsense," an Eshuvani man complained. The way his words slurred together suggested he was low-born.

A single set of footsteps grew louder.

"I already told you why he doesn't want to flatten the building." The tension in the woman's voice suggested she'd happily eviscerate the man if they were in the same room. "If someone's not left to raise suspicions against the humans, it's all no good. We've spent too much time setting this scenario up. Best if it's one of the children. That will raise a lot of sympathy. We already know that ridiculous secretary and the ..."

Vadin nodded. He heard enough. All the woman's consonants were too hard, not just the trailing ones. That often happened when someone of the lower social classes overgeneralized when affecting a noble accent.

The voice trailed off as the man kept going past them.

Halyuwin gasped and spoke Eshuvani. "I know who that is."

"Which?" Vadin whispered.

"The woman. That's Teviya Gren."

"The *kiat*'s–" Vadin stopped himself and lowered his voice. "The *kiat*'s assistant?"

He was right. Vadin had met her at one of mother's parties. The pitch was right, and the cadence of the words, and even the snarl, more intense now.

Halyuwin nodded. "I've met her at a few functions. Of course, I've been talking to her a great deal about these meetings to keep the *kiat* informed."

"The 'he' is the *kiat* himself?" The *tura* frowned.

Vadin shook his head. "Possibly, but we don't know enough yet, Your Transcendence." That would, however, explain many things, but not why Halyuwin would have accepted Hawk's Nest as a suitable location. Surely, Teviya and Emyrin hadn't spoken well of their least favorite station. "I just don't und–" No. That wasn't an appropriate question to ask. He was well-placed in the social hierarchy, but not well enough to question the *tura* or his staff.

Halyuwin smiled. "Ask your question, lad."

"It's–it's impertinent."

The *tura* glanced at his secretary. "You don't understand why we allowed the meetings at Hawk's Nest."

He was that readable? Vadin felt the warmth creeping into his ears. "I've no right to ask that."

"I think we can forgive the outrage, given the circumstances." The *tura* nodded once toward Halyuwin.

Halyuwin lifted his chin. "It's neutral territory. The only truly neutral territory in the region. Everywhere else is owned by either a human or an Eshuvani. At the time, we believed that to be of the greatest importance." He sighed. "I've come to question that decision now. There was far mo–"

"–Course, I looked there!" The hunter's voice grew louder again.

The *tura* held up his hand, and Halyuwin pressed his fingers to his lips.

Vadin sat with his back to the wall. The cold tiles offered meager relief to the pain in his shoulder, but they'd warm from his body heat too fast.

Ω

A split second after the loud bang from a gun, a solid grip on the back of Amaya's shirt hauled her back from the opening into the next exhibit. She fell back against Patrick. The front of her shirt came back hard against her throat.

He set her upright. "Sorry 'bout that. I remembered seein' one o' yer guys doctorin' yer arm, only I couldn't remember which one."

Amaya tugged the front of her shirt away from her neck. "That's all right. A pinch in the collar is better than a bullet in the face." She pointed to the bullet hole in the wall.

"Y'got that right." He smirked.

Another shot impacted the far wall about a foot from the first.

She drew a deep breath. "You with the pistol. This is the *kiandarai*. Disarm and come into the open with your hands clearly visible. Noncompliance will be deemed willful defiance of *kiandarai* directive."

"No way." Conner Florentine laughed. "You come into the open. I've got you trapped. They fired me because of you, and now you're going to get yours."

Conner? Yes, he'd been a loose cannon. Certainly, he'd shown pathetically bad judgment. Perhaps injuring or killing a mere "twig" was an acceptable "accident," an insignificant bit of "collateral damage." According to his partner, none of that was new, but to join with the group plotting against the *tura* and governors? That went well past unprofessionalism and immaturity.

And, naturally, Conner's foolishness was now her doing and grounds for justifiable homicide. That part, at least, fit in with his "it's everyone else's fault" mentality. Amaya sighed and shook her head. "Then you'll have to come get me. We can stay here quite happily for a long while."

That was definitely against protocol, but the protocol didn't include any instructions for how to deal with "loose cannons" in a museum with blocked doors.

Two more shots hit the cinderblock wall behind her.

Patrick tapped her shoulder. "You know this guy?"

"Yes." She looked down at her right arm. "He's the former police officer in Las Palomas who put the bullet across my arm trying to shoot past me."

Patrick snickered. "Uh-huh. The guy's a bale o' hay short of a cattle ranch. He can't be carryin' endless ammo. Let 'im blow it all, and he'll be easy pickin's."

"Let's see if we can encourage him. Go along with me." Amaya drew a deep breath. "So, have you two played Stellari?"

"Can't say I have? That anythin' like poker?" Patrick asked.

"Not entirely, but you may find some similarities. I've got a set in my pocket. Would you be interested in playing a couple rounds?" Amaya's right knee cracked as she crouched and used her knife to peek around the corner.

The edge of Conner's sleeve was visible behind the display of Texan World War Two medal recipients. His arm was not likely to be in that sliver of cloth, so she'd be wasting a dart if she tried for him. He wasn't the only one with limited ammo.

"Well, sure, I'm game. Honey bunch, you want to play a round or two? Might be a good way to pass the time." Patrick pulled Jackie further back from the edge of the opening.

"Um, sure. Why not?" Jackie frowned and looked up at her husband. "We can sit right here on this rug."

"Very good. First, take these coins and toss them on the floor." Amaya angled her knife.

In the reflection off her knife, Conner's arm was more visible for a moment before disappearing.

Patrick pulled a handful of coins out of his pocket and dropped them.

The sound was all wrong and there were way too many of them, but Conner wouldn't know that.

Conner huffed. "Amaya, I'm going to give you to the count of three to throw down your weapons and come out. One, two…"

"We're a little busy right now, Conner." Amaya kept watching the reflection. She spoke at a normal volume. "Each of the coins is something different. The picture on both sides will help you identify them. This is the—"

"Three!"

He spun out and fired a couple more shots. He pulled the trigger again, and it clicked. Amaya leaned around the corner and fired three darts as he retreated toward the medal display again. All three hit his leg. Conner struck the ground like a powerless avicopter.

She kept her gun trained on him and waited for him to move. He stayed still. After sheathing her knife, she helped Patrick collect the dropped coins.

"Nicely done, ma'am." He pocketed his coins. "Is there really a coin game like poker?"

Amaya smiled. "There is a coin game called Stellari, but it doesn't have much to do with poker."

"If you're up for a round, we may havta play it later to satisfy my curiosity."

"That can be arranged. Wait here, in case he had an accomplice nearby." She left them behind the wall and stepped out, checking all directions with her gun tracking her eyeline.

When she reached Conner, she confiscated his gun and checked him for other weapons. A pouch full of ammunition joined the gun. She pulled out handcuffs and secured him before checking behind the rest of the displays for any other potential hazards. There was no one in the reconstructed World War II F2A. The uniform and parachute displays were clear. Even the janitor's closet and restrooms were unoccupied.

That just meant the fourth floor was safe for the moment. Whatever other threat was planned against them had to be more involved that just Conner Florentine. He didn't have the background to collapse the façade.

She returned to the governor. "Ed."

"Go, Amaya."

"Fourth floor is clear." She glanced back at Conner.

"Good. You might want to leave Governor and Mrs. Farrell up there and get to Nurinyan or Vadin if you can. Nurinyan's getting shot at, and Vadin's hurt."

Patrick leaned closer. "Nothin' doin', Sergeant. Used to be a sheriff's deputy. Did it for twenny years, an' I ain't one for sittin' on my hands."

Ed blew out a breath. "That's up to you and Amaya to work out, sir, but what about your wife?"

"This guy's out cold. He ain't much threat to a skeeter."

Amaya shook her head and stepped back from Patrick. "We have to find a safe way down first, Ed. We'll negotiate who's doing what afterward."

"All right. Keep me updated," Ed said.

Patrick held out his hand. "If ya gimme that boy's six-shooter and ammo, I can be more useful than a tick on a hound."

Amaya hesitated, but he had a point. If he had been a deputy for twenty years, she was better off with his experienced help, provided he didn't charge like a cattle stampede. She handed over the gun and ammo pouch and led the way to the stairwell. When she pushed on the door, it didn't budge.

Patrick stepped in past her and threw his greater weight against it. The top corner opened a finger-width then slammed back closed. He tried again and got the same result.

He stepped back and scratched his head. "Somethin's blockin' it."

Amaya went to the elevator and pried the doors open. Patrick grabbed a free-standing trash bin nearby and held it between the doors. Amaya let them close until they rested on the ends of the bin. The elevator car was all the way at the bottom of the shaft.

In the darkness, it had a lot in common with the mine in Michigan. Essien had died there when his knot had failed. A chill washed through her and tears burned in the corners of her eyes. This wasn't that mineshaft, and there was nothing she could've done to help Essien then or now, but if she didn't descend this shaft, there would be more deaths. There was only one option. She drew in a deep breath and held it for a moment.

Patrick leaned on one of the doors and looked down the hole. "Don't suppose you have a rope in that backpack."

"No, this is mostly medical gear." She stepped back from the elevator and looked at the parachute stretched out along one wall. "How upset do you think the curator would be if we used the parachute cords?"

"He'd be 'bout ready to spit nails, I reckon, but them fellas need a hand and we ain't gonna fly down that shaft for sure." He pulled a pocketknife out and extended one of the blades. "I'll either buy 'im some new cord or find 'im another World War Two 'chute. Let's check it out."

Amaya followed him to the display.

## Ω

Nurinyan willed his too-fast breathing to slow before he hyperventilated. He stood between the governor and open space in front of them. The bole of the fake tree was not the best cover in the world. No two darts had come from the same direction. So far, the worst had cut through the sleeve of Nurinyan's shirt but missed his arm.

He looked along the path of the shot and saw nothing. "Ed, I cannot see de shooter. I am going to go hunt him down."

"Do not leave the governor." Amaya sounded a little preoccupied, but there was no sternness to her words. "What keeps the shooter from getting around you and taking out the governor or his family?"

"She's right." Ed voice was almost lost under the sound of a vehicle driving by. "Stay with them and find better cover if he's getting too close."

"Get here soon, Amaya." Nurinyan sighed.

He had to get the governor's family out of sight from all directions. He looked up at the fake tree. The ladder built into the face of the trunk led up to a low-walled platform. As long as everyone stayed down and the suspect didn't find a way to get up high, they should have decent concealment up there.

Nurinyan glanced back at the governor. "When I say, get up in de tree and get down."

A dart whizzed past him and smacked into the wall.

"Go!" Nurinyan stepped in front of the ladder and returned fire along the same trajectory.

He kept firing as quickly as the Model Five pistol would load the next dart until all four of his charges were up in the tree. He backed up until he hit the trunk. The rough plastic was colder than any natural one. A dart struck his arm.

Nurinyan winced and ran behind the tree. He pinched the fletching on the dart and pulled it out, but his arm was already going numb. "Ed, de family is safe in de tree, but a dart hit my arm. It is useless now."

Ed drew a breath through his teeth. "All right. Do what you can and stay under cover. Amaya's looking for a way down to your level."

A dart flew past him. Nurinyan ducked. A second one hit his side.

Ω

The throbbing pain in Vadin's shoulder turned his stomach. He sat against the wall in the restroom and listened as the man stalking them walked around. The cold tiles had already warmed up from his body heat.

The barely audible voice came nearer. "–didn't set the charge right. There's a gap in the side door. They must have gotten out that way."

Teviya groaned. "You said yourself it's too small an opening for a grown man."

"It is now. What if they blocked it up to make it look like they didn't escape?"

"What if you're just too incompetent to find out where they're hiding?"

A loud thud echoed. "Just engage the *kiala*'s tracking circuit and guide me to them. When that last charge blows, it'll be time for me to leave whether I've ..." The voice trailed off.

Vadin's collar tabs lit up like a brightly colored constellation.

He gasped and tapped the code to disable the tracker. "Mark, my tracking circuit has engaged, and it will not shut down."

"Take 'em off and pitch them as far away from you as you can." Mark spoke quickly but softly.

Vadin fumbled with the clips.

"I've got it." Halyuwin pushed Vadin's hand away and unclipped both tabs.

Vadin reached for them with his uninjured hand.

Halyuwin pulled them out of reach. "You can't hold the door and toss them. I'll do it."

His Transcendence nodded. "Carefully."

The older man scurried around to the door and listened. He pulled the door open and tossed the collar tabs away then let the door drift closed as he scurried back. "Now, hopefully, your *kiand* or the police will get here before our pursuer figures out where we're hiding."

Vadin nodded. "But we're completely out of contact." He was too new at this. If the attacker found them first, could he actually do enough to protect the *tura?*

"Can't be helped, lad," Halyuwin said.

Ω

Amaya finished the last knot in the parachute cord and tested all the knots with solid tugs while Patrick secured one end around a support column.

She joined him. "I don't like the idea of leaving your wife here alone. Those darts will only keep Conner down for half an hour total, and we've spent about half of that."

Patrick glanced back at Conner and the extra parachute cord. "I'll hog tie 'im with the last of the cord, but you got two boys in trouble, and you can't get to both of 'em in time. I'll go back up the guy who's pinned, but the one who's hurt is gonna need yer medical help and quick like."

Yes, but if something happened to the governor while under her care … She sighed and rubbed her forehead. And yet he was right. She couldn't help both and couldn't get back up. "All right. If you're both agreeable."

She drew her dart pistol and pinched the clips holding the trigger guard on. The clip snapped, and she removed the guard so a human's hand could reach the trigger.

"Mrs. Farrell, do you know how to fire a gun?" Amaya crouched next to where the governor's wife sat on a bench.

Patrick snickered. "She keeps me honest on the gun range, t'be sure."

Jackie blushed. "Yes, I know how."

"This is a dart pistol. There's very little recoil. Do not shoot more than three darts at a coherent target. The fourth is often fatal." Amaya offered her the gun.

She took it, aimed at the wall, and fired. "You're right. Not much recoil at all. Thank you."

"You've got twenty-one shots left." Amaya stood and tapped Patrick's shoulder. "Let's go."

He led her aside. "Thanks fer givin' her a gun, but what're you gonna use?"

"Either Vadin's gun, my knife, or my wits." As she recalled, there were a number of throwable things on the ground floor displays. She went to the elevator shaft and picked up the rope.

Recollections of the mine shaft floated up in her memory. This elevator shaft was as dark as the one Essien had tried to descend by rope. He'd died.

If she didn't succeed in her descent, Vadin and Nurinyan, along with the people they were guarding, might not survive, either. Tears burned in the corners of her eyes, and she pinched the bridge of her nose.

"A little high-shy?" Patrick asked.

"Not particularly." She drew a deep breath and held it for a moment then blew it out. "I was involved in a mine rescue a couple months ago. It was physically and emotionally difficult in many ways."

Before he could ask for more details, she stepped off and descended into the darkness.

Thirteen

Nurinyan's eyes snapped open, and he shook his head. He had to stay awake. He would be completely useless if he fell asleep, and then what would happen to the governor and his family? "Amaya, can I use a stimulant to counteract two tranquilizer darts?"

"Yes, but it's risky." Her voice echoed through the comm. "It might cloud your thinking or unsteady your hand, but that might be better than going unconscious. Help is coming, but the option is open to you. Consider the situation and the likelihood of being able to maintain a reasonable defense."

He slid off his backpack and opened the pouch containing the pre-loaded syringes. "I'm going to use one. I should have fired from cover instead of stepping out."

"We'll debrief and analyze later, Nurinyan. For now, deal with reality." Something near her creaked.

"Message received." But much easier to say than to act on. He used his teeth to tear open the foil packet containing the stimulant syringe. The foil had a weird, bitter taste.

He injected the stimulant into the back of his deadened hand. Maybe he'd regain some use in that arm.

A dart struck the wall nearby.

"You aren't even making this interesting for me, *Kiandara*. Shoot back or something." The man's voice came from somewhere to the right.

Nurinyan grabbed his backpack and pistol and scooted around to put the trunk of the fake tree between him and the voice.

"Or is it a matter that you cannot use your gun anymore?" The man chuckled.

"Why don't you come find out?" A strange warmth radiated from his numb hand through his arm and across the rest of his body.

The sleepiness didn't abate so much as he got a rush like guzzling a couple stiff, caffeinated drinks. His left hand shook.

Oh, yes, that was exactly what he'd needed. He rolled his eyes.

"Just stay where you are, *Kiandara*, if you can even move anymore. Your troubles will end soon." The man's laughter bounced off too many walls to get a fix on the location.

Footsteps came nearer. Nurinyan gripped his gun tighter. He didn't relish racing three of his shots to one of the suspect's, but that might be the one chance any of them had. At his best, he could do it, but compromised and shaky? Not likely.

"Hold it right where you are, mister." Governor Patrick Farrell's sturdy drawl was loud and steady. "Drop the gun. Face down on the floor. Now, or I'll put a shot right 'tween yer horns."

Definitely not protocol-based phrasing. Nurinyan smiled and repeated the warning in Eshuvani, with a few syntax changes.

"You stupid human. Do you think you can defeat an Eshuvani?" the voice answered.

Nurinyan leaned around the bole of the fake tree. An Eshuvani man stood about three strides away, staring down the Texas governor about five strides from him perpendicular to where Nurinyan sat. The governor's cover behind a skinny cartoon scientist statue was not the greatest, but the suspect's cover behind a map kiosk shielded him only from the human. The kiosk left him wide open to Nurinyan, though. He fired three shots. One dart missed the target and hit the kiosk, so he went for a fourth shot and hit.

The suspect started to turn toward Nurinyan but collapsed.

Nurinyan blinked hard and lowered his gun. "The suspect is down."

Patrick ran over. "Good shootin', son. Anybody hurt?"

He shook his head. "No, but I was hit by two darts. It is hard to stay awake."

"Well, you rest easy now. Gimme some cuffs an' I'll go secure the suspect." Patrick crouched nearby.

Nurinyan powered down his gun and slid it into the holster. "I am surprised to see you here."

Patrick braced himself with a hand on the tree trunk. "Well, 'Maya wasn't real keen on the idea, but Vadin's hurtin' purty bad, and options were mighty short. I used t' do yer job, er somethin' like it."

"I understand." Nurinyan sat up straighter and pulled a pair of handcuffs out of his pocket. "Do you know how dese work?"

"Yep. Saw yer *kiand* use 'em earlier." He walked over to their downed attacker and secured him. "Sam, you and yours up a tree? Come on down now."

Their steps thudded on the tree's ladder. Nurinyan slumped back against the rough plastic of the tree trunk.

"Good. I felt a little silly hiding up there," Sam said.

"Ah, don't let it eat on ya, Sam. Yer job was pertectin' yer wife an' kids, an' you did that jus' fine."

Nurinyan let his eyes drift closed to rest for a few minutes.

Ω

Judging from the volume of the voice, the suspect had walked past the men's room twice after the tracking circuit had been engaged. Vadin hoped help arrived before the suspect figured out what should have been a too-obvious hiding place. In the meantime, Vadin listened and tried to gather his strength. If they were discovered, protocol demanded he at least try to defend the dignitaries, wounded or not. He had more training than they did in the art of self-defense. Maybe not much, but some.

"According to this, you should be standing on their toes." Teviya's voice sounded distant.

"Yes, well, I–Oh, very clever of them," the man said.

Vadin sat up straighter and strained to hear.

"What?" Teviya asked.

"I found the collar tabs, but they're not attached to the *kiala*'s shirt." A loud thud sounded. "Only a few places they could be now: restrooms, custodial closet, or stairwell."

Teviya growled. "You haven't checked those yet?"

"Checked those first."

"But didn't think to look again? Nah, why would you? People don't move around, right? Moron."

"Watch it, Gren, or I'll come visit you when I'm done here."

"You wouldn't dare."

"No?"

Rest time was over. Vadin pushed himself up from the floor and drew a sharp breath through his teeth as the movement exacerbated the pain in his shoulder.

Halyuwin reached for him. "What are you doing?"

"There's only one way in or out of this restroom. I'm the only one with any combat training. Amaya is on the way, but we have no way to tell where she is right now. If I can't take him out, maybe I can at least keep him off you until help arrives." Vadin stood painfully and pressed his back to the cold tiles on the wall by the door and waited.

The muscles in the back of his neck tensed.

The door burst open.

Vadin fired twice. One dart hit the suspect's arm. The other hit the door. Vadin rushed through the door before the spring-loaded hinge pulled it closed. He stopped in the large open space in front of the restrooms. The nearest display cases and exhibits were seven or eight strides away. Too far for his attacker to hide behind. Movement to his right drew his attention. He brought the dart gun around. A heavy kick struck his wrist, sending the gun flying into the wall.

The Eshuvani man was muscular, bulky for his height. The dart Vadin had fired was uselessly lodged in his watch.

The man sneered. "Is that where they are? I'll have to pay them a visit once I've dealt with you."

The man closed in. Vadin stayed between his attacker and the door and bided his time. The moment the man was within range, Vadin launched a kick at the man's gut. He caught Vadin's leg and shoved. Vadin fell back against the wall hard. The pain in his shoulder surged. The world around him whirled.

His attacker smirked and pulled out his own dart pistol.

Ω

Amaya dropped down into the elevator car from its roof. As dark as the shaft had been, the car was darker. Infrared goggles would be useless in this space. The walls around her would all be the same heat level.

She reached ahead of her and shuffled forward until she found a wall then followed it around until she came to a different kind of surface with round bumps. That would be the floor selection panel. She slid her hand further until the wall recessed. And that would be the door.

Amaya found the crack where the doors came together and pulled them apart. Light bled in through the narrow space in a second set of doors. She pried those apart enough to squeeze through and exited into the ground floor.

She listened closely. "Mark, what was Vadin's last known location?"

"Men's room."

Amaya recalled a map of the ground floor and turned left. A dart pistol fired. A man grunted, and Vadin cried out.

She came around a display wall showing the range of wild buffalo for a given era.

Vadin lay on the floor on his back. His right arm was bent at the elbow and pressed hard against his chest. A heavily built Eshuvani man stood over him. A tranquilizer dart stuck out of his watch crystal. Vadin kicked but his target dodged and took aim.

Amaya snatched up a fist-sized iron ball from a cannon display and threw it like a fast-pitch baseball. The ball hit the man's side. He flinched hard and spun toward her. Vadin rolled up onto his left side and scrambled out of range. He looked at a dart pistol against the wall and edged toward it.

"Stop where you are. Down on the ground. Now. Noncompliance will be deemed willful defiance of *kiandarai* directive." She circled around to the right so she could keep an eye on Vadin.

The man sneered and pivoted to track her, putting his back to Vadin. "Why? So I could be tried for attempting to kill a peace officer and get sentenced to execution? I'd rather take you down with me."

He charged at her. Amaya sidestepped his attempt and gave him a shove. He caught himself on the edge of a display and came back more slowly.

She slipped her backpack off and set it on the nearest glass-encased display table. The extra weight would tire her faster.

He stepped toward her, and she let him close the distance.

When he threw a punch, she leaned aside. The shot passed her arm. She ducked the follow-up punch and hopped back to evade a kick.

"You think you can make me mad enough or tired enough to do something stupid? I'm better trained than that." He settled into a half-crouched combat stance.

There were other ways.

She kept dodging while he threw combinations of punches and kicks. She glanced behind her. Too many more steps, and she'd be up against the wall. He panted hard and winced with every inhale. When he drew his knife, she went for her own.

"Amaya, down!" Vadin yelled in English.

She dove to the floor, almost clipping the corner of a display case. He fired five darts. Their attacker collapsed.

Amaya rolled onto her side and slid over to the downed Eshuvani.

Pressing her fingers behind his ear, she felt for a pulse. The pulse was slow but steady. The comm crystals on his collar were dark.

Amaya blew out a breath and pulled handcuffs out of her pocket. "Vadin, you have to stop scaring me like that."

"Sorry, two went wide." His smile made it through the grimace.

"Well, you're shooting off-handed, you're wounded, and you're not a specialist. We'll forgive you." She secured the suspect and retrieved her backpack. "Does he have any friends?"

He set his dart gun next to the door frame of the men's room but left it armed, a prudent choice until they knew for sure that they were no longer facing attackers. "We only ever heard the one and his accomplice. Over the comm system, not here."

She strode across the room to Vadin's side and crouched.

"All right, son, we're almost there." Patrick Farrell's voice echoed oddly at first and leveled out.

She leaned back to look around the partial wall blocking her view of the elevator doors. The governors of Texas and Oklahoma led Sam's wife and kids out of the stairwell. Patrick was supporting Nurinyan who looked ready to collapse into a nap at any moment. Young David's arm was in a dark gray sling.

Amaya returned her attention to Vadin and pulled her viewer out. "Let me get you stabilized before I check the rest of this floor."

Patrick helped Nurinyan sit nearby. "I'll take care o' that, 'Maya. You look after th' injured. Stairs are clear t' the third floor. Second and third floors are clear. After I check this floor, I'm goin' after Jackie, and then we can figger out how t' get those other two down here."

Sam looked around. "Where's Rinyulin?"

"He and Halyuwin are in the men's room." Vadin tipped his head back to look at the door. "I guess they don't need to hide there anymore."

"I'll get them." Sam slipped past Amaya and went in.

Patrick headed off down the hall.

The viewer chimed.

Amaya held it up to her eye and scanned Vadin's shoulder. His clavicle was cracked in two places, and that had misaligned the pulley in his shoulder. Much of the soft tissue was banged up, too. All that, and he could move around without passing out from the pain. Impressive. Let no one criticize his persistence. "Nurinyan, are you hurt?"

"No, I need a nap." He yawned.

"What happened to David's arm?"

"Piece of glass hit him. He responded well to regenerative. De sling is just a reminder."

"Good." She set the viewer aside. "You did quite a job on your shoulder, Vadin. What hit you?"

"A rock de size of my head, but it hit me, not Halyuwin." He closed his eyes and tipped his head back. "What did I do?"

The restroom door opened, and Amaya shifted aside to let the gentlemen exit without tripping over her. "The good news is nothing broke completely. You have cracks in some of the bones, your shoulder is misaligned, and there are more than a few damaged tendons, ligaments, and muscles. It's probably going to take two or three regenerative treatments to repair it all, so I'm going to open your shirt, apply the gel, and immobilize your arm. I'll have to reset your shoulder after the first treatment repairs the cracked bones."

"All right."

While Halyuwin stood over her shoulder and watched, Amaya tugged open the snaps on the seams of Vadin's shirt to reveal the heavy black bruises marring his chest, back, and shoulder. She pulled out a packet of gel and a pair of plastic gloves and slid the shears off her belt.

As she tugged the gloves on, Vadin drew his feet in closer and leaned forward.

Amaya scooped the gel out of the packet and spread it over his collar bone and shoulder blade. The gel sank into his skin but little visibly changed. She revised her estimate to three or four days of treatment. She dug an elastic wrap from her backpack to secure Vadin's arm.

Patrick came back down the hall. "No one that way." He dropped into a crouch next to her and whispered, "Curator's gonna need a coroner." He stood up. "Sam, whaddya know about rope work?"

Sam stood and shook his head. "Not much, but I can help you get the guy from the third floor down."

"I'll have Vadin stabilized by then, and I'll help you with the fourth floor." Amaya glanced up at the two governors.

"That'll do jus' fine. Come on, Sam."

The two of them went off toward the stairs.

By now, the gel should have done all the repair work it was going to do on Vadin's injuries. Amaya unsnapped the other side of his shirt and started binding the injured arm to Vadin's chest. "Ed, the hazards are cleared, as far as we know."

"As far as you know?"

She glanced at the human children and switched languages to Eshuvani. "Something about this still isn't settling correctly."

"Bring it into the open." He matched her choice of language.

Amaya looked at the debris-clogged side door. "They barricaded themselves in here with the intention of going on a killing spree and then what? Wait until Las Palomas excavates an exit? How did they plan to get out?"

Halyuwin went to one knee and pointed. "That one–" He glanced at the children, who probably didn't know Eshuvani anyway, and lowered his voice. "That one over there mentioned a pending explosion that would immediately precede his departure."

She twisted around to look at Vadin's attacker.

"You know, Amaya, that bomb Orinyay and I found this morning was in a trash bin by an external wall. That may be what he referred to. It wasn't complicated, but it could have easily blown a hole big enough to get through." Jevon chimed in.

Ed drew a breath between his teeth. "Could be, but let's not let the sun get too much further away from us. We'll work on that hole in the side door. If you can, see what you can do from the inside."

Amaya finished immobilizing Vadin's arm and snapped together all the parts of his shirt that would still close. "We'll get everyone to the ground floor and work on the debris. Oh, and Ed, you'll need a coroner for the curator."

He sighed. "Message received."

She supported Vadin's head and back as he lay down. "Rest now."

Halyuwin tapped her shoulder and waved for her to follow him. They stopped several strides away. "I wish to apologize."

"Sir?" She arched an eyebrow.

"I received some grossly incorrect information about you. I not only accepted it without question but spread some of it to others." He pressed his fist to his forehead. "The distributor of this information will be properly dealt with, I assure you, and the proper information will be given."

There was no mystery to who was initiating that gossip. "Thank you."

"There's more." He looked back at the unconscious stalker. "We heard this one speaking to his confederate. I know the voice."

A credible witness who could ID another link in this chain? How could they have gotten that lucky? "Clearly enough to make an official report?"

"Oh, yes. I've had many dealings with that one over the last month. I would know the voice of Teviya Gren in a crowd."

Her eyes widened. "The *kiat*'s secretary?"

He nodded once. "The same, and she referenced another man involved. Might be the *kiat*."

"That would explain all." She scratched above her ear. Sure, she and Pavwin had both proposed the theory that the *kiat* was trying to hatch some sort of plot, but she'd never dreamed anyone would have proof. Evidence against Teviya wouldn't touch Emyrin, but that got them one step closer. "With your report and the other random pieces of evidence I have, I'll be able to get the court's permission to search her property."

"Good." Halyuwin clapped his hand on her shoulder. "His Transcendence has excused me from service until I get these two matters dealt with."

She was about to turn away from him but stopped. Vadin's lessons came back to her. If changing the subject of conversation was not permissible, ending it probably wasn't, either.

He drew a deep breath and held eye contact. "I wanted to commend you. When I toured your station the first time, I should have realized that you were not properly equipped for the task we were demanding of you. Four *kialai*? Substandard equipment? One station covering an immense area?" He shook his head. "I was so determined to use the neutral territory that I put us all in a precarious position. I even encouraged one of your subordinates to assume authority over you. As if his noble birth could supercede your years of experience. So worried about protocol and propriety that I was blind to real challenges you were dealing with even without our interference." He paused and leaned closer. "In spite of all that, you, your staff, the *kiandarai* at Falcon's Wing, and the human police kept us safe even when the building literally blew up around us. Thank you."

Amaya waited a moment to be certain he wasn't going to continue. "You're welcome. God empowered us to be sufficient to the task."

Sam and Patrick returned carrying another handcuffed, unconscious Eshuvani. They set him down near his co-conspirator.

Halyuwin gripped her arm. "I have taken enough of your time. As soon as the wounded are situated, I'll go with you to the courthouse. Let's not give Teviya time to get away from us."

"Agreed." She stepped away from him and went to join Patrick.

He sat on the floor and held his hand up. "Gimme a minute to catch my wind, and we'll see about gettin' Jackie and that varmint on the fourth floor."

Ω

Amaya powered down the courier in the parking area of a grocery market half of a block away from Teviya Gren's apartment. She hadn't been in this section of town before. All the trees were precisely placed and trimmed to exactly the same size and shape. Crystal flowers hung from the branches in identical configurations. Signs in shop windows advertised manicures and hairdos at prices rivaling the monthly budget her family had been privileged to. Clothing went for closer to her father's yearly wages. Judging from the number of high-end avicopters and chauffeurs waiting in the parking lots, none of the shops were lacking business. Her makeshift avi stood out like a beggar at a royal court function.

Snatching the court paperwork and her backpack, Amaya hopped out of the courier and jogged over to Pavwin and another *kiandara*, a shorter-than-average woman with long, red hair tied up in a tight bun on the back of her head. That shade was common enough among humans but almost unheard of among the Eshuvani. Had she won the genetic lottery or was her *kiand* particularly lenient on that part of the protocol? Amaya shouldered her backpack as she went.

"Grace be unto you," the *kiandara* said.

"And peace from God, the Father of our Lord." Amaya embraced the woman.

"Amaya Ulonya *Kiand*, this is Inniya Curan *Kiandara*, a cryptographer I borrowed from Shark's Bay for this little excursion. If we do find the records we anticipate, I doubt Teviya was so good as to write them in standard language."

Excellent thinking. She'd been so preoccupied that getting a cryptographer hadn't even occurred to her.

He pointed to the papers. "Search permits?"

She held the documents up. "And conditional arrest warrants in the event we find what we expect, both here and at the headquarters."

"Good." He nodded toward the building. "Let's go. I have people watching the back door, and we haven't seen her come out. Shark's Bay loaned us another pair to watch the front while we go up."

"Excellent." She followed him across the greenbelt to the apartment complex's parking lot.

The glass-fronted building was laser-etched with detailed images of landscapes and landmarks from around the world. Although Amaya identified them all, she hadn't visited any.

Pavwin glanced back. "How many of yours are down after this morning?"

The glass door opened at their approach.

"Only Vadin, and he'll be out for a few days while he recovers from a particularly bad injury. Nurinyan was groggy for a while, but he was coming out of it by the time we got home. Orinyay and Ishe have driven themselves to exhaustion handling the day's calls, so I had to leave Nurinyan and Jevon to take over for them. Thank you for helping with this." Amaya stepped in and looked around.

The foyer floor was intricate tile work in various types of granite with colored LEDs embedded in patterns that might look interesting when viewed from above. The elevators along the walls were manned by operators in expensive, well-tailored suits. The excessive use of precious metals and gems was all at once mesmerizing and disgusting. She couldn't deny that the artistry involved was amazing to behold, but at the same time, the value of the materials used in the floor alone would have supplied the entire neighborhood she'd grown up in for a decade or more.

Inniya chuckled and clapped Amaya's shoulder. "You seem on a different planet, Amaya."

She smiled. "I grew up on the opposite end of the socio-economic strata. I've never seen this much wealth in one place."

"All this ostentation does take some getting used to." Inniya directed them to the uniformed operator standing at attention near the elevators. "We seek Teviya Gren, please."

The operator tapped a few times on his large, digital-readout watch. "This way please. Shall I announce you?"

"No, thank you." Pavwin stepped into the lift. "We prefer the element of surprise."

"Ah, yes." The operator's smile looked a little tight.

Slipping out of the erect posture Amaya had gotten used to seeing in Vadin, Inniya leaned closer to operator. "We'll be discreet, of course."

The smile turned somewhat more genuine. "Of course."

Right, because the upper echelons couldn't possibly stand the prospect that there might be crooks in their midst. Anything that caused reality to intrude into their carefully structured universe would be wholly unwelcome. Amaya hid an eyeroll by turning away from the operator as she moved to the back of the elevator.

The digital floor readout climbed at the rate of a floor per second and stopped at ten. She consulted the paperwork in her hand. Teviya had apartment ten-thirty-two.

When the door opened, Amaya stepped out. The etched glass floor of the hallway gave her the impression of walking on clouds.

Pavwin planted one foot and slowly brought the other one to match it. "Oh. I did not anticipate this."

Amaya offered her hand. "It's easier in the middle where the etching is denser."

"Do you want to wait downstairs?" Inniya slipped past him while reaching behind her head to resituate one of the pins holding her red hair in a bun.

He blew out a breath and moved to the middle of the hallway, keeping his eyes fixed straight ahead. "I'm all right, but I would've sent someone else had I known about this."

Glowing crystals embedded in the wall pointed them toward the right.

Amaya took the lead and walked, checking door numbers until she reached a ruby-encrusted, gold-plated door with the right number etched into it.

"I'm thinking she doesn't afford this place on a secretary's salary." Pavwin went past the door and leaned against the opposite wall.

Amaya drew her dart gun. "She has a sponsor?"

Inniya nodded. "Yes, but it may not have anything to do with the conspiracy. There are a lot of men and women in complexes like this who are here because some wealthy person enjoys their company and wants them nearby." She tapped the door chime, which played a ten-second tune Amaya didn't recognize.

That would become tedious after a while, but she supposed there was an option to switch the tune or rotate through a collection.

Footsteps ran closer. A motor whirred overhead. Amaya glanced up at the lens of a camera. Footsteps retreated.

Inniya pulled out a small metallic box. "Get ready."

She pressed the box against the door and tapped a button. The box whined until the lock popped and the door opened.

After powering up her dart pistol, Amaya rushed into the room with Pavwin and Inniya close behind. She took a quick, cursory check of the immaculate living room decorated in green and gold brocade and hurried to the door on the other side while Inniya headed through the kitchen to another door. Pavwin stayed to guard the apartment's one exit. Amaya drew her knife and used the blade to peek into the well-appointed bedroom decorated in red gauze, gems, and gold. A suitcase sat on the bed with several belongings piled nearby. A brilliant orange dress with sequins hung over the back of a red velvet armchair. Teviya crouched on the far side of the bed with a Model Six dart pistol in hand.

## Fourteen

Amaya drew a deep breath. "Teviya Gren, we have court permission to search all property belonging to you or in your possession. You have no way out. Discard your weapon and come into the open with your hands clearly visible. Noncompliance will be deemed willful defiance of *kiandarai* directive."

"You think I don't know why you're here?" Her laugh sounded a few protons short of a stable atom. "I've got just what I need for you."

Pavwin snorted. "It would be foolish of you to try a gun duel with a marksmanship instructor, Teviya. Amaya can likely get all three shots off accurately before you can aim."

"Maybe, but I'm not shooting tranquilizers. I only have to hit once."

Toxic loads? Not surprising. Teviya had been part of a plot to barricade them in the museum while three of her conspirators went on a killing spree. Amaya blew out a breath. Although Pavwin was right about the imprudence of Teviya trading darts with a trained marksmanship specialist, there had to be a less risky way to do this.

Pavwin stepped forward. "I can have one of the guys downstairs bring up tear gas."

Teviya laughed. "You wouldn't dare. This room shares ventilation with all the others on this floor."

"So, we evacuate this floor first." Amaya shrugged. "She's not going anywhere, so time isn't critical."

"That won't settle well with the management. Tell them, Inniya."

Amaya glanced at the *kiandara*. "And that's important?"

Inniya sighed and nodded. "My *kiand* places a high priority on such things as keeping our 'clients' happy. Pretty much anything that would hint that we're here to apprehend someone, even if we have the correct court paperwork, would not be agreeable. The more invisible we are, the better."

Ridiculous. Yes, they served the people, but changing standard protocols to avoid upsetting people? Hardly prudent. The protocols existed for a reason.

Well, as Pavwin had said, her training should give her a clear advantage.

"You two get clear of the shot path through the door." Amaya checked the power level of her gun and adjusted to balance shot speed with the close range. She removed the trigger guard and put on a pair of lightly armored gloves. A dart, especially fired at high power, could still get through if it hit right, but the tightly woven material made that prospect much less likely. "This is your last warning, Teviya. If your gun is armed with toxic loads, you'll be in enough trouble with the court even if we don't find documentation about the conspiracy. If I have to shoot it out with you, the judge will be unfavorably disposed. Discard your weapon and come out with your hands clearly visible. Noncompliance will be deemed willful defiance of *kiandarai* directive, which is punishable by a fine or time in prison or both."

She checked the path of fire and verified Pavwin and Inniya were out of range. Her guts unsettled, and she drew a deep breath to calm her nerves.

Teviya scoffed. "Go eat an ice cu–"

Amaya spun into the doorway and squeezed the trigger three times. The first two darts struck Teviya's hand. The third landed to the right of her trachea. Teviya jerked the trigger. Amaya ducked back to safety outside the door. The return shot went high and thunked into the wall above the door.

"Did you get her?" Pavwin asked.

A muffled thud came from the bedroom.

Amaya nodded. "Twice in the gun hand and once in the neck."

Inniya started forward.

Amaya held up her hand to stop the *kiandara* and used her knife to peek into the room. All three darts had landed, and that should have incapacitated her, but certainty was better than assuming. Teviya's head, arm, and shoulders were visible past the end of the bed. The gun had bounced a full stride away.

"Clear." She sheathed her knife, took off her gloves, and reassembled her pistol before following the other two into the room.

Pavwin picked up Teviya's gun. "I'll test the load in these darts."

For the secretary's sake, Amaya hoped she'd been bluffing.

When Inniya dumped over the suitcase, an electronic notepad fell out onto the pile of clothes.

Amaya secured Teviya and carried her to the forest green couch in the other room. The secretary's bright orange hair and partially removed make-up didn't match her black shorts and green shirt. Amaya pressed her fingers behind Teviya's ear and confirmed a strong pulse.

"I've found what you're looking for, I think." Inniya came out of the room, notepad in hand.

Amaya looked over Inniya's shoulder at columns of what appeared to be random characters.

"It's a ledger of some kind." Inniya glanced back at her. "The code looks pretty straightforward, but I'll need a couple minutes to crack it."

"I'll leave you to it." Amaya patted Inniya's shoulder and joined Pavwin in the kitchen.

Gold faucets and a gold sink glowed with the LED-embedded tile countertop.

Pavwin held the test vial up toward the light. "Definitely not the standard tranquilizer load." He handed her the vial.

She studied the test strip against the light and read the key embedded in the side of the vial. "Nightshade derivative?"

He nodded. "And a potent one at that. You would have been justified in a fourth shot."

"Maybe, but I dislike being the executioner." She gave him back the vial.

He patted her shoulder. "As it should be."

"I've got it!" Inniya clapped her hands once. "It's a straight substitution code. I'll have it translated shortly."

Amaya smiled. "She's quick." When her collar tabs chimed, she tapped a blue crystal. "Amaya."

"Dispatch. We apologize for the disruption of your comm system earlier. We had received an order from the *kiat*'s office to disable those four while you were on a sensitive assignment. The *kiat* informed us that no such order came from him. We're looking into the source of the false request."

Amaya leaned out of the kitchen and looked at Teviya, unconscious on the couch. She had a real good guess. "Thank you for restoring service. Message received." She tapped a crystal.

"So, the idea was to isolate you from contact and trap you in the museum with the killers?" Pavwin led the way back into the living room.

"Yes. She must not have known the human system was active and Hawk's Nest is linked into it." Amaya sat on the squashy couch.

Pavwin turned one hand upward and unrolled his fingers. "Either that, or she discounts the effectiveness of humans."

"Very likely. Do you believe Emyrin's claim of innocence?"

He snorted. "Do you?"

Amaya smiled. "Not for a second, but that does suggest he's stalling for time. We can use that."

Inniya tapped the notepad. "All right. It's translated."

"What do you have?" Amaya leaned forward.

"This first page is a list of people's names, their skills, payoffs, equipment she supplied, and other comments." Inniya chuckled and covered her mouth with her hand. "She didn't have much respect for this guy Wylin Leonan. Described him as an 'emotional disaster.'"

Amaya nodded. "I'm afraid that I'd have to concur, especially after he'd let his grief get too far."

To think she'd almost let her own grief get too far. She'd been furious with Talin for forcing the issue, but really, if he hadn't made her continued service dependent on completing the Rite of Final Memorial, would she be any better off than Wylin?

"She made similar comments about his brother Maran." Inniya tapped the screen. "Second page starts more of a diary. Plans to undermine the humans and wipe out Las Palomas started almost a year ago, just after the Buffer Zone station was first suggested. It's the usual rhetoric. 'Humans are holding us back' and 'restore the old, old glory of the Eshuvani' and 'why should we be sharing resources with these primitives.' If you needed conspiracy evidence, here's all you need and more."

Pavwin leaned on the back of the chair and looked over Inniya's shoulder. "Any word of other *kiandarai* in on the conspiracy?"

"Not exactly, there was a list of collar tabs stolen and a comment about how that would possibly implicate the original owners. Nothing listed in the top part where she details her accomplices. There are some veiled references to a 'boss,' and that might be Emyrin. Maybe." Inniya turned off the electronic notepad. "If you're going to see him next, I'll take Teviya to the courthouse."

Amaya sorted through the warrants and permits and handed over the ones relevant to Teviya. "I have the necessary paperwork to challenge him here at his apartment or at his office."

Inniya pocketed the paperwork. "If you two are going to challenge the *kiat*, you'll need a third *kiand* with you."

That could get tricky. Protocol required that arresting a *kiat* took the consensus of three *kiandai* or *kiati.* Reasonable, or otherwise someone who had to make difficult and unpopular decisions could be hampered by false or exaggerated accusations. She and Pavwin needed a third *kiand* or a *kiat* even with the court paperwork in hand.

"What about your *kiand,* Inniya?" Amaya asked.

"Maybe some time after the sun implodes." She snickered and shook her head. "A secretary, sure, no problem there, but the *kiat?* Your evidence was enough to convince the court, but it's too circumstantial for him to 'risk political suicide.' Before he'd take actions against the *kiat,* you'd have to pretty much catch him at wrongdoing and get him to swear out a confession. Even then, it's a maybe."

"Perfect." Pavwin rolled his eyes. "Timoran at Wolf's Teeth, perhaps." He reached for his collar tabs.

"Only if you know his code off hand." Amaya caught his wrist. "I strongly suspect at least one dispatcher is in league with this conspiracy. Recall the issue I had with getting the input of a pediatrician."

Inniya scowled. "That means any and all radio contact could be overheard."

"We don't have time to go door to door." Pavwin rubbed his forehead. "Any way to code the transmission?"

"Not that would go unnoticed." Inniya tucked the notepad into her backpack.

Amaya gasped. "The courier pilot is a *kiand.* He served on the frontiers."

"Old Sotril?" Inniya laughed and covered her mouth with her hand. "Does he even count?"

Pavwin smiled. "Of course, he does. He still has his rank and the protocol specifies three *kiandai* or *kiati* to arrest a *kiat*. There's no mention of whether the *kiandai* have to be serving in a station." He grabbed Amaya's arm, just missing the healing injury. "Call and request pick-up. The questionable repair status of your avicopters is legendary, so even if he is listening in, that shouldn't raise suspicion. We'll meet Sotril downstairs, brief him on the situation, and see if he's agreeable."

Amaya nodded. She pressed and held two of her dark blue crystals.

"Dispatch."

"Amaya Ulonya *Kiand*." She tried to inject a little annoyance into her voice. "I need a courier at my location. Please. Two passengers. No cargo."

"Message received."

The connection clicked off.

Inniya picked up Teviya. "Come on. Down the service elevator for us."

Amaya let the others lead the way while she checked all the appliances and secured the apartment. She caught up to them at an elevator half-hidden behind a gold and glass wall. This "service elevator" with mere steel and etched glass was still more ornate than the dumb waiter system where Amaya had grown up. She hadn't even known powered elevators existed until after she'd joined the *kiandarai*.

Inniya smirked. "Just how far on the other end of the socio-economic scale were you?"

This again? Why was it so hard for Inniya to fathom that some people weren't born in the lap of luxury? "Just this side of the poverty line." She held the door open for the others and pushed the button for the ground floor as she stepped inside.

The smirk faded. "I'm sorry, *Kiand.* I guess I'm being a little insensitive. You kind of get used to all this decoration after a while."

She hoped that marked the end of the mild humor at her expense. Surely there were funnier things in Inniya's world. "Peace. My family had little, but we were content."

The elevator landed at the ground floor with hardly a jolt. Amaya held the doors open for the others and followed them out the back. Inniya took Teviya to the waiting avicopter from Falcon's Wing. Amaya and Pavwin hustled around to the front, arriving as Sotril landed a gray and white courier in the parking lot. They joined him.

Sotril grinned and scratched his head. "Both of you need a ride? Lose your avis somewhere?"

"Not exactly," Pavwin said.

"We needed to get you here without alerting unfortunate listeners." Amaya stepped up into the passenger seat and explained the conspiracy details.

"Lemme see those warrants." Sotril extended his hand toward her.

Amaya offered them to him. As much as they needed to get moving, she could appreciate that he needed to verify they were following protocol. If he agreed to help them, he'd share whatever consequences were coming.

He studied them carefully. "Tricky business, challenging a *kiat*, but I done it before, and I'm not afraid to do it again. It's been a while since I done field work, though." He slapped the brace wrapped around his knee with his heavily scarred hand. "If there's any rough stuff, you two youngsters will have to handle it."

Pavwin gripped the elderly pilot's shoulder. "Leave it with us. You can supervise."

"That I can do." Sotril winked and got his cane from the holder he'd rigged to the back of his seat from a piece of pipe insulation and a ragged, little chunk of reusable tape. "Let's go."

He secured the avicopter before they headed back inside.

The elevator operator looked them over with obvious disdain, spending particular time on Sotril's cane, gnarled hand, and creaking leg brace.

As they stepped into the car, Sotril leaned closer to the operator. "If you take a hologram, you'll have more time to study the details."

The operator shook himself. "Yes, sir. Sorry, sir. What floor?"

Amaya glanced at the warrant. "Seven, please."

She watched the floor numbers race up and stepped out onto the etched-glass floor. Pavwin hesitated a moment, but Sotril bounded out to the center. Amaya led them to the left and stopped at a gold door encrusted with emeralds. She tapped the door-chime. Rushing waves and seagulls responded from inside. Amaya shook her head. Emyrin's love of the sea had carried to his home.

Pavwin smiled. "What is it with him and oceans?"

"Grew up in a desert's the way I hear it," Sotril replied.

There was no noise from within.

"He may not be here." Amaya slipped her backpack halfway off. A peek with her infrared goggles would solve that mystery.

Pavwin caught her arm with one hand while he slipped a sleek, new-model pair of infrared goggles out of a small pouch on his belt. His were half the size of hers. "Mine are handy." He put on the goggles and powered them up. "No heat source big enough to be a person."

"Then let's check out his office and be quick about it." Sotril jerked his head toward the elevator. "No sense in pinning the floor down here."

Amaya led the way back down to the ground.

Ω

As Sotril set his courier avi down in the training center parking lot and powered down systems, Amaya slid her backpack over her shoulders. She twisted around in the seat to look at both of her companions. "Ready?"

Sotril grinned. "As ever."

Amaya hopped out and waited for the others before continuing to Emyrin's office.

Pavwin nodded. "Let's hope he hasn't destroyed the evidence."

"I'm sure he's workin' on it, but it takes time and we haven't let him have much of that." Sotril clapped a hand on Pavwin's shoulder.

Amaya glanced at them. "Judging from what Dispatch said, I think he'll be more likely to try to cover this whole situation as Teviya's doing."

"Sounds like." Sotril snickered. "I'm not convinced she's that clever, and she won't have the access to do what we all know has been done."

Pavwin angled his path away from them and darted around to the front.

Amaya would have liked to approach the building faster, but Sotril was already hobbling as quickly as they could expect. She kept his pace and rolled her shoulders through their range of motion to dispel at least some of the tension. They approached the limestone building from the back. A sturdy door the same color as the stone walls was set near one corner. Amaya scanned all around them and kept her hand on her pistol. She reached the door first and leaned her back on the rock. Sotril stood at the door's opposite side, leaned across, and grabbed the door handle. Amaya drew a deep breath to quell the jittery nerves unsettling her stomach. She nodded once to Sotril, and he eased the door open. Amaya drew her knife and used the flat of the blade to peek down the hall.

"Clear," she whispered.

She kept her gun in hand and crept down the corridor. The lighting was the blue and green swirling blobs that reminded her so much of disorientation training. Sotril followed a couple steps behind. The clicks and squeaks of his brace and the soft thud of his cane on the floor were the only sounds.

Amaya glanced back at him.

"Sorry," he mouthed.

She nodded once. Although Emyrin's office was probably not sound proofed, such soft noises weren't likely to carry through the walls or door. There wasn't anything to do about it anyway.

They reached Emyrin's office door. Amaya passed her hand over the sensor, and the door slid open with a soft hiss.

"Oh, what is it now?" Emyrin slammed something on his desk. "My secretary takes a day off, and people think they can just stop by to chat?"

Amaya led the way into the room. The first thing she noticed was a change in the artwork on the walls. The nautical theme was the same, but the actual pictures showed a different assortment of fish and coral. The ceramic fish in the front room had made their way here.

"Go away, Ulonya." Emyrin snorted. "Come back when you have a proper appointment."

Sotril creaked in behind her. "Shame on you, Emyrin. Didn't your parents teach you it's impolite to call someone by their surname?"

"What is this?" Emyrin glared at them. "The two biggest wastes of *kiandarai* training in my office at once?"

"Emyrin Koral *Kiat*, I have a search permit from the court of Woran Oldue giving us permission to search all property belonging to you or in your possession." Amaya produced the paperwork from her pocket and placed it on Emyrin's desk.

The door hissed open again and Pavwin entered. "Move away from your desk and into the middle of the room please."

"What is this?" Emyrin stood and planted both fists on his desk.

"Evidence has been found suggesting a link between you and the recent criminal activity in Las Palomas and the Buffer Zone." Pavwin drew his pistol. "Move away from your desk and into the middle of the room please. Refusal to comply will be deemed willful defiance—"

"This is ridiculous." Emyrin rolled his eyes and moved around to the open area in the middle of his office. "If you really had any evidence, you would be arresting me, not searching. You know what this is? Harassment. You're looking for vengeance because Hawk's Nest isn't state of the art."

"State of the art?" Sotril laughed and took Emyrin's dart pistol and knife. "From everything I hear, it's state of the junk pile. Don't think your new decorations escaped notice, either. Used station funds on that, didn't you?"

Emyrin's ears turned bright red.

Amaya willed Sotril to be more careful. Emyrin was a powerful man, and they hadn't found any hard evidence.

While Sotril kept an eye on the *kiat* and Pavwin searched the rest of the room, Amaya planted herself at the computer. The screen was set for Emyrin's height, requiring her to tip her head back a little further than normal. She flipped on the power switch for the monitor. A countdown timer was in the last few seconds of a major file deletion.

She checked the discard bin in the corner of the screen, but it was empty.

A smirk flickered across Emyrin's face.

He hadn't gotten away with anything yet. Amaya tucked her left foot under her to bring her up to the proper height for the screen.

The hard drive's main directory was just as pristine. The one remaining file folder was the usual day-to-day business of overseeing a few dozen *kiandarai* stations. She opened all the files and scanned through them to confirm titles matched contents.

"Find what you're looking for?" Emyrin sneered.

Maybe she hadn't, but his attitude told her there had been something to find.

"You keep a very organized computer." Amaya left the computer for the specialists who might be able to recover the deleted files. Someone as tradition-minded as him would have paper backups. Amaya turned to the desk. Unless he was arrogant enough to keep the paperwork in his desk, they'd need to make another trip to his apartment.

Keeping an eye on Emyrin, Sotril backed toward the desk.

Amaya stood and leaned closer.

The elderly *kiand* shielded his mouth with his hand and whispered, "He tensed for a moment when you turned to his desk."

"I'll check it," Amaya whispered in his ear. "Can you or Pavwin check Teviya's?"

He nodded and made his way to Pavwin while keeping Emyrin in sight. While Sotril and Pavwin talked, Amaya opened the top drawer of the desk. She rifled through meticulous piles of pens, pencils, and other supplies. Sotril left, and Pavwin took over guarding the *kiat*.

"There's nothing you need in there, and you're just making a mess for me to deal with later," Emyrin snapped.

Amaya turned one hand toward the ceiling and unrolled her fingers. "If there's nothing here, the search will end quickly and turn up nothing."

She pushed that drawer closed and tugged open one of the side ones. A few dozen files were suspended from rails on the sides of the drawer. Each folder was named for one of the *kiandarai* stations. They showed expense reports, budgets, personnel assignments, and equipment lists. Station after station had budgets that exceeded ten times the amount she'd been allotted, even accounting for starting midyear. Hardly a surprise.

Amaya grabbed Hawk's Nest's folder. Maybe his comments would be revealing.

His notes detailed her incompetence and lack of judgment. Some of the comments mirrored reports from Halyuwin.

She compared the length of the drawer to the side of the desk and pulled the drawer until it hit a stop about a third of the length too soon. "That's odd."

"Hm?" Pavwin kept his gaze on Emyrin.

"The drawer is too short."

Emyrin rolled his eyes. "Don't be stupid."

She lifted up on the drawer, slid it completely out, and set it on top of the desk. The back third of the drawer had a metal-hinged, built-in box. A magnetic lock sealed the edge opposite the hinge.

"Where's the key, Emyrin?" Amaya opened one of the other drawers.

"That's personal information in there. Nothing you need." Emyrin planted his hands on his hips.

"We'll determine that for ourselves." Pavwin scooted around closer to the door. "Sotril, check the desk drawers for hidden compartments."

Sotril laughed. "Thought they were sneaky, eh?"

Pavwin leaned against the doorframe. "The key, Emyrin. The courts will not look favorably upon you if we have to force it."

"Find the key yourself."

"I've got a lock breaker." Pavwin snapped open one of his belt pouches.

Amaya traded places with him. "If there's nothing in there, Emyrin, why are you so secretive?"

"A man is entitled to his privacy!" He jabbed his finger at her to punctuate each word.

Pavwin took out a two-centimeter square, dull metal box from his belt pouch. He set the box on the lock and flipped a tiny switch. The lock breaker hummed until the lock popped. Moments later, the lights dimmed for a moment until another loud pop came from further down the hall.

Amaya smiled. Sotril must have rigged his own lock breaker with the building's electrical system.

Pavwin flipped the lid and arched an eyebrow.

He withdrew a set of files. "One for each of our mysterious names matched up with one of the criminals." He flipped one open. "Assignments, skills, payments, reassigned comm numbers."

Sotril's creaky brace came toward them, and he stepped into the room. "This'll do. Maps of the museum, an aquarium, and the airport with notes for how much of what sort of explosive to put in various places."

"I know nothing about maps." Emyrin glared at the old *kiand*. "My secretary's desk is not my responsibility. That was an illegal search."

"No, we had a court permit to search her property, too," Pavwin said.

"If that's not enough for you, how about this?" Sotril sorted through the papers. "A letter with your signature on it requesting funds from Earth Liberation Group."

He wanted to eradicate humans from their own planet? Of course. Then Eshuvani wouldn't have to wait for human tech to catch up. They wouldn't have to share the planet's limited resources. Amaya pulled out handcuffs. "Emyrin Koral *Kiat*, I have a warrant for your arrest. You are charged with treason, conspiracy, and affiliation with a known terrorist group."

Sotril looked around and muttered, "Not to mention terrible decorating sense."

She cuffed the *kiat* and removed his equipment belt before leading him away.

## Fifteen

Amaya left the courthouse with Vadin in tow. A week after the *tura*'s visit, Emyrin's and Teviya's trials were finally over. Their remaining accomplices had been found, tried, convicted, sentenced, and executed already, and the two masterminds would join their co-conspirators soon.

She climbed into the avicopter and set her backpack behind her seat. As usual, the temperature inside was much hotter than outside.

Vadin settled into the seat next to her. "I feel sorry for them, actually."

"Oh?" Amaya flipped the switches to bring systems online and triggered the ignition. "What part of their actions was not their own responsibility?"

Blessed cold air erupted from the vents in the dashboard.

"I don't mean they didn't get what they deserved. The courts were just, and justice is without mercy, but at least with Emyrin and Teviya, they were only homesick in a way."

"Homesick?" She pulled back on the lever to lift off and aimed for Hawk's Nest. "How can you be homesick for somewhere you've never been?"

Vadin turned one hand skyward. "Maybe homesick isn't the right word. Some of our people wish we had our own world."

"Wishing and dreaming are fine. Trying to oust humans from their world–"

They passed over the headquarters building. Workers carried boxes out to a cargo hauler avi. Whoever was replacing Emyrin apparently didn't agree with his decorating preferences. That gave her hope for their new leader.

"I know. I know." Vadin twisted toward her. "No level of homesickness excuses what they did. I'm just saying I sort of understand. Maybe Earth Liberation Group and those who agree should be trying to design a new generation ship with the resources on Earth."

Amaya nodded. "That would be more constructive."

When Hawk's Nest came into view, three new avicopters sat in the front parking area. Two were the gray and silver of the current *kiandarai* color scheme, but the third was gray and white, an official message-courier.

Vadin pointed. "We have company."

"A lot of it, apparently." Amaya glanced at him.

"Do you think it's the new *kiat*?" he asked.

Amaya smiled. "He's only been here a couple days. With so many things for him to do in Woran Oldue, why would he visit the red-headed step-child of the *kiandarai*?"

His eyes narrowed. "Red-headed step–what?"

He really needed to work on his human slang.

"That's a human idiom. Use the context. What do you think it means?" She tapped the remote to raise the hangar door.

He bit his upper lip and stared out the front windshield for a few moments. "The least desirable or most problematic?"

"Very good." She landed the avi in its bay and powered down before she grabbed her backpack and hopped out.

"That should be Amaya and Vadin." Ishe leaned around the corner from the dispatch desk and waved.

Vadin waved back and looked at Amaya. "Think they've been here long?"

Amaya shook her head. "No idea, but I'm sure Ishe has kept them suitably entertained." If nothing else, they now knew all the gossip of Woran Oldue.

He snickered.

In the foyer, a *kiat*, judging from the copper collar tabs, sat playing Stellari with Ishe. The *kiat* had brown hair graying near the temples. His eyes were a piercing dark green. He picked up one coin and flipped another over.

Ishe groaned and looked back at Amaya. "You two must have learned from the same instructor."

Amaya set her backpack down and looked at the score sheet. She might have to challenge this *kiat* to a game some time. Based on the score for this round, they might be equals. "It's called experience, dear one. When you reach my age, you, also, will be able to solidly defeat the average *kiala*."

"Maybe." Ishe updated the computer's readout of who was at the station. "Orinyay and Nurinyan are still stranded at their last call and trying to fix the generator on the courier. Jevon's recruited Ol' Sotril to do some part-scavenging and he will meet them out at their location if they can't get the dumb thing to work."

"I understand." Amaya clapped Vadin on the shoulder. "You and I will be busy."

"I need the practice."

The *kiat* rose. "Grace be unto you."

"And peace from God, the Father of our Lord." She clasped the *kiat*'s right arm and embraced him. "I am Amaya Ulonya *Kiand* and this is Vadin Tara *Kiala*."

The *kiat* embraced Vadin. "I am Rollin Jivara *Kiat*."

"Welcome to *Uloniya Varoosht*." Amaya gestured to the chairs lining the foyer wall. "What brings you to the Buffer Zone?"

Rollin sat in a wobbly chair. "I received a donation earmarked for this station, which is curious enough, but I also received the budget requests from all the stations and saw that yours came in four times the next highest. I had to come see what was happening out here. Ishe introduced me to the station, and I find you didn't request half of what you need."

Amaya looked around the foyer. "Funds are not endless, so I requested what was necessary and omitted conveniences."

He cocked an eyebrow. "You have a very austere definition of necessary. Unfortunately, I can't afford to give you the budget you requested, as much as you need it. Nevertheless, it will take us a few years to get the job completed, but I do intend to bring this station up to modern code, starting with the escort and light cargo avicopters in your parking lot. They are refurbished but only two and three years old, respectively, and in excellent working order. Those are from the earmarked donation meant for this station."

Those were meant for Hawk's Nest? And the station would be gradually brought up to the protocol's operational minimum? Less creative engineering and making do with substandard equipment would still be a while coming, but her new superior officer recognized the problem and planned to do something about it. A warm rush radiated through her body, and her heart was full.

"Whom do I thank for the gift?" Amaya looked out the window at the two avis.

"One of the conditions of the donation was anonymity of the donor." The *kiat* stood and tugged downward on the legs of his trousers. "I must go. Serve with diligence."

Amaya walked to the door with him. "Serve with diligence."

The dispatch computer chimed.

"Hawk's Nest," Ishe said.

"Dispatch. Las Palomas relay. Medical emergency involving Eshuvani tourist. Eastern Division, El Pasto Verde Park, south entrance. Las Palomas already on site. Assist."

"Message received." Ishe updated the computer.

Amaya retrieved her backpack. "Let's try out one of the new avis."

Vadin chuckled. "We might actually get there faster."

"Ishe, move the other to Bay Four in the hangar."

She grinned. "You got it!"

Amaya gestured for Vadin to precede her out the front door.

Originally from Michigan, Cindy Koepp combined a love of pedagogy and ecology into a 14-year career as an elementary science specialist. After teaching four-footers — that's height, not leg count, she pursued a Master's in Adult Learning with a specialization in Performance Improvement. Her published works include science fiction and fantasy novels, a passel of short stories, and educator resources. When she isn't reading or writing, Cindy is working as a tech writer, hat collector, quilter, and crafter.

Other books by Cindy:
*Remnant in the Stars*
*Lines of Succession*
*The Loudest Actions*
*Mindstorm: Parley at Ologo*
*Condemned Courier*
*Like Herding the Wind: Urushalon Part I*

Anthologies
*Medieval Mars*
*Avatars of Web Surfer*
*Victorian Venus*
*Hero's Best Friend*
*A Chimerical World: Tales of the Seelie Court*
*Aquasynthesis Again*
*Friends Like These*
*Rise and Rescue, Vol. 1*
*Warrior's Tribute*

Cindy can be found on the web at: ckoepp.com

CPSIA information can be obtained
at www.ICGtesting.com
Printed in the USA
BVHW041602110520
579510BV00003B/133